Spirit Trilogy

Book One
Spirit of the Mountain

Book Two
Spirit of the Lake

Book Three
Spirit of the Sky

Spirit of the Sky

Paty Jager

Windtree Press
Beaverton, OR

SPIRIT OF THE SKY

Contact Information: info@windtreepress.com

Windtree Press
Beaverton, Oregon

Visit us at http://windtreepress.com

Cover Art by Christina Keerins

PUBLISHING HISTORY

First Published by Wild Rose Press in 2012

Published in the United States of America
ISBN 9781940064888

Cover Art images:
Background photo by Paty Jager
Other images from Canstock and Dreamstime

Dedication
This book is dedicated to the people
who inhabited the Wallowa country
and held it dear to their hearts.
Special thanks to:
Jade Black Eagle and Red Wolf

Disclaimer
The daily activities and beliefs of the Nimiipuu in this book are factual—the spirits, other characters, and situations that evolve are only factual in the imagination of this writer/storyteller.

Glossary of Nimiipuu words

Anihm ---winter
Blackleg ---Blackfoot
El-weht--- spring
Heel-lul--- winter
Himiin (He-meen) wolf
Hi·sqi--- bad luck
Hoplal --- autumn
Imnaha --- Area along the Imnaha river in NE Oregon
Keeh-keet --- an edible root
Kehmmes --- an edible root
Kouse --- an edible root
Nimiipuu (Ne-Mee-poo) The People (Nez Perce)
o`ppah--- a smoked bread made of kouse
Pe`tuqu`swise ---Crazy One
Qe`ci`yew`yew --- Thank you
Sa-qan   (Saw-kawn) bald eagle
sekh-nihm---autumn
so-yá-po (so-yaw-po) White man
Thlee-than --- an edible root
Tiw`et   (Tee-wat) male medicine doctor
Txiyak---power of the spirit
Weippe --- meadow where root gathering and races were held
Wewukiye (Way-woo-keya) bull elk
Weyekin (Way-ya-kin) guardian spirit

«»«»«»

Ná-qc
(1)

Big Hole Montana, 1877

Sa-qan's heart raced with anxiety. Her wings faltered as she circled above the devastating scene. The large number of soldiers moved with stealth through the growing light of day toward the Nimiipuu camped many moons from their beloved Wallowa country. The same soldiers who would soon invade the camp of her sleeping people had given Young Joseph and the other chiefs no choice. It was either move to a reservation under a treaty they did not sign or dash for freedom. They chose freedom and now must fight to survive.

She screeched out a warning, but no one would heed the call of a bald eagle. Short of showing herself to the Nimiipuu in mortal form, she could do nothing but hover over the carnage as the white soldiers first shot an unarmed old man checking his horses, and then charged into the sleeping camp spraying bullets into everything—women, children, the old—it did not matter to the soldiers if they were warriors or not. They called the Nimiipuu savages, but the Wallowa band had only killed those who tried to harm them on their flight from the soldiers forcefully taking their home.

The violence sickened Sa-qan. She was a spirit of the Nimiipuu, but she was useless against this many. Her wings weakened with each slain Nimiipuu. *What can I do?* She pleaded to the Creator.

Warriors stumbled from their tepees, scrambling for cover and weapons. The celebration the night before now scoffed their good luck in finding a peaceful place to rest. With each spark and crack of a rifle and swipe of a sword their safety vanished.

Sa-qan landed on a rock on the hillside. Her chest ached. Screams, war cries, and rifle blasts echoed up the ravine. The acrid smoke of burned gun powder, stench of fear, and tang of blood filled the crisp morning air. She couldn't call upon Wewukiye and Dove. Her brother and his wife kept watch over the forked-tongued leader of the soldiers, Cut Arm. His large group of soldiers were in pursuit, crossing the mountain pass, Lolo, the Nimiipuu had traversed seven suns earlier.

Her keen eyesight sought Dove's daughter, Girl of Many Hearts. The child had come to this earth nine summers earlier after a so-yá-po, White man, raped her mother. Wewukiye had helped Dove, a mortal at the time, and fallen in love. But their working together to prove the so-yá-po's deceit had ended Dove's mortal life and the Creator gave her the gift of being a spirit. Sa-qan caught a glimpse of Silent Doe, the child's adoptive mortal mother, pushing Girl of Many Hearts into the willows along the river bank moments before the woman collapsed.

Dove's daughter needs me! Sa-qan swooped down the hillside, spread her wings, and hovered at the top of the willows. Her body dissolved, changing to smoke, then restructuring into a mortal form. She dropped into the knee-deep, cold water beside Girl of Many Hearts.

"Shh…" she whispered into the child's ear, hugging the small body close. She would not allow the soldiers to harm the child. Going against the Creator's rule to not show herself in mortal form ticked at Sa-qan like an irritating woodpecker, but she saw no other way to save Dove's daughter. She'd sworn nine summers ago after Dove became a spirit that she, Sa-qan, would always be there for Girl of Many Hearts when Dove was not around to care for her daughter. The mortal girl had become the child she would never have.

Splashing at the river's edge heightened Sa-qan's need to protect the child. With slow movements, she eased the child deeper into the cold water careful not to make ripples that might cause the tall, stiff weeds to reveal their hiding spot. She used her spirit *txiyak*, power, to fill the child with warmth. Her sharp sight watched for movement in the reeds. The rustle of the reeds behind her drew her attention. Would the soldiers try to surround a woman and child? A slight breeze fluttered across her tense face.

The wind.

A deep voice cursed and splashing grew nearer.

Girl of Many Hearts stiffened in her arms as water rippled past their still bodies.

The plants parted, revealing the contorted face of a soldier squinting down the length of a rifle pointed at them.

Girl of Many Hearts squeaked.

Sa-qan drew the child behind her, using her body as a shield. As a spirit she could not be killed by a mortal's bullet.

A man dressed in buckskin pants and a soldier's shirt with leader markings appeared behind the soldier pointing the rifle at them.

"No, Private! Leave them be!" The command rang with authority. The man's dark eyes, shaded by the brim of a hat, narrowed, staring at her. "We're only after the warriors. Go." He pushed the soldier from the water and stepped closer.

"Are you a captive?" He held out his hand not holding a weapon. "I can help you. Take you from this." His voiced dropped to a deeper, calming tone.

Sa-qan met his gaze. Should she let him know she spoke his tongue? The compassion in his eyes was a harsh contradiction to the violence still raging through the village. She shook her head and pressed Girl of Many Hearts farther into the river.

He took another step forward. "I can help you. We're going to keep after these people until they give in. I know the army. They don't give up." The sorrow and weariness in his tone puzzled her.

She thought all soldiers thrived on attacking and harassing the Nimiipuu.

"I can get you away from this now, before it gets worse." He took another step.

His nostrils flared as the stinging scent of burning hide filled the air along with terrified high-pitched screams.

"Damn!" The soldier lunged out of the river and ran toward a group of teepees being lit on fire.

Now was her chance to save Silent Doe. Sa-qan led Girl of Many Hearts back to the edge of the river and instructed the child to stay out of sight. Keeping an eye on the soldiers burning the dwellings, Sa-qan crawled to Silent Doe and dragged her into the river. Tears glistened in the child's eyes at the sight of the only mother she knew. Sa-qan's heart went out to Dove who after becoming a spirit was not allowed to have contact with her only child.

"You must not tell anyone you have seen me or of what I do." Sa-qan clasped the child's hand, drawing her young gaze to her eyes. "One day the truth will be revealed, but for now, it is our secret. A secret between us and the Creator."

The child nodded slightly, but her brow wrinkled in puzzlement.

Sa-qan placed her hand on the entry and exit wounds of Silent Dove and chanted quietly. Healing the woman would weaken Sa-qan, but it was necessary. Silent Doe had to keep the child alive. She, Sa-qan, could not live among the Nimiipuu. Even though many tribes and bands had come together for this escape from the soldiers, she would not go unquestioned. Her moonbeam-colored hair and eyes the color of sunshine would not put her in favor. Her two qualities would mark her a spy for the so·yá·po.

Silent Doe's eyelids fluttered and slowly opened. She was strong of heart. This helped the healing. When the woman stood in the water next to them, Girl of Many Hearts wrapped her arms around her mother. The fighting had moved down the river bank and up the hillside.

"How?" Silent Doe stared, her gaze moving from Sa-qan's eyes to her hair. She sucked in air and nodded. "Wewukiye. You are of his band?"

Silent Doe had been present at the birth of Girl of Many Hearts and knew Sa-qan's spirit brother and his deep love for the child's birth mother.

"Yes. He is my brother." Sa-qan nodded toward the area opposite the fighting. "Go there and wait. The warriors will drive the soldiers away and the leaders will find you." She patted Girl of Many Hearts's head and dove into the river, swimming to the far side. She needed cover to regain her strength and return to her bald eagle form to monitor the fighting.

Spirit of the Sky

«»«»«»

Lieutenant Wade Watts yanked the torches from the men's hands. "You're killing women and children. Go after the warriors!" The dwellings weren't catching fire quickly due to the dampness in the early morning air and the fresh hides stretched on the frames. Those that caught fire gave off a foul odor. Even more discomfort curdled his guts. The men were easy targets for the marksmanship of the Indians. His odd assortment of troops were lucky if they could hit the horses the Indians rode.

Stories told by the few survivors of the 7th Cavalry's run-in at Little Bighorn and the way the Indians surrounded the troops sparked through his mind as he ordered the men to drop the torches and head for cover.

A small contingent of soldiers had fallen back from an unseen onslaught by the Nez Perce. A bullet buzzed past Wade's ear. He bent, hoping to make his over six foot frame a smaller target and dodged strewn bodies of men, women, and children as he hurried to catch up to the others. War and combat no longer surged his blood and fed his adventurous side. It only saddened and sickened him ever since Custer's ill-fated campaign. He'd been lucky that day. His commanding officer had sent his troop to guard a supply depot.

This campaign could have been avoided. If only his government would have listened closer to what the chiefs asked for and relented a little, they could have all come to a mutual agreement. But instead, he had to control a bunch of killing-crazed soldiers and civilians. Only a handful of the men under him had ever fought Indians before. The rest didn't include the Nez Perce as part of the mortal race. His head pulsed and his gut soured stepping over a small child. The carnage took him back fourteen years to his first battle in the war. He'd been sixteen and torn between the ways of his southern roots and the belief all humans deserved to be free. In the end he followed his conscience, and saying good-bye to his family, had fought against his brothers, cousins, and friends. His side had won, but the only winners were the government and the freed slaves. The men who'd fought in the war and the families torn apart or dead—they became the biggest losers.

11

He stared at the child's body, his mind replaying skirmish after skirmish he managed to walk away from. Not so true for many of the men and boys he fought beside. How could men do this to other men?

"Lieutenant? You hit?" Sergeant Cooper, a man who'd been beside him since the war between the north and south, hurried around the dead bodies. "Sir, we gotta get out of here if we want to keep our scalps."

"Why did the men do this?" Wade unleashed his rage. "Women and children aren't a threat!" He couldn't calm his voice or his anger. "Why the hell did they do this?"

"Lieutenant, sir. We need to follow the others."

The man studied him like he'd caught a bullet to his chest and his guts hung out. The flash of a corporal he'd witnessed in just such a display weakened his knees.

Cooper grasped his sleeve and pulled. "I seen a squaw fire on our men. She picked up the rifle after her man was shot. She killed one of ours before we shot her."

"Self-defense. She was shooting to save her own life." Wade fought the bile rising in his throat. This whole mess could've been avoided if only the officers higher than he would listen. He hated killing. Had ever since he returned from war and saw his family…He squeezed his eyes shut and wondered again how he, the traitor, had survived that war and his family perished.

Bullets sprayed the ground around them. His years of staying alive kicked in. He jerked Cooper to the ground by the scruff of his neck, and they both crawled toward a bush for cover. How did things get so turned around? They'd caught the Nez Perce unaware, yet the soldiers were the ones retreating. From his cover, he watched soldiers making their way up the hillside they'd stealthily descended in the dark to surprise the Indians.

Cooper gurgled next to him. Wade rolled to his side. Blood gushed from a wound in Cooper's neck. Life drained from the sergeant's eyes at the same rate blood covered the ground. No time to grieve for a man he'd called a friend for fifteen years.

Wade crawled out from under the bush and ran up the hill. He ducked behind trees, calculated the direction the bullets came from, and worked his way toward his retreating regiment. Fifty yards from soldiers hastily digging a trench, a warrior rushed from behind a tree.

The knife in the warrior's hand slashed Wade's arm, shooting pain and igniting his anger. Rage fueled his counter attack. He grabbed the assailant's arm holding the weapon. They fell to the ground wrestling for control. The downward slope of the hill carried their struggling bodies away from his chance of help. Jagged rocks pummeled his body as they rolled, knocking out bursts of air from him and his assailant.

His head cracked against a rock, ringing his ears and fusing his concentration on being the victor. He would not die here. Wade twisted the sharp blade and rolled, slamming his body into their hands gripping the handle. The warrior's eyes widened as the blade sunk into his chest.

Wade didn't wait to see if the impaling had been lethal before springing to his feet and scrambling for cover. Behind a clump of willow shoots, he evaluated his situation. He'd lost his rifle, pistol, and side knife in the struggle, and suffered a wound. He pulled the neckerchief from his neck and wound it around his arm, tightening it to stop the bleeding. He studied the area and found himself nearly back in the village.

The scuffle landed him an unhealthy distance from his men. His arm throbbed. He bit down on a corner of his mustache and peered into the sky. Only mid–morning. How the hell had this day gone so wrong? He could head east and not look back. He'd be a casualty of war. Let the others chase the Nez Perce for God knew how long and come up with more casualties than the Indians. His conscience wouldn't let him. He fingered the insignia on his shoulder and knew he couldn't walk away. He'd walked away from his family before the war to join the side he believed in. Now the cavalry was all he had.

Wade battled the urge to race up the hill and join the others. Most of the Indians had dispersed, leaving a small contingent to keep the soldiers busy. The only way he saw a possibility of rejoining his troop was to wait until dark and slip between the warriors holding the soldiers on the side of the hill.

Wailing from the village began low and sad, building to an ear-aching chorus and standing the hair on his arms. He sat, hidden in brush, but with a fair view of the village.

Wade watched the women begin dragging off the dead and

tending the wounded. He stared at each one, hoping to glimpse the blonde-haired woman. She had to be a captive. Why hadn't she allowed him to save her? Was the girl she shielded her child? Gradually, the area filled with more warriors as they one by one came back to help take care of their families.

They took care of their own but left the soldiers where they'd dropped. He didn't witness a single scalping of the dead soldiers. The day wore on. Sporadic gun fire kept the soldiers on the hill as the villagers gathered and moved out of the river basin in a southerly direction.

He had to tell Colonel Gibbon the Nez Perce were moving out.

Wade stood. The sound of rushing water swooshed in his ears and the world went black. He hugged a tree with his good arm until his senses became balanced and the world focused before him swathed in sunshine.

The neckerchief sported more red than its original yellow color. He'd grown weak from loss of blood, but he had to get to Gibbon. He pushed off the tree, and using the bushes and gullies started a slow ascent of the hill, trying to circle around hidden areas where Indians could lay in ambush.

Lepít
(2)

Sa-qan perched in a tree halfway up the hillside. She had witnessed the soldier who saved Girl of Many Hearts's life fighting with a warrior. Her heart sat in her chest like a hard cold stone, knowing her allegiance should have been with the warrior. She had willed the soldier to endure, and he had come out the victor. She grieved the loss of another Nimiipuu life, but she did not wish the soldier to lose his life today when he had saved her niece. Now the soldier worked his way up the hillside. His wound clearly weakened him. If he met a warrior, he would not be the victor this time, and she did not wish to watch. Could not root for him, again, without suffering even harsher guilt.

She launched off the limb, sailed to the village, and up the draw following the escaping survivors being led by young Chief Joseph and Chief White Bird. Frog, Joseph's brother, remained with the warriors holding off the soldiers, leaving Young Joseph to deal with Frog's wounded wife.

The Nimiipuu traveled into the night, only stopping long enough to give the wounded care before pushing forward. Sa-qan continued her vigilance, waiting to hear from the Creator or her brother. With Wewukiye and Dove following Cut Arm who travelled many moons behind the Nimiipuu, Sa-qan found communication with her brother difficult. She couldn't relay Dove was needed here to protect her daughter, or that they'd lost many to the soldiers.

She feared they would lose many more. What would the Creator think of her if she allowed more deaths? But she was one and could do little to stop the madness in the so·yá·po soldiers. They were determined to wipe out the Nimiipuu. Her heart bled with the knowledge. Why couldn't they learn to live alongside one another? The Nimiipuu had done this for generations with many other tribes. Why were the so·yá·po so greedy?

Her keen vision scoured the land below. Her wings faltered at the sight of a small group hidden in a grove of trees. A mile ahead she watched the main group continue. These left behind would be the people unable to keep up due to their wounds. She searched the castoffs trying to determine who remained behind to care for them.

Swirling lower and lower, she counted seven bodies. Two old men, three children, and two warriors. She landed on a tree limb and surveyed the small group. The warriors would be needed to help battle the soldiers, the children to continue their people.

Sa-qan quivered with anxiety. She had to heal them. It was her responsibility.

An old woman shuffled out of the trees, dragging a water bag. The woman's gait proved she could barely take care of herself. The water bag dragging along the ground showed her bones too weak to carry the vessel. This woman could not care for them all by herself. And if the soldiers followed, how would she protect them?

Fear for the small group propelled her motives.

Sa-qan studied the group, peering first at the old woman and then the wounded. Did she enter the old woman and heal them or appear as herself and help the woman? She watched the woman administer a drink to each. Her hands shook, and she could barely raise the warriors' heavy heads.

They all had life-threatening wounds. She, Sa-qan, could heal the warriors quickly but would then be left weakened. If she entered the old woman, in a weakened state she would be a prisoner in the woman's body if trouble arose.

Guilt plagued her musings like the rumbling of thunder over the mountains of her home. She had to help. But she could not allow herself to be imprisoned in another's body.

The two warriors must be saved swiftly and sent on with the rest. With her decision made, she raised her beak to the sky, and for the second time after years of refusing to use her mortal form, she changed to smoke and into a Nimiipuu maiden. No time for misgivings, she walked confidently through the trees and into the middle of the injured.

"Who are you?" The woman shot to her feet and teetered.

Sa-qan held the woman's arm, steadying her. "I am Sa-qan, and you are?"

The woman's wrinkled face reminded her of the ravines she had flown over following the Nimiipuu.

"I am Summer Cloud. You are not of this tribe. How do you speak our tongue?" The old woman's suspicious tone caught the attention of a warrior. He tried to rise up on an elbow.

"I am of the Nimiipuu. My people live far north." Sa-qan moved to the warrior, easing him back down and sending healing warmth through him. "I heard of our cousins' troubles and wish to help."

"There is a tale of Nimiipuu who live in the cold who have hair the color of sun and eyes the color of a summer sky." The woman squinted, staring into Sa-qan's eyes. "Your eyes are the color of *hoplal*, autumn, leaves, and your hair the white of a moonbeam."

"There have been many intermarriages among my people." Sa-qan moved to the next warrior, feeling his forehead and taking stock of his injuries. He would require more time to heal. She would heal him slowly so the woman didn't become more suspicious.

"How did you find us? Why are you alone?" Summer Cloud leaned over her shoulder, watching.

Sa-qan finished infusing the warrior with healing and moved to the children. "I am alone because I have been separated from my family. I heard the noise of the soldiers fighting your band. Circling the noise, I came upon you and these inured people." The small girl would require much of her txiy̓ak, her power. The two boys were badly wounded but not to the extent of the girl.

Sa-qan touched the child's forehead, searching within the girl for strength to heal. Tears burned Sa-qan's eyes. She blinked and jerked her hand from the child.

She had never held emotion for another in all her years as a spirit. Confusion muddled her thoughts and shot fear to her chest. She did what the Creator expected of her and felt nothing other than nurturing of the Nimiipuu and her brothers. Now, for just one brother and his wife since their oldest brother became mortal and left this earth with his mortal wife.

The sudden emotion of sadness for this child and the tear slipping down her cheek numbed her thoughts and froze her in time. Back to her eleventh summer and the passing of their mother to the earth. She was a good woman, a loving mother, and too forgiving a mate. What would have become of her had she been alive when their father behaved so greedily and cowardly?

"I fear she will not make it." Summer Cloud's raspy voice entered Sa-qan's thoughts.

"She has many wounds." Sa-qan shoved her thoughts aside and ran her hands over the dried blood of the child's wounds. Could she spare the power to help this one? The warriors should be the first to heal.

The old woman nodded and shuffled over to one of the old men. Her gentle touch proved the man to be her mate. That is why she remained.

"Do you have healing herbs?" Sa-qan asked. She could strengthen the herbs healing if she chanted over them.

The woman nodded and shuffled to a small pile of supplies at the base of a pine tree. She picked up the blanket tossed over the top and held up a leather bag. "This is all I have plus that of my daughter."

"She is well?" Sa-qan took the leather bag and knelt to see what would be of use to the wounded.

Summer Cloud shook her head. "My man and granddaughter"— she nodded to the girl—"are all I have left. My daughter and her other child are of this earth." She had greater reasons for staying with the wounded than any other. Two were her family.

Sa-qan knew the loss of family. Even though one brother had been a mortal for many summers and she'd watched him age as he had not done as a spirit, his passing had left a large hole in who she was. Wewukiye was fun and loving, but he did not sit and talk with her like he once did. Not since he took Dove for a mate.

"This one needs bark."

Summer Cloud stole into Sa-qan's sad thoughts, bringing her back to her mission. To help the Nimiipuu. Sa-qan wrapped her hand around the willow bark, closed her eyes, and chanted to intensify the healing powers of the bark.

"What are you doing?" the woman asked, standing beside her.

"Asking the Creator to help these people heal." Sa-qan glanced at the increasing shadows. Night closed in on the small group. "I will gather wood. We will need a fire to boil the bark and cook broth."

The woman's heavy gaze weighed on Sa-qan as she walked between the trees gathering dried limbs and twigs for the fire. Summer Cloud started the fire and set out the other herbs by the time Sa-qan had a large pile of wood collected.

The woman boiled water in a metal trader's pot and added the bark. Sa-qan knelt in front of the herbs and one by one placed a hand on each, chanting to increase their healing powers. She leaned back against a tree and rested, waiting for her txiẏak to replenish. She watched Summer Cloud raise each person and either help them drink or dribble the tea between their lips. The warriors slowly showed strength, raising their heads and moving their arms and legs.

Darkness hovered at the edges of the small fire when Sa-qan's body sung with txiẏak again. She made the rounds of the injured, checking to see that they each had a blanket and placing her hands on them to once again add her healing powers. Summer Cloud had curled up under the blanket with her mate. Sa-qan returned to the base of the tree and studied the old man and woman. What would it be like to have a man, a mate, to talk with, share secrets, and be held?

She shook her head. Where had that come from? She had never craved a mate like her brothers. She was a loner. Up in the sky, watching everyone below and living through them, you had to be. And she would never forsake the privilege of being a spirit to the Nimiipuu. The Creator had given her and her brothers new life as spirits.

Several times during the night she checked on the injured and placed her healing hands upon them. By morning, the warriors sat up and asked for food. They watched her warily until Summer Cloud admonished them for not being thankful she came along to help. The old woman bent over the fire cooking up stew from dried fish.

"I am going for a walk," Sa-qan said and headed into the trees. She needed to return to the sky and see where the soldiers were and how far the Nimiipuu band had gone. Once out of sight of the small camp, she shifted to smoke and floated into the air, becoming a bald eagle.

Spreading her wings, her heart soared. She loved the freedom of floating through the air. She scanned at the trail toward the abandoned camp and spotted a small group of warriors racing the direction of the band. If they veered to the right they would encounter the wounded she left and perhaps help them reunite with the rest. Her healing would make them able to travel again.

We have seen the devastation. Wewukiye's sad words filled her mind.

Where are you? she asked, hastening her pace.

At the edge of the village. Cut Arm is here.

Her feathers ruffled in distaste. The leader of the soldiers acted superior to the Nimiipuu and put words on paper that were not true. He talked one way and acted another.

She quickly circled above the village and spotted a regal bull elk alongside a slick beautiful cow elk. Dove, while taking on an animal that could keep up with her husband, had refused to change her name. Sa-qan landed in a tree next to them. They watched her intently.

"What happened here?" Wewukiye asked, tapping a hoof to the ground.

"The soldiers attacked while the Nimiipuu were sleeping. Many women and children were killed."

"Girl of Many hearts?"

The fear in Dove's voice and eyes validated Sa-qan's decision to use her human form to save Girl of Many Hearts.

"She is fine. I had to use my mortal form when Silent Doe was injured."

Dove stepped forward, her eyes glistening with concern.

"Do not worry. They are both fine and traveling with the band. Joseph is keeping all well." Sa-qan peered at her brother. "It would be best if you catch up and watch over the band. I will watch these soldiers and let you know what they plan."

Wewukiye nodded.

"Thank you for helping Girl of Many Hearts." Dove rubbed her head on Sa-qan.

Her sister's show of affection and gratitude warmed her like flying close to the sun. "She is Nimiipuu and family." Sa-qan waved her wing. "Go, our people are moving quickly to get away from the soldiers."

"*Qe`ci`yew`yew*, Thank you, sister." Wewukiye winked, pivoted, and charged through the trees, Dove in his wake.

Sa-qan lunged into the air and soared up above the camp of the soldiers. Many hustled around burying bodies, tending the injured, and setting up tents. Her heart lurched at the sight of Bannock scouts digging up Nimiipuu dead and desecrating their bodies. *How dare they treat the human vessels with such disrespect*!

She dove, raking her claws across their backs and snatching clumps of hair. One shot at her, but she soared into the sun, disappearing into the glow. Her heart pumped, spurting anger and exhilaration.

The emotions barely registered before shame engulfed her, sending her spiraling toward the earth. Sa-qan caught her body in an updraft and floated, settling her mind and sifting through the reactions that flowed from her unwanted and unchecked. She never did things without thinking them through and weighing the good for the people from her actions. To have disregarded her position and attacked settled heavy and sour in her stomach. This and the emotions that swarmed her when she healed the girl confused. She did not lose control or live by emotions. She was neutral to all but saving the Nimiipuu.

Sa-qan landed in a tree on the side of the hill above the trenches dug by the soldiers. Her mind raced to make sense of her careening emotions. Why did she act so? These emotions had never surfaced in her since the day the Creator made her a spirit.

Her gaze came to rest on the dark haired soldier who saved Girl of Many Hearts. A man tended the wound on his arm. He'd removed his hat revealing shoulder length, wavy, black hair. Hair grew on his upper lip, not in an unappealing or unruly manner. She had noticed his dark brown eyes, much like a Nimiipuu, when he asked her to come with him.

How could one with his concern for others be part of a group who killed? Warriors knew how to kill, but they only retaliated when their families were attacked. The soldiers killed anyone and for no reason other than the Nimiipuu did not heed the words of their so·yá·po leader. The soldiers set up camp and continued to take care of the dead and wounded.

The men giving orders entered a tent. The dark-haired soldier entered, and shortly walked out and down to the village.

«»«»«»

A shadow moved over Wade as he left the strategy meeting. He glanced up and spotted a bald eagle. If only he could be that carefree. But reality squashed any hopes of ever being carefree again. The army only cared about catching up to the Indians and killing the warriors so there would be less hassle moving the women and children to the reservation. He found his loyalty to the military tested by this campaign. He always followed orders without compunction, but General Howard had made this a personal vendetta. Vengeance should never be a reason to carry out orders. General Howard had taken the Nez Perce flight as a snub to his authority.

The gentle slope of the hillside carried Wade down to the river. The backdrop of the ravaged village behind the placid stream mimicked the campaign and started the tic in his eyebrow to return. He waded through the cold water wondering how the women and children had managed to remain hidden in the reeds of the frigid stream. The sight of the blonde woman and the girl clinging to her came to mind. He smiled, remembering the woman's firm stance while facing down the barrel of the private's rifle.

He wandered into the village hoping he didn't see the blonde woman, yet searching for a clue as to who she was and how she ended up a captive. Her intelligent golden gaze and slight tilt of her head, as though she had understood and was fearful to speak, remained forefront in his thoughts. Her memory was more welcome than the mutilated bodies of women and children.

Colonel Gibbon strode across the village toward him. "Lieutenant Watts. I need you to muster a group of men to follow the Nez Perce's trail and report back to General Howard with their whereabouts."

Wade stared into the man's weary face. They'd known each other several years, both being stationed at the same fort. Before yesterday's attack, Wade had thought highly of the colonel. The fact he couldn't control his troops didn't set well. "I—"

The colonel cut him off. "You're the only experienced man I trust to keep the men you take from giving away your surveillance."

"I'll gather the appropriate men and be on my way." His gut squeezed with reproach for continuing after the Indians. They only wanted to live in peace, but his loyalty to the military compelled him to follow orders. He'd been doing it for so long, he couldn't comprehend not.

Wade tapped men on the shoulder he knew and respected, ordering them to follow. He wished Cooper had made it. He'd been a good man to have by his side.

Colonel Abernathy stalked out of Gibbon's tent and stopped in front of Wade as he tied his bedroll on his mount. "Don't go letting any Indians get away like you did this morning."

Wade didn't even glance at Abernathy. He may be higher ranking but the man had the conscience of a rock. It was Wade's bad fortune the private he told to stand down from the woman and girl cowering in the river was in Abernathy's platoon. The private must have been disappointed he'd missed out on killing two Indians to have reported the incident to his colonel.

"I saw no need to kill a woman and child. If you trained your men correctly they'd know the difference between a warrior and a woman." Wade swung up into his saddle.

"Why you—" Abernathy reached toward Wade.

"This is no way for two officers to behave." Colonel Gibbon's voice rang with reprimand.

Abernathy could have burned holes in Wade's forehead if he let the man get to him. Instead, Wade saluted Gibbon. "My scouting party is picked. We'll leave as soon as the supplies are loaded."

Within an hour of the colonel's order they had supplies and were mounted, heading after the running Indians. The platoon of fifteen men moved out at a steady traveling gait. The Bannock scout Wade brought along discovered where the Nez Perce had stopped. The minimal rings of charred sticks and many small areas of packed dirt proved the Indians spent a brief time here.

While their horses rested, Wade sent the scout to discover which direction the Nez Perce headed next.

Hair on his neck vibrated, giving him the sensation someone watched. Wade scanned the trees and higher elevations with his spy glass. Nothing.

The sensation continued to plague him as they mounted up and followed the Nez Perce's trail. An eerie impression forced him to turn in his saddle every five minutes. The private next to him started picking up his jitters. Wade cringed, realizing his nervousness not only made him a threat to his men but had rubbed off on at least one trooper. Not a good attribute for an officer.

Wade mentally flogged himself, straightened in the saddle, and called two men forward. "Drop back and scout our back trail. Make sure there isn't anyone trailing us."

The men saluted and disappeared back the way they'd traveled.

"Lieutenant, you think them Injuns is following us?" Chester Trainor, a young private placed in Wade's troop over a year ago, asked.

"It's best when following your enemy to make sure you have all sides covered." Wade stared forward. He didn't need the man becoming paranoid because of his actions.

"This was my first Injun encounter, sir."

Wade could sense the man wanted to talk about the skirmish, but he wasn't in the mood. "You're bound to see more before we get the Nez Perce onto the reservation."

"That's what I don't get, sir. Why aren't them Injuns wanting to go to the reservation? I mean it would be better than gettin' killed."

He studied the private. The man hadn't been out west long enough to venture into an ill-run reservation. Wade had firsthand experience while stationed near the Omaha reservation. If the Indian agent wasn't honest, the Indians didn't receive their allotted meat and clothing. And the sickness…It riled his gut as much as the last skirmish.

"When we get this campaign over, I'll send you to a reservation, and then you can tell me what you think." He spurred his horse into a trot and pulled away from the private. Since sixteen, he'd witnessed more sorrow and cruel behavior than one person should have to deal with, and little happiness. Over half his lifetime had lacked any joy.

The morose thought hammering at his mind did little to aid him in leading his platoon onward, knowing this assignment also held no joy.

Mita
(3)

Sa-qan followed the dark-haired soldier and the others he commanded. Their path pursued the retreating Nez Perce. She circled in the air ahead and found the small group of wounded she had helped still resting in their copse of trees. Fear the wounded warriors would be found sped her flight. She had to hide the warriors. And hope if the Bannock scout arrived before the dark-haired soldier he didn't kill them all. Setting the outcome of the encounter on the hopes the dark-haired soldier would save them festered in her chest like maggots on a dead fish. Too many times the so·yá·po had proven they could not be trusted.

She landed out of sight of the injured and changed to mortal form. Hurrying into the camp, she startled the old woman and the warriors regaining strength. One pointed a rifle at her. The tip of the weapon wobbled in his weakened condition.

"There are soldiers coming. The warriors must hide." She grabbed the rifle aimed at her. The warrior glared at her as she locked elbows with him, drawing him to his feet.

"I will protect you," he said, shoving at her and reclaiming his weapon.

Warriors were stubborn, but they had not met a stubborn spirit before. "You cannot kill all that are coming. They may not kill the injured children and old men. But they will kill you. Hide!" She slipped her arms through both warriors' arms, leading them to the far edge of the trees. With quickness and strength neither wounded warrior possessed, she took their weapons and pushed the two warriors toward a pile of bushes. "Crawl in there and do not move or make a sound."

"Give us our rifles," the strongest protested.

"No. I will hide the weapons. If we do not fight them they are less likely to hurt us." She believed the dark-haired man would let them be. The compassion he had shown saving Girl of Many Hearts and the way he offered to help her even though he believed she were not a Nimiipuu fluttered hope in Sa-qan he could be trusted. There were good and bad Nimiipuu. The dark-haired soldier was a good so·yá·po. Her instincts and the rapid beat of her heart sung this to her.

"We had no weapons ready when they slaughtered our women, children, and old people. When the warriors slept." The warrior attempted to take the weapons from her.

"No, I will not allow you to get yourself killed. The band needs you when you are well." She ran to the opposite edge of the trees and slid the rifles into an empty log.

Sa-qan returned to the camp, pulling up the blankets the warriors had used and covering the children. "Go about as you were. Do not let the soldiers know we have seen them." She knelt next to the girl, soothing her forehead, using the touch to slip a small bit of healing power into the child. Not knowing the outcome of the soldiers' visit, she did not dare use up too much of her txiy̓ak.

The Bannock scout entered the camp. He ran his horse close to the sick and nearly knocked the old woman off her feet. The scout spun his horse and tossed a malicious smile at Sa-qan. Anger at his attempt to harm others burned like pine coals in her stomach.

"Leave!" she shouted.

He forced his horse toward her, sticking out a moccasin-clad foot to kick her.

Sa-qan grabbed a downed limb, jumped to her feet, and swung the limb, knocking the man to the ground. He bound to his feet and lunged. She side-stepped and slammed the stick against his back. The viciousness of her swing astounded her. If she were not saving the lives of Nimiipuu, shame would have bathed her for her actions. She feared the scout more than the soldiers. The Bannock tribe had not been friends of the Nimiipuu for many summers. They wanted the Nimiipuu horses and good grazing land.

Her moment of indecision left her vulnerable. The scout grabbed her from behind, wrapping one arm around her throat while the other secured her middle. She had the strength to dislodge him but to do so would bring suspicion.

The soldiers rode into the area. The dark-haired soldier slid from his still moving horse and advanced on them.

"Release her!" he ordered, pulling a pistol from his belt and aiming it at the scout's head.

The arms around her released and shoved her into the soldier. Before her mind caught up, a strong hand held her by an upper arm, and she gazed into the concerned eyes of the dark-haired soldier. Tingles raced up her arm, setting her heart to fluttering.

"Did he harm you?"

His intense gaze and firm, yet gentle, hold on her arm scrambled her mind. Words stuck in her dry throat. She shook her head in slow motion, her gaze riveted on the full line of hair above his mouth. She had never witnessed this so·yá·po trait up close.

"Lieutenant, this looks like wounded being cared for."

The dark-haired soldier dropped his gloved hand and peered around the small camp.

"So it does." He returned his attention to her. "Are the rest of your group close by?"

She did not dare let on where the main group could be headed. Instead of answering, she continued to stare as though she did not understand.

"Private Trainor, see that there are proper rations left for these wounded. Private Marks, take half the men and scout around. The rest of you keep that damn Bannock from killing anyone." The lieutenant grasped her arm and led her away from the others.

Sa-qan did not fear the man. He could not hurt her. Her txiyak made her invincible to harm. The way his touch and concern sparked her body left her mind spinning with interest and dread. She knew he held more kindness than the other soldiers, but the suspicious glare Summer Cloud shot her compelled Sa-qan to struggle against the man's restraint. It would not do well to have the woman suspect her of consorting with the enemy.

"I'm not going to hurt you. I just want to talk where we aren't overheard." His hold lessened. He continued to lead her away from the others but close enough they could be seen.

He released her and stepped back, leaving a good arm's length between them. "Now, I'm pretty sure by the flashes of intelligence in your eyes when I talk to you that you understand. I also believe you're a captive."

She shook her head. Where had he come up with that?

"You're not a captive? Then how come you have blonde, near-white hair and eyes yellow as my scarf? I haven't seen another Indian with that coloring in my years of traveling." His piercing gaze nearly moved her feet back a step.

Sa-qan squared her shoulders and glared back at him. She would not let his concern weaken her. She cleared her throat. The last time she spoke this man's tongue she had taken over a trapper's body to save a young Nimiipuu maiden from being attacked by another trapper.

"I am a proud Nimiipuu. I come from a band to the north."

Wade almost jumped out of his skin hearing the woman speak. Her soft lyrical tone and stressed pronunciation warmed a hidden chunk of ice deep in his heart. A smile ruffled his mustache. The last month he hadn't had much to smile about, but this woman's poise and grit along with her angelic voice felt like a gift.

"See, that isn't so bad. Now, if you are from the north, why are you here? Is your tribe joining with this one? If so, where?" He watched indignation spark in her luminous yellow eyes.

Her hands fisted on her hips. Defiance raised her chin and flashed in her eyes. "You are like all so·yá·po. You know nothing of our people. You only want to kill us because you do not understand us." Loose strands of hair wiggled in the breeze, but her body remained unmoving, her eyes blazing, her full lips twisted in disgust.

"I don't want to kill your people. But the Army has orders to put the Nez Perce on a reservation, and I'm part of the army. When you shoot at me, I'm going to shoot back. It's nature. We all want to survive."

Her head tilted slightly to one side and the tight line of her lips relaxed. "Do you fear the Nimiipuu? Is that why the so·yá·po leaders wish to hunt us down and cage us?"

"So-ya-who? No, I don't fear you." He didn't have time to argue the reasons. They each carried their convictions. "I need to know where the rest of the tribe is."

She folded her arms and stared at him. Her belligerence should've made him angry, but it only increased his interest.

"Okay, I see you're not going to help." He grasped her arm to lead her back to the camp. The soldiers gathered around their horses watched. Wade released his hold and walked to his horse being held by Private Trainor.

"Did you see to their supplies?" He swung up into the saddle.

"Yes, sir."

He glanced at Private Marks. "Did you find anyone else?"

"No, sir."

"Did you happen to find the direction the main group is headed?" His gaze wandered to the young woman. She stiffened at the private's affirmation.

"You two"—he motioned to the last two men in formation—"ride back and let Howard know we found a group of wounded children and old men and which direction we're headed." The two spun their horses and headed back the way they'd traveled.

Wade sought the Bannock scout. He didn't need the man returning and causing harm to these innocent people. The scout was tucked neatly between two privates. Nodding to the two, Wade raised his arm and ordered, "Move out!" He couldn't stop his gaze from lingering on the blonde woman. She stood tall and stoic, and her gaze, while not warm and inviting, held less animosity as he rode away.

"Did you learn anything from that light-haired squaw?" Private Marks asked, riding up beside Wade.

He shifted in his saddle and glared at the private. "No, I didn't learn anything from that light-haired woman." The most important thing he'd learned from an old Indian at his first western station—the Whiteman's use of the word squaw angered the Indians. "She speaks English but wasn't willing to tell me anything." He had to admire her loyalty though he still found her story hard to swallow. She had to have been captured as a small child and truly believed the Nez Perce were her family. It was the only thing that made sense.

Wade urged his mount into a trot, setting the usual trot/walk gait the cavalry followed. He turned his thoughts to his conversation with the alluring woman. She said little but her actions, dark coloring, white hair, and unique eyes remained vivid in his mind. The warmth of her skin penetrated his gloves as he led her away from the others. Alone with him, her strength never wavered. She had his admiration. He hoped she, and the wounded with her, found a way to avoid Howard and return to the reservation on their own.

His motives were not all gallant. If she returned to the reservation, he could find her and learn more about her.

«»«»«»

Sa-qan helped the warriors return to the group. Their angry faces and refusal to accept her help proved they would not soon forgive her forcing them to hide. "You would have been taken prisoner or killed had you had shown yourselves. Now you can live to help our people."

She stared the direction the soldiers left. The warriors needed horses to catch up to the band. "Tonight I will find you horses. Tomorrow you will travel around the soldiers who just left and rejoin the band."

"What about us?" Summer Cloud asked. "Did the hairy-mouth leader not say Cut Arm is coming?"

Sa-qan held back a snicker. Yes, the lieutenant had said the leader of the soldiers was coming. "I will hide you where you will not be found. When you are well, you may either follow the path of the band or return to your homes. The soldiers are hunting for our warriors. They will not come for you at your home."

"And you? Where are you going?" Summer Cloud stared at her.

"I will continue on to help where I am needed." Sa-qan spread her hands on the closest warrior's leg wound, sending healing powers into him. She moved to the other warrior, touching his chest wound with her fingers, sending warm healing deep into his injury. He watched her with wary eyes but soon fell asleep on the bed of blankets.

Sa-qan ignored the old woman's curious stare and knelt by the children. She used the last of her txiẏak to heal them. Her weak body slumped against a tree. She could fight her weariness no longer and slipped into a trance to rebuild her powers and ready her spirit to catch up with the band.

«»«»«»

Sa-qan took flight long after the sun disappeared. She searched for horses for the warriors. A herd finally appeared. They grazed not far from the lieutenant's camp. She did not like stealing from him. He had shown compassion for her people, but the warriors needed horses. No others proved close enough to return to the wounded warriors by morning.

Shifting to smoke, she drifted among the animals until she found two swift ponies. She slipped their tethers loose and entered one, coaxing the other to follow. Slow, quiet steps carried them out of sight and hearing of the soldiers. Once she no longer feared detection, she picked up speed and raced back to the camp of the wounded. Out of sight of the camp, she withdrew from the horse and changed to mortal form.

She waited at the edge of the forest allowing the horses to eat and rest until the sun began to rise. The warriors would be well enough to ride. She entered the camp leading the horses.

The most skeptical of the warriors jumped to his feet and walked to her. "How did you come to get a soldier's horse?"

"I found them unattended. Perhaps they ran off during the fighting?" She handed the ropes to the warrior. "Gather food and water and catch up to our people."

The other warrior stuffed supplies given to them by the soldiers into a leather pouch, and Summer Cloud handed him a water bladder.

"I do not know you, but I believe you are a spirit of the Nimiipuu." The warrior swung up on the horse and nodded to her.

"*Qe'ci'yew'yew*, thank you," the other warrior said, from his horse's back. They spun the animals and set off at a lope.

Sa-qan stole a moment of satisfaction. She rarely took pride in what she did as a spirit. Pride was a selfish emotion best not heeded. But having someone acknowledge her help after all the generations of selfless attention to the Nimiipuu, she basked in the joy. Her mind snatched onto the pride and elation, dissecting why she now experienced them. Her season upon season as a spirit these emotions never surfaced.

"Why are you frowning?" Summer Cloud asked, stepping next to her.

"I have changed…" Sa-qan walked away from the woman. How was it she felt sorrow for the sick child, elation at the lieutenant's presence, pride over the warriors' gratitude? What is happening to me?

"We will stay here two more days before traveling to the reservation. My man and I believe we will be safer at the reservation until Joseph can come and get us and take us back to the Wallowa Country." Summer Cloud waved a hand toward the old men and children.

"It is best. I will send good wishes to the Creator for your safe travels." Sa-qan stepped to walk away.

"And you? Where are you going? Back to your family?"

She stopped and stared into the woman's faded eyes. Summer Cloud's gaze revealed she suspected powers in Sa-qan.

"I will follow and help the Nimiipuu. It is my gift."

Summer Cloud nodded. "It is as I thought. May the Creator always walk with you."

Sa-qan smiled. If the woman only knew. "May the sun guide you with warmth." She hurried into the forest, shifted to smoke, and back into her bald eagle form. She must catch up to the Nimiipuu and continue to help with their journey.

Pí-lep

(4)

Wade stalked back and forth in front of his men. "What do you mean two horses are missing?" He glared at the group, who avoided his gaze and shifted nervously. His control nearly snapped at the sight of the smirk on the Bannock's face.

"It looks like they came loose and wandered off," Private Marks answered.

"Then get out there and find them. If they wandered off they can't have gone far." He waved his good arm and waited as the men clambered onto their horses and rode out, leaving Wade and Private Trainor standing by a smoldering campfire.

"What if they can't find the horses?" Trainor asked, kicking at a rock.

"You'll double up on two horses." He didn't like the idea of two men riding on one horse. It would slow them down and be hard on the animal. The best alternative would be to leave two men here to wait for General Howard. Five years ago he would've made this decision. Ordered two men stay and the rest move on without wasting time searching for the missing horses.

But he valued lives, even those of slightly reformed criminals, more than he had five and ten years ago. Marks and Trainor enlisted to see the West and live out the stories they read in dime novels. Half of his small group chose this life over going to jail for crimes from stealing to murder, and the other half being immigrants fresh off the ships barely spoke English.

Wade wiped a hand over his face, trying but not succeeding in, swiping away the tiredness he couldn't shed over the past year, and even more so since having his arm slashed open the other day.

He sat, taking the cup of coffee the private offered. Hard tack and coffee were the best he could offer his soldiers on the trail. Staring into the cup, he watched coffee grounds float to the surface. What he wouldn't give for a full course meal and a glass of whiskey. The good stuff. Not the rot gut sold from a tent near the fort.

"Lieutenant. Sir. How do you think those horses got loose?" Private Trainor clutched his rifle and watched the open area ahead of them.

"Tired people don't tie knots as well." He sipped the harsh black brew and wiped his mustache releasing coffee grounds. A hot bath would be welcome, too. Loosen his saddle sore muscles and layers of dirt on his skin.

"What if them Injuns snuck in and let them loose?" The warble in the man's voice caught Wade's attention.

"Trainor, if it had been Indians, they would've taken all of the horses." He dumped out the remainder of his drink and stared at the private. "Are you afraid of the Indians?"

"N-no. Well, I'd rather not fight one. I don't mind being hunkered down behind something and shooting at them, but they're fierce in hand to hand fighting."

"I know." Wade rubbed a hand up and down his throbbing arm. He had a sizable gash that still oozed to remind him of how well they fought. "But you have to put aside your fear if you're going to be of any use to the rest of us in a fighting situation. You do what you have to do."

"Like Sergeant Cooper?"

Wade sighed, deep and long. The ache in his lungs rivaled the dull thud of his heart. Cooper was a good man. His wife and children would miss him. As soon as he returned to the fort, he'd send out a correspondence and the man's pay to his widow.

"Yes. Cooper was a good man. I fought beside him many years and can easily say we were friends." Of all the ways for the man to go.

Hiding under a bush. But life always seemed to throw oddities at Cooper.

"What do you tell his kin?" Private Trainor continued to peer into the distance.

"The truth. He died with honor doing his job." Wade stood, stretching his good arm and back. The horses couldn't have gone that far. He dreaded bouncing on the horse all day, but he would rather be on a horse than sitting in this canyon more or less defenseless.

Two horses appeared, running fast toward them. Instinct grabbed his rifle and flung his body to the ground. Wade used a rock to hold the barrel. Movement to his side brought the realization the private still stood.

"Get down!" he ordered Trainor.

A shot rang out before the man moved, and his body crumpled to the ground.

Damn! Another young, good man gone. He didn't have time to mourn.

Two warriors raced through the camp on army issue horses. Horses the others now searched for. Wade discharged his Henry at the retreating marauders as fast as he could cock the gun.

The horse in the rear spun around and charged back at him.

Wade rose to his knees, aimed his rifle at the warrior's chest, and pulled the trigger.

Click.

Jammed!

He stood, holding the gun by the barrel like a club, and waited for the warrior to race by.

The horse bore closer; pounding hooves matched the pounding in his head. It was either him or the Indian.

He raised the gun to swing. The sweat and dust of the horse mingled with the tang of fear on his tongue.

He swung.

The horse dodged.

The force of his swing carried him on unsteady feet toward the retreating horse.

The animal slid to a stop, pivoted, and the warrior faced him. He raised a rifle.

Spirit of the Sky

The bullet slammed into Wade's shoulder, forcing him to spin. The blast ricocheted in his ears as he fell to the ground landing on his wounded arm. Pain shot through his body, drowning him in blackness.

«»«»«»

Sa-qan flew toward the soldier's camp. A group of soldiers along with the Bannock scout followed the trail of the horses she'd stolen the night before. She did not see the lieutenant among them. Why did he not follow the horses as well?

The crack of gun shots rippled the feathers on her neck. She soared toward the sound. Fear sprouted in her stomach and balled in her throat at the sight of the warriors racing off, and two bodies unmoving lay near the campfire. The clothing on the one told her she had found the lieutenant.

Guilt riddled her thoughts. She stole the horses the warriors rode. If she had not taken those animals…She dove, landing near the lieutenant. She peered at his chest; it rose and fell in an erratic cadence, but he lived. He could be healed.

Sa-qan flapped her wings and walked to the other soldier. She recognized the young man who gave the wounded food. His open shiny eyes and gaping wound left little doubt he was no longer of this earth. He could not be healed.

Her attention focused on the lieutenant. She could not heal him all at once. She needed time. If the shots brought her here, the soldiers would return. To heal the man she had to take him away. But where? She scanned the area. The camp stood at the base of a ravine with a river wandering through it. Halfway to the top of the steep ravine her keen sight spotted a flat area. With the injuries to his arm and chest she didn't dare carry him in her talons.

Smoke wrapped around her form, and she swirled into a mortal. She squatted next to the lieutenant, scooped him into her arms, and stood. A quick glance around proved they remained alone. Long strides carried them toward the side of the ravine, and she began climbing. Her strength, though more than that of a mortal man, began to drain with each step, from the weight of the lieutenant. The outcropping came into sight. Relief flowed through her spent body, giving her steps renewed vigor.

She placed the man against the cliff and peered down at the camp. The other soldiers had returned. One gestured wildly as several dug a hole and others scouted the ground around the camp. They would find the horses' prints but not her steps. As a spirit she never left a trail. The disappearance of the lieutenant would plague them, but she refused to allow him to die from her actions. Once he was well, he could do as he pleased.

Using her weakened txiẏak, she stopped the bleeding and sat down next to the lieutenant. Rest would strengthen her. She studied his strong, square jaw, straight nose, and wide forehead. His black hair did not hang straight like a Nimiipuu. Dark, short pieces, damp from sweat curled along his hairline and longer hair had contours like bark on a pine tree.

She leaned close, sniffing. The scent of male, gun powder, blood, and something pleasant mingled in the air around him. The pleasant smell fluttered her insides with a peculiar warmth.

The sound of racing hooves drew her attention to the canyon below. She crawled to the edge and peeked. The group rode back the way they had come. A new pile of dirt marked the resting place of the young soldier. The soldiers no longer followed the Nimiipuu. Without that threat she could concentrate on the lieutenant.

Once she regained her strength.

Sa-qan returned to the man and sat. She leaned her head back, chanting for renewed strength and wisdom.

《》《》《》

The sun hovered directly overhead. Sa-qan placed her hands on the lieutenant's cheeks, gauging the life still in him. He had not regained consciousness. His life beat strong and warm on her palms. He would heal quickly. Her fingers strayed to the ends of the hair on his lip. Thick and soft. She pushed stray strands from his forehead. His hair resembled a soft, rich beaver pelt.

The rhythm of her heart increased as her hands lingered on his face.

What are you doing? Heal the man and feel nothing more. She

worked the fasteners of his shirt free and exposed the blood crusted shirt underneath. The tiny fasteners on this shirt taunted her fingers. She tore his shirt open, exposing a large hole in his upper right chest. She slid her hand around his side, leaning near him, searching for an exit wound. The heat of his skin and firm muscles under her fingers triggered a flash of fire in her body.

She sat back on her heels, staring at him. How was it touching his skin gave her a fever? She was a spirit. They did not become sick or experience such things. Contemplating her reactions to the man did not heal him. Without an exit wound the bullet remained in his body. It had to come out or her healing would not last.

Sa-qan settled him flat on his back on the ledge. Her fingers and the man's knife would have to be enough to remove the bullet. Water would be needed for cleansing.

She changed into a bald eagle and leaped off the ledge, floating on spread wings down to the camp area. The soldiers had left in a hurry, leaving behind many items she could use for the lieutenant. She changed to mortal form, filled a canteen with water, and stacked it with other useful items on an outstretched blanket.

Smoke swirled around her, and she changed back to an eagle. She flew back to the cliff ledge grasping the sides of the blanket in her talons. The man remained unconscious. She changed back to a maiden and drew the man's knife from his belt. The wound no longer bled from her first healing, but the bullet had to come out.

Her chant of a steady hand for her and good health for the lieutenant filled the air as she worked the tip of the knife into the wound and searched for the bullet.

Blood flowed, again, obstructing her view.

The lieutenant moaned and started to fight. She flattened her palm on his shoulder, taking away the pain and easing him to sleep.

The knife sunk deeper into his body. The blade connected with the hard object she sought. Her stomach squeezed with concern. Blood gushed and the blade cut more of his flesh as she wrestled the bullet from his body.

Finally, the bullet lay on the ledge beside her. She placed a palm over the wound and chanted for his life blood to still and his body to renew.

Soon the blood no longer trickled down his shoulder. Sa-qan used the knife to cut away his undershirt. She wet a blood-free piece of the shirt and washed the dried and new blood from his body. She marveled at his muscles, much like a warrior's. She thought all so·yá·po were lazy and let their bodies turn soft. The lieutenant had firm smooth skin, and a sprinkling of dark curly hair on his chest running down his flat belly.

She folded the blanket and placed it under his head. He would need nourishment. She, as a spirit, did not require it, but mortals must replenish their bodies with food. Rummaging in a leather pouch produced a hard bread and leathery meat. She thought back to the many summers before she became a spirit. Her mother had boiled meat such as this in water to make soup. Sa-qan plunged her hands back into the pouch and brought out a tin cup. This would work to boil the water, but a fire would be needed.

The side of the cliff offered little wood. Trees in the bottom of the canyon would have dead limbs and bark. She shifted into an eagle, grasped the man's outer shirt in her talons, and leaped off the ledge. In the cover of the trees, she filled the shirt with twigs, limbs, and bark. The sleeves barely met over the wood piled in the garment. She clutched the material in her talons and returned to the ledge.

On the ledge, she struggled to remember another childhood lesson—starting a fire. She squealed with delight watching a spark catch the bark. She leaned forward, blowing on the small glow until smoke feathered toward the sky and a flame licked at the bark and twigs she placed on top. She placed the cup of water and meat over the flame and waited.

«»«»«»

Pain. Wade's mind struggled to ignore the ache and spasms as a gentle hand raised his head and pressed something to his lips.

"You must drink to regain your strength."

He knew that voice. So soft and lyrical. Not one of the fort prostitutes. He forced his eyelids to rise. Who was this woman? Where was he? The struggle with his memory and opening his eyes sucked his energy.

"No, do not go to sleep. You must drink."

The forcefulness of the voice drew his eyelids up. He stared into the amber eyes of the captive woman from the village. "How?"

"No words. Drink." She pushed a tin cup to his lips.

The meaty flavor of the broth surprised him. She didn't relinquish his head until he'd drunk the whole cup.

"Where am I?" He tried to shift his head to see the lay of the land, but she slipped her hand from under him, and his head sank into something soft.

"You are safe and healing." She placed a blanket over his body and disappeared from his line of sight.

His stomach muscles tightened as he tried to sit up. His left arm worked to push off the hard ground, but pain shot up his right arm and pierced his right shoulder, roiling his stomach.

"Hellfire!"

Hands pressed on his left shoulder. "Do not try to rise. Give the wounds time to heal."

Wounds? He had a gash on his arm from wrestling the warrior during the skirmish…another wound? The flash of two warriors on Army-issue horses caught in his mind. Trainor dead. His gun malfunctioning. Taking a bullet in the shoulder and passing out.

"How did you find me?" He listened, hearing only the whoosh of the wind. "Where are the others?"

"I was traveling to catch up to my people when I heard shots." She sat down next to him, her shoulder and one side of her face within view. "I found you and the other. He was not of this earth anymore."

"Did you bury him? He was a good young man. He deserved to be buried."

She glanced down at him. Something in her eyes…Respect?

"The other soldiers put him in the earth."

"Where are they?" He swiveled his head, but he only saw a cliff wall on one side and the woman on the other.

"They have left." She stood, walking away from him.

"Left? They wouldn't leave me. We don't leave wounded."
Private Marks wouldn't have left him with only a young woman and no weapons. The two warriors who did this could come back.

"I had moved you before they arrived. They could not find you."

"Moved me? Why? I need to be with my men." Dizziness and fatigue swamped his head. He fought the anxiety rippling up his spine. "Where am I?"

She knelt beside him, placing a hand on his forehead. His body relaxed, and warmth flowed through him.

"You are safe. You will come to no harm with me. Rest and heal." Her soft words sang in his head as his mind closed down and his body relaxed. Why wasn't he anxious anymore? Why did her touch soothe? Where the hell were his men?

Pá-xat
(5)

Sa-qan paced the ledge. She had retrieved three more loads of wood and filled every possible thing that could hold water. The lieutenant slept through the rest of the day and all through the night, only waking long enough for her to force him to drink more soup. She knew he would soon be strong enough to sit up and realize they camped on a ledge. He would ask questions. Ones she could not answer.

Wewukiye, where are you? The band must have moved even farther off for her to not be able to communicate with her brother. In their generations of helping the Nimiipuu as spirits she had always been the one her brothers came to with problems. Now it was her turn to ask for guidance.

The Creator had stopped communicating with her since she chose to save Girl of Many Hearts in mortal form. The Creator had always been with her, helping her guide her brothers and the Nimiipuu. Fear for herself and those she helped trickled through her body, causing her arms and legs to shake.

This scared her even more. Never had fear or any other emotion been a part of her existence as a spirit. What was happening? *Why have you abandoned me when I need you the most*? She questioned the Creator.

The lieutenant pressed up on his good arm and scanned the area. His dark gaze roamed over the stockpiled supplies and then to her.

"Where are we? Are we alone?" His raspy voice urged her to pick up the canteen and kneel beside him.

"We are on a ledge above the canyon where you camped." She held the canteen to his dry lips. He drank heartily and leaned back, closing his eyes.

"Are we alone?"

"Yes."

"Why did my men leave me with you?" His eyes opened, and his piercing stare revealed a man full of confusion.

"They could not find you." She plugged the canteen and shifted to find the hard bread.

He clutched her arm, stopping her from turning away. "Why couldn't they find me?"

"I arrived right after the warriors rode off. I feared they would return, or worse the soldiers would return and think I shot you. That is why I hid you." His hand on her bare arm singed like a red-hot rock. Sa-qan jerked from his grasp.

He rose up again and peered over the edge of the ledge. His gaze connected with hers. "How did you get me up here all by yourself?"

"It was not easy. You are a big man." She retrieved the hard bread and held it out to him.

The lieutenant took the offered food and waved his hand. "And all this stuff?"

"Many trips." His constant questions irritated. She should have left him to his own people.

He would have died. Her healing qualities saved him. His wounds were beyond what his own people could have healed. Her belief he was a person who could help the Nimiipuu displaced any other objections to help him. The respect she had witnessed in his eyes led her to believe he did not see her people as animals to be slaughtered for fun.

"Could I have some more water? This bread is dry." His voice grew in strength as did his body.

She handed him the canteen.

"What's your name?" he asked after taking a drink.

"Sa-qan."

"Saw what?"

"It means bald eagle."

"Your light colored hair is about as white as a bald eagle's head. But who would name a girl bald eagle?" He shook his head and chewed some more, watching her.

His attitude toward a name The Creator bestowed upon her prickled annoyance across her shoulders.

"You look more like a Sadie, Susie, or—" Wade let the images of past women by these names fade. This woman was different in so many ways he couldn't compare her to others.

Wincing, he drew his body up, sitting with his back against the side of the cliff.

"Is your name Lieutenant?" she asked, once again changing the subject.

"Sort of. My military name is Lieutenant Wade Watts. My civilian name is Wade Andrew Watts."

"You have many names. You must be a good soldier. Only the bravest warriors have many names for all their brave actions."

She turned from him but not before he noticed her cheeks tinge a deeper red.

"I'd prefer it if you called me Wade. And I'll call you… Angel. I have a feeling you saved my life and with that white hair you look like an angel."

"I am Sa-qan. I do not want a so·yá·po name."

She folded her arms across her chest, pushing her breasts up, displaying a portion of their soft mounds through the neck opening in her buckskin dress.

"What is so·yá·po?" He did his best to try and pronounce the word the same as Angel.

"It is how we call the White man."

"Angel has been used as a name for women, but it means a spirit who floats in the clouds and delivers messages from our God to the mortals on earth."

Her body straightened, and her eyes narrowed, peering at him intently. "This is a name for a woman, a spirit, who flies?"

"Yes. Why does that make a difference?"

She smiled and his heart leapt into his throat. He thought her beautiful from the first moment he saw her standing in the river fiercely protecting the child, but watching her tense face relax and smile, he was smitten. A light and pleasing calm washed over him for the first time in a very long time. He could only bask in the moment briefly. *They were enemies.*

"I am from the sky, and I watch over the Nimiipuu." She nodded her head and flashed him with yet another smile. "You may call me Angel."

"Only if you call me Wade."

She nodded. "Let me check your wounds. You have moved around."

"Why are you taking such good care of me when your warriors left me for dead?"

Her sunshine gaze peered straight into his eyes. "You saved my niece at the village and the wounded from the Bannock scout. You do not have the thirst to kill like the other soldiers." She bowed her head and removed the blood encrusted bandage from his shoulder. "The Nimiipuu need you."

Her touch warmed his body, tingling the areas around his wounds. He glanced at her small, delicate hands hovering over his injuries. He shut his eyes, and then opened them. Her hands shimmered as if in a fog. His pain subsided, in fact, his body felt well rested.

A soft lyrical chant rose from her lips as she continued to hover her hands over his wounds. Her eyes remained closed, her light lashes resting on her sun-kissed cheeks. He'd never seen a woman as beautiful as this. He had to learn her true origins and return her to her family.

"Tell me about your childhood," he said.

Angel's chant faltered when he spoke, then faded. Her eyes opened, and her lips turned down in disapproval.

"You will be well enough tomorrow to climb down and wait for your soldiers." She leaned away from him, sitting on her heels.

Wade studied his wounds, from the angry red scar of the knife gash to the dark red indention of the bullet hole.

"How? How long have I been on this ledge?" Confident he hadn't been unconscious for several weeks he glared at the substantial healing of his wounds.

"Two suns." She stood and walked to the edge of the ledge.

"Two days?" He ran a hand over his arm and shoulder. Still a bit tender but otherwise healed. "How did I heal so quickly?"

"I know healing secrets." She kept her back to him as she stared out across the canyon.

"Were they taught to you by the Nez Perce?"

She gazed at him over her shoulder. Her eyes narrowed slightly resembling a cornered mountain lion. "Yes, my people have many healing ways the so·yá·po do not know."

"Are you sure they are your people? Could you have been abducted as a baby? Your coloring—"

"Is as it should be. My brothers both have the same color hair. We are of the Nimiipuu to the north. I am Nimiipuu. Why do you insist I am not?"

Wade ran a hand over his face. The prickling of his beard growth irritated as much as her insistence she was an Indian. "Couldn't your brothers have been abducted as well?"

She spun and stalked toward him. "I am Nimiipuu. I love my people and will do everything I can to save them from your people. Do not make me one of your people. My heart is with the Nimiipuu and will never be with the so·yá·po."

Sa-qan stared down at the man. The so·yá·po name he gave her earlier, expressing her true essence, gave her reason to think they could be friends. She wanted him to help her people. But his insistence she was not Nimiipuu raised her anger. He acted like all the rest, trying to change the Nimiipuu into a people they were not.

He held up his hands in surrender. "I see you won't be swayed. I just…nothing." He pushed up against the wall using it to lever his body to stand. When he stood, a good head taller than her with his broad shoulders leaning against the cliff, her body sagged remembering his weight as she carried him up to the ledge.

"Do not move around so much." She grasped his arm to keep him away from the edge of the ledge. She did not need him toppling off after she had healed him. Clinging to his strong arm, her stomach swirled like being tossed around in a storm. Her feet tangled, and his arm wrapped around her middle, keeping her from tumbling over the edge.

"Whoa, watch your footing."

His long, hard body pressed against her as he held her tight. Her heart beat like the cadence of a summer thunderstorm. She had never been held in the arms of a man. Tranquility and safety flowed within her, calming her heart, and sending sensations of heat and desire coursing through her body.

Something stroked her arm. She glanced down. His other hand moved up and down her arm, caressing. She tried to step away, but he continued to hold her, his chin resting on her head. His chest pressed against her with each intake of his breath, causing her body to yearn for something. Something she had feeling only he could help her find.

"Angel, I haven't held a woman other than a soiled dove in so long I forgot what one felt like." The sadness in his voice stalled her thoughts. "I was still a boy when I joined the army. I thought by going off and joining the North I was fighting for a good cause."

She detected his need to unburden his journey and remained locked in his safe embrace.

He snorted. "When I think of all the good men killed…what a waste." He sighed. "I'd never been keen on taking over my father's plantation, but when I rode back after the war…"

He swallowed loudly. "There was nothing left but the graves of my parents, sister, and two brothers. The slaves were all free and gone, the house and buildings burned."

His raspy voice laced with hurt tugged at her heart. He'd lost so much in one moment. Just like Summer Cloud had lost her daughter and grandson.

"There was nothing left for me, so I joined the cavalry. They needed officers out here, and I was looking for a place to belong." His hold slowly released, and he stepped back. "Sorry, you didn't need to know all that. I don't know why…I just needed to get it off my chest."

"It is good to cleanse the mind and body. We do it in the sweat lodge. The old man or woman of the sweat lodge chants and talks of things that ease your mind." Sa-qan stared into his sad eyes. His hard and lonely life dulled the dark pools. She knew the hardships that plagued him. Surrounded by and serving people you cannot get close to. She for fear of being discovered as a spirit, and he for fear he would lose them.

He raised an arm and sniffed. "I could use a bath."

"Tomorrow when you leave the ledge you can wash in the river."

His gaze flowed over her. "What about you?"

"I will rejoin my people."

"The wounded up the canyon?" He waved his good arm in the direction they had both traveled.

"No. The others need me now."

Sister, what are you doing with a so·yá·po? Wewukiye's question broke into her thoughts.

I will tell you tonight when he sleeps.

I will go nowhere until then.

Sa-qan stared at Wade. He watched her intently. She shook her head.

"You're not going to answer me?" he asked, taking a step toward her.

"Answer what?" She stepped away from him. Had Wewukiye seen them holding one another? If not, she dare not give him anything to lecture her about.

"How do you plan to catch up to the Nez Perce? You don't have a horse…do you?" He reached out, and she stepped away, his fingers grazed her arm sending her skin skittering.

"No, no horse."

"You'll never catch up with them. You should wait with me for General Howard."

"No! He speaks untruths and breaks promises." Did he believe in Cut Arm?

"He's doing what he's been ordered to do." Wade took another step toward her. His steps no longer wobbled. His body healed.

"How can he follow orders to kill the Nimiipuu? We are people, flesh and blood just as you. We are not so different if you took the time to learn instead of trying to change us. When we do not change your leaders say kill them." Her heart beat with contempt for a people who could care so little for others.

"We tried to live with the Indians, but they stole horses, took cattle, and stole food, not to mention killing." Wade stood toe to toe with her. His dark eyes blazed with indignation, his fists while clenched at his sides, showed his anger. She did not fear him. Instinct told her he would not harm her.

"The Nimiipuu have only killed those that provoke. They steal to eat and live when your people do not keep their promises. That is why they do not wish to live on a reservation. Your people promise a good life, then we see what those you promised get. None of the promises—only poor meat and disease. We are better to live where we were born." She nodded. "I have seen how those on reservations live."

He ran a hand through his hair and stared over her head. "I've seen some atrocious things at some reservations I've come across, but that isn't the government's fault, it's the crooked men in charge of the reservations."

"Can you promise a good man will be at the Nimiipuu reservation?" If there was hope the people could be spared, she would work to bring this slaughter to a halt.

He gazed in her eyes. The sorrow in the depths of his eyes stirred her heart. He cared what happened to the Nimiipuu.

"I can't promise a good man would be in charge of the reservation. I can't even promise you there won't be more bloodshed even if you're people were to surrender. They've got Major Howard in a fit." He raised a hand and cupped her cheek.

The warmth of his palm and softness in his eyes required extra effort to remember he was the enemy.

"Stay with me until my men return. I'll take you to the nearest town, and you can survive this chaos. No one will condemn you for being kidnapped."

She knocked his hand away. "I was not kidnapped. I am Nimiipuu!" His concern for her people compelled her to melt into his arms one moment, and then he insulted her and her people the next. She could not remain around him. Her senses became muddled.

Sa-qan scrambled down the side of the cliff. She needed distance. She needed to think and speak with Wewukiye.

"Angel! Come back. You'll get hurt."

Rocks clattered and rumbled. She glanced over her shoulder. Wade tumbled down the cliff behind her.

`Oylá-qc
(6)

Sa-qan's heart jumped into her throat. Rocks tumbled toward her. She shoved them away, clearing a path to Wade's still body. Blood covered his head and shirtless chest. She picked him up in her arms and carried him back to the ledge.

"Crazy man," she said, placing him back on the blanket and assessing his new injuries. A large gash on his head gushed blood down his face. She stopped the bleeding and placed her hands on his ribs to heal anything he might have hurt inside. Her fingers dipped into the contours of his muscles. He was such a fine figure of a man; why did he have to be a so·yá·po and not a Nimiipuu?

Is the soldier dead? Wewukiye's words in Sa-qan's head startled her from her thoughts.

No. I will make him sleep, and we can talk.

I will meet you by the river.

Sa-qan wet a section of Wade's undershirt and cleaned his head and face, removing the blood and dirt. Her fingers lingered, skimming over his nose and full lips. His face pleased her. Touching the soft skin of his lips sent shivers up her arms and bees abuzz in her chest.

The bugle of a bull elk reminded her Wewukiye waited by the river.

She sighed, stood, and shifted into a bald eagle. Sa-qan dropped off the ledge, opened her wings, and sailed down toward the river. What should she tell her brother about the man on the ledge?

Wewukiye stood as regal as ever beside the river. His large antlers and thick brown coat shimmered in the sunlight. Sa-qan landed in a tree not far from the riverbank. Her brother walked with grace and elegance as he joined her.

"Why have you wasted time with a soldier?" He did not give her a chance to ask about his wife and her daughter, Dove and Girl of Many Hearts.

"I do not feel I am wasting time saving a man who does not view the Nimiipuu as animals. By helping him I am giving our people a voice in the soldiers." She peered down her beak at her brother. He would not make more of this than it was. By saving the man she could save the Nimiipuu.

Wewukiye stared back. "I saw you in mortal form embracing the man." He tipped his head and peered closer. "You have always said to stay away from mortals, especially while in mortal form. You lectured both Himiin and I when we showed ourselves. How is it different for you?"

"This is the only way I know to help. To stop the soldiers from killing." She hopped to the ground and paced, avoiding his eyes. "This soldier stopped another from killing Girl of Many Hearts. Later, when I healed two warriors and children, he stopped a Bannock scout from hurting us." She spun, peering into her brother's eyes. "He does not want to kill us all. He is only following his duty."

Wewukiye walked close and lowered his head, gazing into her eyes. "You cannot feel anything for this man. He is the enemy. He is not Nimiipuu."

"I—I do not feel anything."

Wewukiye snorted. "It is in your denial. Come with me now. Get away from him before you cannot think like a Nimiipuu or a spirit."

"I plan to return to the band tomorrow. Last night I saw the soldiers with Cut Arm coming this way. I will help the soldier down here by the river and then I will leave."

"If he is well enough to travel he no longer needs you."

Wewukiye's insinuating tone dug into her like a stick in her ribs.

"He was healed until he fell down the cliff just now." She stood tall and glared at her brother. "I will remain with him until tomorrow." She spread her wings to return to the ledge. "Dove and Girl of Many Hearts are well?"

"Yes," he said through clenched teeth.

"Good. I will see them tomorrow." Sa-qan jumped in the air and flapped her wings, ignoring the niggling that her brother was right. She should leave now and not allow the soldier's words and actions to sway her judgment of him or those chasing the Nimiipuu.

«»«»«»

Wade opened his eyes. The bright sunlight blinded him. He blinked and focused on a bald eagle flapping its wings to land on the ledge. The color of its head reminded him of Angel's hair. His mind cleared, and he stared into the bird's eyes. The held a familiar gentleness.

I must have hit my head hard. He squeezed his eyes shut, then opened them. How did he get back on the ledge? The eagle flapped its wings and jumped into the air, disappearing over the edge.

Angel had stormed down the side of the cliff, he'd gone after her, and slipped…He remembered knocking rocks loose and…Oh God, could Angel be lying below hurt? Wade scrambled to his knees and bracing against the cliff, stood.

"Angel!" He wobbled toward the edge. "Angel!" If something happened to her…he couldn't bear the thought of another person's death on his hands. Especially not her. The more time he spent with her, the more he didn't want anything to happen to the feisty woman. "Angel!"

"I am here. Do not fall off the cliff again."

Her soft voice drifted to his ears as her head appeared above the side of the ledge. The frantic beating of his heart slowed. Dizziness swept through his head and weakened his legs.

Angel grasped his arm and led him back to the blanket. "Sit. You are not strong."

"Are you all right?" He traced his fingers over her face and down her arms seeking wounds. "Did the rocks I knocked loose hit you?

53

How did I get back up here?" He gathered her into an embrace. His heart raced faster when she didn't fight his arms drawing her close.

"The rocks did not harm me. You are lucky you were not hurt worse." Her arms wrapped around him, and her head snuggled against his chest.

Bliss. He could hold this woman in his arms and be content for the rest of his life. They argued but it wasn't fighting. Coming from two different places, they tried to make the other understand their point of view. And then this—the comfort and belonging he experienced when she wrapped her arms around him.

"I still find it hard to believe you're an Indian"—she stiffened and started to pull away—"but, I'll stop arguing with you." He grasped her chin, tilting her face into view. The uncertainty in her eyes jerked his protective instincts out.

"I don't want anything to happen to you. The thought the rocks I dislodged could have hit you…" He smoothed his thumb back and forth across her soft cheek. "I could never live with myself if I caused you any kind of harm. You've done so much for me."

"You could never harm me."

The sincerity glistening in her eyes made him wonder if she held any of the emotions raging inside him. He dipped his head, touching her enticing lips. Soft. So soft. He brushed his lips gently across hers. Her body stiffening brought the realization she'd never been kissed.

Wade lifted his head only enough to peer into her eyes. "Thank you for healing me and saving me again today." He placed another chaste kiss on her lips and gazed at her, again. His body ached to deepen the kiss and explore her essence.

She relaxed in his arms. "I helped you for saving my niece. You have a good heart."

"I saved you, too. You stood between the rifle and your niece." He drew her tighter. "All that death could've been avoided. I'm glad I came along and you and your niece were spared."

Her small hands grasped his face. "These feelings you have are why I saved you. You can help my people. You are more than a soldier. You can talk to the leaders." Her eyes searched his before they closed, and she pressed her lips to his.

He had to tell her he didn't have a chance in hell to change the minds of the higher ranking officers. Her mouth pressed to his, muddied his thoughts. He pulled her tight and skimmed his tongue along the seam of her lips, coaxing her to open and share more.

Her lips parted, and he slipped his tongue in. Desire unlike anything he'd ever experienced before rocked him as if the earth shook. And her taste. Sweeter than sugar and twice as addictive.

Her tentative exploration of his mouth stilled his movements.

Angel's fingers slid into his hair, holding him in the kiss. A sigh floated in the air. The last time he'd kissed an innocent woman he'd been just as innocent. The day before he headed to war, he and Jenny Small kissed behind her barn. A heated coming together of two youths who hadn't a clue what they wanted.

Wade renewed his side of the kiss. He knew what he wanted. To show her she meant more to him than saving his life. Since the first time he saw her, she'd been foremost in his thoughts. Never had a woman plagued him so. He'd take the comfort she gave and hope when they parted tomorrow it would be enough to get him through this latest campaign.

Her palms pushed against his chest. His arms tightened, unwilling to let her go.

"No." Her soft, calm voice along with her breaking their kiss slammed the reality of their situation back into his head.

He released her and stepped back. His warm lips buzzed from the contact. "I'm sorry. I didn't—"

She placed two fingers on his lips. "You did nothing wrong. Rest while I make soup." Her plump lips and heightened color on her cheeks were a reminder they'd just kissed. Her gaze drifted to his lips before she walked to the small fire pit and knelt.

"I can help," he offered, taking a step.

"No. It is best you stay there and I stay here." She didn't glance his direction but set to the task of enticing the coals in the fire to catch on the bark steeple over the white ashes. Her pursed lips blowing on the ashes shot heat through his body. The kiss they'd shared would be burned in his memory.

"You never did explain how you plan to catch up to the band when the army hasn't made it yet." This was a good topic to chill the yearning growing in his body.

She poured water from the canteen into a tin cup and tossed in two pieces of dried meat. "I have my ways."

Her confident tone curved his lips into a smile. "I would think to catch up with the tribe you would need wings."

She peered at him over her shoulder. Her eyes twinkled, and her lips tipped in a sassy smile. "That is a good idea."

He shook his head and smiled. He liked this playful personality, but he also liked the serious Angel. The one who stood up to him when he questioned her about the tribe.

Sa-qan ducked her head as if studying the soup and touched her lips with her fingers. She never knew kissing could heat a body so and leave one almost floating off the ground, much like flying. The safety she experienced in Wade's arms blossomed with the touching of their lips. Happiness, greater than she had ever experienced before, swirled in her chest. The last time she remembered wanting to giggle from happiness happened before she became a spirit.

How could she be this happy when the existence of the Nimiipuu grew more and more threatened? This thought sucked the happiness from her. She studied Wade sitting against the cliff, his eyes watching her. A goofy smile peeked out from under that soft patch of hair on his upper lip. The contrast of the short prickly hair on his cheeks and the softness of the long hair on his face had surprised and pleased her.

She liked too many things about this man. And had too many reasons to stay away from him. She would leave tonight when he slept. He had enough wood and water to last him until Cut Arm arrived.

Sorrow replaced the earlier elation. Even knowing it was best to leave, her decision weighed heavy. She enjoyed talking with the lieutenant. Sa-qan touched her lips again. She enjoyed many things about the man.

The water boiled, changing the liquid to light brown. The meat plumped. She pulled it from the water and using a rock and Wade's knife, cut it in bite-sized pieces. She returned the cut meat to the soup and placed the cup out of the flames to cool.

Her hands fluttered on her lap with nothing to occupy her.

"How come I never see you eat?" Wade's brow wrinkled in a frown.

"I eat when you are sleeping." Now that he was healed she would have to be more careful. He was more perceptive of what went on around him.

He continued to watch her closely. "When do you sleep?"

"In between caring for you."

"I've been a lot of work." He ran a hand over the hair on his lip.

"No more than any other wounded warrior." She knelt beside him. "Is there a name for the hair on your face?"

His hand smoothed the hair once more. "This?"

She nodded. Her fingers itched to reach out and touch the softness of it one more time before she left.

"Mustache." His gaze hovered over her face. "Do you like it?"

She nodded. "Nimiipuu men do not have hair on their faces. Why do you have scratchy hair here"—she touched his prickly cheek—"and it is soft here?" Her finger trailed over to the mustache.

"If I allowed this part to grow"—he captured her hand, placing the palm on his cheek—"it would be as soft as the mustache."

Sa-qan scrunched her face. "You would look like an animal if all of your face had hair."

"I agree. That's why I usually shave. But as you know I've not been up to the task lately."

Her palm heated from the wet kiss he placed in it. The heat of his breath, softness of his mustache on her fingers, and the glimmer in his eyes lit a warm glow in her chest.

"You will forever be in my memory." His deep voice and sincere gaze quivered her insides.

"Your soup is ready." Sa-qan stood, pulling her hand from his and putting distance between their bodies again. She knew only what she saw of animals and the Nimiipuu mating. But she grew certain the internal fire burning in her core had to do with wanting to mate with this man. She must leave as soon as possible. The consequences of going so far with a mortal were shown to her firsthand through her brothers. First Himiin becoming mortal to be with Wren, and then the anguish Wewukiye struggled through when he thought he had lost Dove.

She would not allow a mortal to come between her and the Nimiipuu. That would not happen to her. Her life was protecting the Nimiipuu, not a soldier—the enemy.

Sa-qan placed the tin cup in his hands and walked to the edge. "I am leaving now. When you feel strong enough, walk down the cliff. Cut Arm will be here in one sun."

"Where are you going?"

His tone caused her to glance over her shoulder. The worry lines framing his dark eyes stabbed her with guilt. "To my people." She watched her feet as she stepped off the ledge.

"It'll be dark soon. Wait until morning when it's safer." His voice followed her down the slope.

I must go now.

Emptiness poured into her soul with each step. But she could not remain with him and protect the Nimiipuu.

Far down the cliff side where he could not see her, she shifted into an eagle and soared into the sky. She flew one pass over the ledge and wished she had not. Wade sat alone and sad, sipping the soup. Her wings faltered. Pushing her emotions deep inside where they would have to struggle to emerge again, she flew toward the Nimiipuu. They were all she needed.

`Uyne'-pt
(7)

Wade slept fitfully. How would Angel catch up to the Nez Perce? She couldn't travel fast enough on foot to catch them. And the fact she could be found by warriors, civilians, or soldiers…his mind played tricks on him all night as he dreamed of the many disasters she could encounter.

Even though he doubted she knew when General Howard and his regiment would arrive, he'd spent the greater part of the morning slowly descending the cliff. How the hell that small woman managed to get him on that ledge stumped him. He doubted he could've carried her up there without having to stop many times.

He'd lugged his saddlebag and personal items down off the ledge. His strength ebbed while descending the cliff, but now, as he stood by the river it slowly returned. He found a spot with easy access to the water to wash and shave. No one would believe he was shot at close range three days ago. The bloody hole in his shirt and the red circle in his shoulder were the only proof he had of the wound. How Angel healed him so fast added another puzzle to the woman.

His stomach growled. He dug in the saddle bag and pulled out hardtack. Chewing on the biscuit brought back moments with Angel. Good memories didn't come often to him. She had given him light in a life that had become dark. A knot formed in his throat, and he choked on the dry food. His eyes burned from unshed tears. How could one person—the enemy—bring him such joy? One thing he knew for sure, if he ran across her again he would not let her go. Her insistence she was Nez Perce put her in danger.

He smiled and ate the remaining biscuit, replaying every moment he spent with the extraordinary woman.

The sounds of an advancing unit drifted through the canyon fifteen minutes before he caught a glimpse of the forward garrison. The scouts must've gone through before he made it down the cliff. Otherwise they would have noticed him struggling on the cliff side.

His heart stopped. What about Angel? Would she be able to hide from the scouts?

"Lt. Watts? Your men said you'd been killed." General Howard reined his horse up alongside Wade.

"Nearly killed, sir. As you can see, I'm well and have been awaiting your arrival since I'm a cavalry officer without a mount." Thoughts of Angel couldn't scatter his thinking. Especially if he planned to keep her safe.

"Corporal Smith, ride to the back and find a suitable mount for the lieutenant." General Howard dismounted. "The rest of you water the horses."

Howard walked up to Wade, scrutinizing his uniform. "A shoulder wound. Well enough to ride?" Howard waved his only arm toward the hole in Wade's uniform.

"Yes." He wasn't going to tell Howard about his nurse. The general would ask questions he couldn't or wouldn't answer.

"Have you seen any Indian activity?"

"Only the two who shot me and Private Trainor and the wounded my men and I came upon a day's ride from here. You should've passed them." He hoped they hadn't been brought along.

"We didn't see any wounded where Private Marks indicated you encountered them." The general studied him as he sent up a silent thank you. He'd hoped the group had managed to move on. If Angel had worked her healing magic on them they should've been able to travel.

"How is it your men thought you dead when you seem to be in better health than most of my men?" Howard accepted an opened canteen handed to him by an aide.

"After being shot I must have been delirious and wandered off, I guess. All I know is I came to and found a fresh mound of dirt I suspected covered Trainor and my belongings scattered. Without a mount, I rested and nursed my injuries." The lie set heavy and sour in his belly, but he'd never disclose his infatuation with Angel or the fact she was headed to the Nez Perce. Instead, he prayed she had a safe journey and stayed far from skirmishes he knew were yet to come. If even a quarter of the Nez Perce had as strong beliefs as Angel, heaven help the Army.

"I see." Howard still watched him intently.

Smith rode up leading a sorrel gelding.

Wade tied his saddlebag on behind the saddle and mounted. The strong animal under him gave him the mobility he desired. He'd spent too many years on the back of these animals to want to join the ranks of the infantry.

"Thank you, General. I'll go find my men." Wade saluted the officer and rode through the ranks peering at the faces, searching for his men.

"Lieutenant Watts?" Private Marks shot out of line, his horse stopping next to Wade's. "Where did you come from? We thought…"

Wade told Marks the same story he told the general.

"You look rested." Jealousy sprouted in Marks's voice.

"I figured it was better for a cavalry man to stay put and wait for a horse than take off walking." He scanned his beleaguered troop. "I wish I could give you all a rest"—the bugle blew to move out—"but it looks like we're on the move."

The regiment moved out. Wade slipped his horse into the formation and studied as much of the regiment as he could see. From the sagging bodies and sporadic conversations of the mounted forces and the wagons overflowing with foot soldiers this campaign had the men worn out. Now he knew why the General was so quick to notice his good health.

The next time they met the Nez Perce it would be interesting to see if their spirits and animals fared the same as these troops.

«»«»«»

Sa-qan followed a trail that sickened her heart. In the path of the fleeing Nimiipuu, White men had been killed. She caught up to the gathered bands and circled above the camp. The makeshift dwellings and poor supplies frustrated her. The once proud and wealthy Nimiipuu lived on meager supplies and hunted for shelter. The wounded lay upon travois ready to be moved if the soldiers arrived.

I am here, she said to Wewukiye.

We are watching from the north.

She circled and found her brother and his wife, in their elk forms, milling around in the tree line. Sa-qan landed in a pine tree and studied Wewukiye and Dove's nervous actions.

"What has happened?" She ruffled her feathers and settled in for an update on the group.

"Lemhi warriors followed the Nimiipuu and cut out almost a hundred horses yesterday." Wewukiye stopped his agitated stomping and stared at her. "And there are those among the younger warriors who have been using the massacre of our women and children as a reason to kill every so·yá·po they find."

"I have witnessed this. It will only anger the soldiers more." She shook her head as her heart ached for her people. "We have to find a way to stop the killing. Someone has to speak to the leaders."

Wewukiye stared at her. "How? We cannot show ourselves."

"But we can enter those that lead." The risk outweighed the outcome. With emotions so high and bodies improperly fed, entering a leader and having them act out of the ordinary could bring suspicion on them from others.

"Who? And what would we have them say?" Dove stepped beside Wewukiye, her big brown eyes shimmering with hope.

Sa-qan knew her sister feared for Girl of Many Hearts and those that kept her well.

"Looking Glass, Joseph, and Lean Elk." Sa-qan studied the two elk. "They are the strongest leaders. Those are the three we will enter. If they are united in not harming the so·yá·po then the warriors will not do so with such abandon."

Wewukiye nodded. "It may work. The three of us cannot keep up with every warrior who has anger in his heart."

"I agree," Sa-an flapped her wings. "I will take Joseph. Wewukiye, you take Looking Glass, Dove, you enter Lean Elk." She thought a minute. "We will bring them together in discussion then have them speak to everyone. That way it will appear more like a combined decision."

"Agreed," Wewukiye said, shifting to smoke.

"I believe this is the only way," Dove said as her body faded and smoke drifted into the sky.

"Me, too." Sa-qan shifted and floated toward the camp, seeking Joseph.

She found the leader of the Lake Nimiipuu surrounded by what was left of his family. She slipped into his body. Joseph's emotions hit her swift and deep. Fear, anger, love, and strongest of all, survival. He would do whatever it took to keep his people alive and prospering. To keep the promise he made to his father of never giving up their home at the Wallowas. His fierce loyalty to his people hummed through his body.

To keep them alive I must make sure no more innocent so·yá·po are killed. Sa-qan fed this thought into his mind.

"I must talk with Looking Glass and Lean Elk," Joseph said, rising and walking toward the center of the encampment. Sa-qan kept his gait unhurried and stopped here and there to allow him to ask after wounded members of the band.

His resistance to her manipulations stuttered his footsteps when Looking Glass and Lean Elk both walked to the center of the encampment. *How did they know I wished to speak to them?* His internal question and suspicious probing of his mind made her wonder if he realized he was being manipulated.

The three leaders greeted one another and discussed their concerns over the young warriors anger and the killing of so·yá·po who did not hinder the Nimiipuu's journey.

Looking Glass called over a young boy and ordered him to have all the warriors in camp come to them.

Our plan is working. Wewukiye communicated to Sa-qan.

Do not celebrate yet. The warriors still need to agree.

The warriors arrived, talking among themselves and eyeing the three leaders standing side by side their arms crossed watching the gathering.

Looking Glass raised his arms. "We are concerned your anger

could cause more pain for our people."

Grumbling and narrowed stares peered at the leaders.

Sa-qan nudged Joseph. All knew he loved the people and cared deeply for their well-being.

"We know the evil and hatred in the hearts of the so·yá·po for our people. It was witnessed seven suns ago when the soldiers swept through our camp killing women, children, and our honored old ones."

Angry shouts and mumbling rolled through the gathered crowd.

"The Nimiipuu do not kill women and children, we have honor. Honor that cannot be stripped from us by the so·yá·po." Joseph peered at the group of warriors. His sadness swallowed Sa-qan, pulling on her txiy̓ak, draining her. "When we kill the so·yá·po men for no reason, we become like soldiers. Warriors do not kill unless they are defending their people. When you come upon a so·yá·po, think: Am I a Nimiipuu warrior or a soldier? Do not kill unless our people are in danger."

"Joseph speaks for your leaders. We must not kill unless the people are threatened." Looking Glass swept his arms open wide. "We must be united in this to reach our freedom."

Some warriors nodded others mumbled and wandered away. Sa-qan drifted out of Joseph, slipping through the crowd, and judging the reactions of the warriors. Some agreed with the leaders, others thought the leaders weak. She could do nothing more, only hope the warriors heeded the leader's words. She hurried from the camp and shifted to a bald eagle, returning to the area where she met Weukiye and Dove.

"Do you think it will help?" Dove asked, trotting up under the tree.

"It will not stop all the killing." Sa-qan remembered the sadness, anger, and desperation in Joseph and realized each Nimiipuu in the camp felt the same. "We can only hope some warriors will think of our people before killing a so·yá·po."

"Wewukiye told me you have made friends with a soldier."

Dove's comment took Sa-qan by surprise. She should have known her brother would not keep anything from his wife.

"Is it wise?"

"Is what wise?" Wewukiye asked, trotting up to the two of them.

"Your sister being friends with a soldier."

He leveled his narrowed blue eyes on her. "It is not wise. I hope you do not plan to show yourself to him again."

Sa-qan had no plans of talking with Wade again, unless necessary to save the people. But her brother's disapproval only made her wish for Wade's accepting company. "I will not seek him out. But should his life be in danger or he can help the Nimiipuu, I will see he comes to no harm."

"You cannot expect anything other than treachery from a soldier." Wewukiye swung his massive antlers and rattled the tree limbs above him.

Sa-qan spread her wings. Her brother would never understand that they may need the help of someone like Wade to save the Nimiipuu. "I am going to see if there are any soldiers nearby." She leapt into the air and soared toward the setting sun. Her head wanted the soldiers to never catch up with the Nimiipuu, but the new emotions swirling in her hoped to spend more time with a certain soldier.

With that thought first in her mind, she soared back toward the ravine to make sure Wade safely climbed down off the ledge. Would she show herself to him if she found him alone? Her heart picked up speed. It was wrong to crave a kiss from the enemy. But the contentment of his arms around her and the bliss of his lips upon hers…she closed her eyes and reveled in the security and happiness his arms brought to her.

Opening her eyes, she scanned the landscape below. She could allow herself nothing more than memories. Wade was the enemy and a mortal. Both entities that could never learn her true identity. She had to keep her distance to make sure that did not happen. Loneliness had not made itself known to her until spending time with the lieutenant.

But she must remain alone and do what the Creator expected of her.

Save the Nimiipuu.

`Oyma`tat
(8)

Wade spent five long days in the saddle with brief rests at night as Howard pressed the troops forward at a grueling pace. Weariness etched the troops' faces as their bodies weaved in their saddles on fatigued horses. The lethargic movements didn't deter the commanding officer.

The company halted, and Wade urged his tired horse up beside the other officers. A path of trodden vegetation from fifty to one hundred and fifty feet wide proved they stood on the trail of the Nez Perce. Grooves in the ground from the travois pulling the wounded marked a path between multiple horse hoof prints. Wade peered into the distance and a cloud of dust could be seen giving away the location of the tribe.

"Is that a signal of some kind?" An officer pointed to a cone-shaped stack of horse droppings.

"They are saying soldiers are lower than horse droppings," one Bannock scout said.

Wade hadn't seen this before and couldn't refute or encourage the comment. General Howard believed the scout and took offense to the reference.

The company continued at an increased speed, pushing the tired animals and men to their limits. Wade noticed fresh earth mounds scattered along the trail. He shook his head, wishing there was a way to convince the Indians to surrender before more deaths ensued. But he knew by the vengeance glinting in Howard's eyes, the general wouldn't take a peaceful surrender. He wanted to prove his might to the Indians.

They camped at a meadow with several streams bisecting the flat areas. The companies and civilian groups of nearly two hundred and fifty men spread out across the meadow, some animals staked between camps, others grazed between the creeks. Some pitched tents while others, too tired to care, slept under the wagons.

Though exhausted, Wade couldn't keep a blonde woman from his thoughts. How could he make sure no harm came to her? Especially when she was bent on staying with the very people they intended to incarcerate on a reservation?

Dreams finally took him from his thoughts but held him captive remembering Angel's warm body and sweet kisses.

A volley of rifle shots woke Wade. He grabbed his weapons and crouched on his blanket peering into the growing light of dawn as men scrambled for cover amid shouts and curses. The sound of stampeding hooves reverberated in the crisp morning air. His blood pumped, and his survival instinct kept him low to the ground as the volley of shots continued. The camp was surrounded. Bullets whistled through the air from all directions. Soldiers grabbed their rifles and dove for the willow thickets along the streams, finding cover wherever they could.

Wade rallied his men, keeping them low as they returned fire.

The exchange filled the air with loud booms, acrid gunpowder smoke, and the tang of fear. The crack and whistle of the volley waned and stopped.

Wade worked his way to the general's tent. Mounted on his horse, the general shouted orders. He spotted Wade and waved him over.

"The heathens stole our mules. Gather your men and go after them."

Wade nodded and strode back to his troop. "Gather your horses, we're going after the mules."

Private Marks returned leading a mount for Wade.

He nodded and climbed onto the saddle. "Trumpeter, sound the chase."

The cloud of dust the mule herd stirred fashioned an excellent flag. The troop headed out at a lope following the billowing cloud.

«»«»«»

Sa-qan watched from above as Wade led a group of soldiers after the animals stolen by the Nimiipuu. A confrontation would happen when they caught up. One she could do nothing about. Fear struck her at the thought Wade would be in the forefront of the altercation. She could not enter his body. Having experienced the closeness they held, he would know she was within him. He must stay alive and well. Her generations as a spirit told her he was the key to the Nimiipuu's future.

Creator, help me. How can I keep this mortal alive to help our people? Frustration over the Creator's lack of communication since the beginning of this journey clouded her mind. *Why have you left me to do this alone*? The Creator's silence worried her. Had he found disfavor with her for showing herself to Girl of Many Hearts? If so would he not have reprimanded rather than ignored her calls? Was his silence confirming her actions or discounting them? Confusion swirled in her head, weakening her wings. Her body plummeted downward before she flapped her wings and caught a breeze to carry her toward the stopped Nimiipuu warriors.

Warriors talked with their arms flailing and their voices rising on the morning air.

"We stole mules."

"It was dark."

"Now we know why the animals were not well guarded."

"What do we do with them?"

"This will slow the soldiers. They need these animals to carry their supplies," Frog said, approaching the arguing warriors. "This will give our people time to get ahead of Cut Arm."

"Horses would be better. They travel faster and are less troublesome." The warrior from Looking Glass's band stood nearly toe to toe with Frog.

"We did not get horses. We will take advantage of what we did steal." Frog waved for the group to continue.

The Nimiipuu started herding the animals, but the soldiers caught up and managed to cut out some of the mules and horses only to lose them back in the herd following after the warriors. Sa-qan wished she could will the horses carrying the warriors to move faster and the soldiers' horses slower. She did not want the confrontation to happen, but knew of no way to stop the soldiers or hide the Nimiipuu.

In an area of timbered rocky ridges a good distance over, the majority of the warriors found cover and shot at the soldiers as they rode into view. Other warriors continued to drive the mules toward the band. The soldiers leaped from their horses and sought cover. Several men led the saddled animals some distance away in the shelter of trees.

Sa-qan found a vantage point in the top of a tree to keep an eye on Wade. Her heart raced erratically when her keen sight noticed the warriors purposely picked off the officers.

The Nimiipuu began creeping forward under the cover of the bushes, trees, and boulders. One by one a soldier of leadership would fall back from a shot that rang out from a rock outcropping close to the soldiers' trenches.

She had to warn Wade. He must not wear the clothing of the soldier leaders. Her instincts did not allow her to hurt a Nimiipuu, but she could not let a warrior creeping toward Wade injure him. If he delivered a fatal shot, she could not help Wade. Sa-qan leaped in the air and soared down to the warrior, snatching the rifle from his hands and carrying it to the waiting Nimiipuu horses. Sa-qan dropped the weapon and flew back to her perch. She shuffled her weight from foot to foot as her mind searched for a way to warn Wade.

The warrior she disarmed remained hidden in the spot where she snatched the gun. His eyes wide. His lips moving. She hoped his chat with himself allayed his fear.

She couldn't disarm every warrior that aimed at Wade. Fear squeezed her chest. How could she save him, other than take him from all of this? That was it. She should have never let him return to the soldiers chasing the Nimiipuu. She should have talked him into…what? He was a soldier as much as the Nimiipuu warriors prided themselves of their status.

Another warrior crept toward Wade's rocky barricade. The other soldiers were slowly withdrawing as well as the majority of the warriors. She had to make the warrior change his mind. Shifting from her eagle form, Sa-qan floated down and into the warrior. With as much stealth as he used to get near Wade's hiding spot, she maneuvered the warrior back to his horse and the retreating warriors. Once the warrior sat on the back of his horse, she slipped from his body and drifted through the trees shifting into an eagle again and watching after her soldier.

Wade maneuvered back to his horse and mounted. The troops gathered their wounded to return to General Howard. Wade found Private Marks helping an injured man onto a horse.

"Private, get our troop and wounded back to the general." Wade pulled the head of his horse around.

Marks put a hand on his leg. "Sir, where are you going?"

"I'm going to follow and see what I can learn. One person can maneuver through their sentries easier than a whole platoon." He shifted his leg, dropping the private's hand. "Tell the general I'll bring back information."

"That's what the scouts are for," Private Marks said. His eyes and tone suggested Wade planned a suicide mission.

"I don't trust the Bannock scouts." Wade nudged his mount forward. The horse proved as tired as he felt, but he'd determined while hunkered down behind that lava bluff there had to be a way to stop the bloodshed. If he could find Angel maybe the two of them could put their heads together and find the resolution.

"Lieutenant Watts. The Indians are retreating."

Wade drew back the reins and shifted in the saddle. Captain Carr watched him.

"Sir, I'm going to follow and see what I can learn."

The captain glared at him through tired eyes. "If I didn't know your record, I'd say you were running."

"No sir, not running. I'm tired of relying on scouts. If the Indians were this close to steal our horses and mules then the whole group can't be that far." They were, in fact, by his calculations heading into the newly formed Yellowstone Park.

"How do you propose to let us know when you've found them?" The captain's body sagged as he continued to hinder Wade's departure.

"I'm not sure, but one man alone can infiltrate the scouts they send out far easier than a party of riders."

"Agreed, but it makes getting information back to us a problem." The captain straightened and kneed his horse into a walk. "I think this is a dilemma best settled by General Howard."

"Not to be disrespectful, sir. But I've already made up my mind. Tell the general I'll be back with news when I have some." Wade dug the heels of his boots into the horse's ribs and loped in the direction the Indians disappeared.

He didn't hear the sound of horses racing after him. That meant Captain Carr had allowed him to chase his folly or what Private Marks dubbed his suicide mission.

Once he loped a good distance from the ambush area, he slowed his horse to a walk and searched the ground for signs of the mule herd and the area around him for straggling warriors. He knew his decision wasn't a wise one by military standards or even by the standards of any sane person. But he had to find Angel and ultimately find a way to help her and the people she believed were her family. His conscience couldn't live with all the killing. He'd had enough.

Wade followed the wide path of trampled grass and bushes throughout the day, resting his horse in secluded areas to avoid being seen by Nez Perce scouts. As the afternoon sun slid lower in the sky, he caught sight of a plume of dust headed northeast. It had to be either the stolen mules or the Nez Perce. He knew how fatigued the troops and their animals had become. What must the Indians be experiencing with their wounded, women, and children to keep moving at a rushed pace?

His horse wobbled under him. Wade stopped, dismounted, and led the poor creature to water. He scanned the area for grass to feed his horse. He'd have to live off of small creatures he could snare and the rations in his saddlebag. Shooting his rifle for food would not only waste ammunition it could signal his location to Nez Perce scouts.

The horse slurped from the trickling creek, and Wade loosened the cinch, tugging the saddle off and placing it at the base of a tree. For the first time in months the tightness in his shoulders eased with each camp activity he performed. He only had to worry about his own safety not that of nearly one hundred men. The relieved pressure didn't lessen his vigilance. Being alone, while having its own virtues, also meant he was the only sentry.

He tied a line between two trees where a fair amount of grass grew and tethered his horse to the line. Setting a snare took less time than scrounging up small dry twigs to make a smokeless fire. The coffee had brewed when a rabbit squealed. Wade jogged to the snare and found a full grown hare caught by the leg. He killed the animal, skinned it, and had it roasting over the fire by the time darkness dropped over his small camp. Roast rabbit would taste a lot better than beans.

Wade leaned back against a tree, his legs stretched out toward the fire. His ears listened to all the night sounds. From years of outdoor living he knew the difference between peaceful night noises and the danger that lurked in silence.

He leaned forward and cut a leg from the cooked carcass. The chorus of frogs stilled. He craned his neck, listening. The sounds renewed. His stopped heart pumped again, booming in his ears.

A twig snapped behind him as a hand settled on his shoulder. Adrenaline pumped through his veins. He grasped the hand, rolled, and landed atop the intruder.

Ku`yc
(9)

Sa-qan gasped for air. She lay on the ground staring into Wade's baffled face. She had not thought what Wade would do when she came up behind him.

"Angel, what…" His grip on her wrists loosened, but remained.

The confusion in his eyes and stunned silence twitched her lips into a smile. "I came to talk with you."

"How did you find me? Are you camped near here?"

She did not mind his hands holding her or his body resting on her hips as he straddled her. The way his gaze slid across her face and hovered on her lips, she wondered if he thought of their kisses as well.

"We must talk." She had to remember why she had followed him. To advise him not to wear this shirt into battle.

"Are you alone?" He released her and touched her cheek with the back of his hand. "You shouldn't be out here by yourself. It's dangerous."

She held his knuckles to her cheek. Heat scorched her skin and traveled down her body to settle in her center.

The horse nickered. Wade's strong arms pulled her to her feet, and he pushed her behind him as he stared into the darkness beyond his small fire.

She clutched his shirt and listened. Before landing she had

searched the area for warriors. None had traveled this far back. "You should not camp on the trail," she said in a whisper. "The warriors check the back trail often."

The horse resumed eating. Wade faced her, wrapping his arms around her.

"Is that how you found me?" His hushed voice warmed her ear.

"I came to warn you not to wear the clothes of an officer when in battle. The warriors know it upsets the other soldiers when a leader is killed." She ran her hands over the fancy decorations on his shirt.

He hugged her tight. "I can't hide what I am. It would look cowardly to the men under me."

"I do not wish anything to happen to you." Her fear for him warbled her words.

"But I have to do my duty. I don't want anything to happen to you either." His hands held her head. "You have ignored all my questions. I need answers."

"I…" She licked her lips and stared into his eyes. His fingers gently caressing the sides of her head weakened her knees. She had to keep her wits about her. To tell him the truth would put her in disfavor with the Creator and possibly hinder she and Wade working together to help the Nimiipuu.

She grasped his wrists and drew his hands away from her face. Any connection with him ignited her body with sensations she did not understand. She led him to the tree where his belongings sat. Sitting, she urged him down beside her.

"Why are you avoiding my questions?" He sat, slipping his arm around her shoulders, tucking her body next to his.

His warmth and strength seeped into her, expanding her heart and bringing a song.

"I cannot tell you what you ask. I am a wanderer. I do not live with the Nimiipuu you chase. But I have seen the fighting and do not wish you to be hurt, again." She snuggled deeper into his arms. What she said held the truth. She could not let him draw more from her.

His warm breath heated the top of her head. "If you don't live with the Nimiipuu why did I find you with your niece in the Nimiipuu camp?" He kissed the top of her head. "And then with the wounded children and old men?"

He would be hard to convince. He had a strong mind.

"It is my duty."

His hand tipped her face up toward his. "How did you find me tonight? Know I looked for you?"

Her heart sung with gladness. "You were looking for me?"

"Yes." His face grew near.

She knew he could not see her eyes in the darkness, but she could see everything about him. And his eyes shone with desire and concern.

"Why did you seek me?"

"To make sure you were safe and to see if together we could figure out a way to stop the killing." His face drew back and his body stiffened.

She placed her hands on his cheeks. "It is not your fault." The sadness in his eyes spoke of more than the soldiers chasing the Nimiipuu. His body held much sadness and pain.

He shifted, securing her back under his arm and next to his side. His heart beat against the hand she placed on his chest. "You're the first person in fifteen years I feel I can talk to." His arm tightened around her. "And in actuality you're the enemy, something I've been chasing those fifteen years."

She pushed out of his arms. The way his hands fell to his side, indicated he gave her permission to harm him.

"I am not your enemy. Did I not heal you and protect you?"

Confusion once again settled in his brown eyes. "Yes. You said because I saved you and your niece. What do you mean you protect me?" He captured her hand. "I should protect you. But when you keep saying you aren't a captive I can't take you back to the camp and keep you safe."

She blew frustration out on a huff. "I am not a captive."

"But you could say you are and be safe." His eyes pleaded.

"I will not lie and leave my people." His concern for her touched her, but she could not leave the Nimiipuu. She would not dishonor herself. She would hold onto her true self. She would not be a coward like her father and save herself over the others.

His eyes grew dark and steady. "What do you call being here with me right now? You have left your people to talk with me." He drew her closer. "Where are they? Why haven't they found me if I am so close you can visit my camp?" He stood, pulling her to her feet. "Take me to them. I'll speak to the chiefs and see if we can settle this amicably."

"I cannot." She pulled her hand from his and spun away, putting distance between them. Showing herself to the old woman and sick and Silent Doe and Girl of Many Hearts could not be helped, but to walk into the camp and ask to speak to the chiefs… The Creator would be most unhappy. Allowing Wade to see her had already broken her trust with the Creator. But necessary. She must help the Nimiipuu. Her instincts told her this was right.

"Why can't you take me to the chiefs?" His arms folded around her, drawing her against his warm, hard body.

She shook her head. "They do not know me." She spun in his arms. "You first thought I was not a Nimiipuu. They do not know me and could think I am not Nimiipuu also."

His arms tightened. "Then where is your family? And how are you surviving if you aren't with the group we're chasing?"

He placed a kiss on her forehead. His mustache tickled.

"I am not alone. I have you and my brother and his wife." Her heart lodged in her throat. She should not have mentioned Wewukiye and Dove. She wanted so badly to reassure Wade she did not think before replying.

"Your brother? Why is he not fighting with the other warriors?" He again held her away from him and scowled in the dark as he tried to see her face.

"He is not a warrior. He is a healer like I am. We do not fight. We try to save the Nimiipuu." Confusion dulled his eyes, again. "You must go back with your soldiers. Lead them the wrong way and let my people gain freedom."

He shook his head. His eyes cleared and his hands tightened on her arms. "I don't agree with the killing and the false promises, but as an officer I won't lead my men or any troops in the wrong direction."

Wade stared into Angel's eyes. He wouldn't allow his infatuation with the woman to sway him from his duties. Her strength fascinated him. He wanted to draw her back into his arms and absorb the strength he'd witnessed in her every time they met.

Her refusal to take him to the chiefs left him powerless to help. And he refused to lead the army astray. They had come to a standoff.

"Where is your brother? I'll take you to him." If he didn't get her out of his camp, his randy body would push him to ungentlemanly conduct.

"I can find him." She took a step, but his hand refused to release her arm.

"You shouldn't be wandering around out here alone." The soft undertone of his voice didn't surprise him. His body had outmaneuvered his brain to lure her into his arms.

"I am safe." The huskiness of her voice matched the desire in his as her body curled back against his.

"For all your strength and intelligence, you're naïve if you think you're safe wandering around here with Bannock scouts, your warriors, and possibly civilians hunting for the Nez Perce." Her curves pressed against him awakening desires he'd left unheeded for years.

"Nimiipuu warriors do not harm women." She inhaled in unison with his hand sliding up her waist and his fingers fanning across her ribs. "And I keep my distance from the others."

Every nerve in his body wanted to kiss her and explore her body. He leaned down to kiss her neck.

An elk bugled in the distance. Angel stiffened and stepped out of his embrace.

"I'm sorry. I shouldn't—"

She reached out stopping his words. "You did nothing. I must go."

The darkness shrouded her features. He couldn't tell what thoughts ran through her head. "Where are you going? Let me escort you."

"Do not worry for me. I will be safe with my brother." She took a step toward him, rising up on her toes. "You are the one who is not safe. Be careful. I wish to see you again." She kissed his cheek and disappeared.

Wade stared into the darkness until his hands and feet tingled from the cold. Replenishing the fire seemed foolish. If she found him, a Nez Perce scout could, too. He rolled up in his blanket and sat at the base of a tree with his rifle across his lap, eating the crispy rabbit.

What did he do now? His objective had been to find Angel. He did and had accomplished nothing. Hell. In his years of military service this was the most worthless and asinine thing he'd done. Rode off in search of a woman in the middle of a damn war. What was wrong with him? Had he finally cracked? Had the last fifteen years of killing and mundane military life finally shattered his sanity?

He shook his head and stared up at the stars. *What are you going to do come daylight? Continue on to be killed or taken captive or ride back to the regiment with your tail between your legs?*

He wanted to put the Nez Perce on a reservation and resign. He'd given enough of his life to his country. It was time to settle down. Holding Angel awoke a desire in him to find a wife and start a family. He had few skills outside of being an officer. That might get him a job as a marshal or Pinkerton. He wasn't cut out for the life of a farmer or rancher. He'd proven that before the war. His father had tried to interest him in growing cotton and crops.

Memories of his childhood flooded through him. Ones he'd shoved to the back of his mind after finding everyone he loved buried in the small family cemetery. From the moment he could talk, his opinions had clashed with everyone in his family. At sixteen, he'd been vocal about slavery and the rights of all people. His family had tolerated it and fended off the neighbors who would've strung him up for his philosophy. He'd struggled with which side to take in the war, fight for his principles or beside his family and friends; none of them said a word when he picked the North. His father had grimly shaken his hand, and his mother cried as he hugged her good-bye. Beth and Barney had hugged him and joked he chose the losing side, but they'd welcome him back after the war.

"Gahhhhh!" For the first time in years, he expressed the futility that overwhelmed him when he arrived back at the plantation and found all his family gone.

Forever.

Pu`ti`m
(10)

Sa-qan heard a yell of frustration. She knew the voice. Wade.

Fear scattered her thoughts. Had a warrior found him? Her heart pounded in her head. She raised her wings to take to the air.

"Where are you going? You just arrived?" Wewukiye glared at her. He had become the clear thinking one lately.

"I must find out what made that noise."

"We both know who. The same person you were with when I called." Wewukiye leaned down, placing his eyes level with hers. "You must stay away from him. His interference with your duty is not good."

"He wants to help the Nimiipuu. That is why he is out here all alone. He wished me to take him to the chiefs so he could talk with them." Her ears strained to seek any other sounds to learn if Wade was in trouble.

"He is using you to find the Nimiipuu so his soldiers can stop them." Wewukiye continued to stare at her. "Why are you not thinking clearly? You are the one who has kept Himiin and I from bringing disgrace to ourselves and the Nimiipuu."

"I am not disgracing myself or my people. I have found a so·yá·po who could help us. Why must you think they are all bad?"

"Since the so·yá·po have spread across the Nimiipuu country

there have only been as many as the branches on my antlers who have listened and spoke for our people. The rest have wished only to rid us of our birth place.”

“This soldier is one who will speak for us.”

Wade’s desire to help the Nimiipuu was pure and his intentions genuine. She believed this as strongly as she believed in the Creator.

“You are feeling too much for this mortal.”

Her body heated as her mind tried to deny the accusation. “I wish him strong because he will help the people.”

“You wish his body strong because you desire him.” Wewukiye stomped his foot and peered down at her. “You fought Himiin and I becoming involved with mortals. Sister, we at least picked Nimiipuu for mates. You are choosing to side with the enemy.” He spun and charged through the trees, leaving her to wonder at his words.

Was she falling in love with a mortal? No. She worried for the man because he was sympathetic to the Nimiipuu. Her heart stuttered as his face formed in her mind. The heat of the path of his hands on her body warmed her thoughts.

The memory of his anguished cry drove her into the air and circling above his camp. He leaned against a tree, weapon ready, his eyes squeezed shut. She landed in a tree and watched as a single tear trickled down his cheek. What clouded his thoughts and brought such sorrow? Every feather on her body ruffled as she fought with herself to stay in the tree and not go to him as a woman.

If she could touch him she would take away his sadness, just as she had taken away his pain as he healed. Wewukiye’s words echoed in her head. Had she fallen for the enemy? Could Wade be using her to get information about the Nimiipuu? She ran the questions he had asked back over in her mind.

Several times he questioned the location of the bands. Could he be hunting for their location to tell the other soldiers? Distrust, as small as the insect that stung the skin without being seen, emerged in her mind.

Wade’s eyes opened, and the anguish she saw in their depths squeezed her heart. His pain had become her pain. Could someone she had grown this closely connected to be using her? Doubts continued to plague her.

She leaped in the air and soared toward the soldiers’ camp. If they gathered close behind Wade she would have her answer to his deceit.

«»«»«»

Sa-qan circled above the camp. Many smoldering campfires and indentions in the ground suggested a large group had left and not toward the Nimiipuu. But as she flew in different directions she witnessed other soldiers converging on the area. Her heart raced as she hurried back to the area of the Nimiipuu. She would warn Wewukiye, and they would find a way to have the scouts discover the other soldiers and warn the people.

On her way, she flew by Wade's empty camp and spotted him trotting along the Nimiipuu's trail.

Fear for him stalled her wings. If a Nimiipuu warrior found him he would be killed.

She had to stop Wade. If he were killed by a warrior she would never forgive herself, yet she could not follow him everywhere to keep him safe. Sa-qan landed in a gulley well ahead of Wade. She shifted to the woman form and started walking toward him. What could she say to make him stop this foolishness?

«»«»«»

Wade wiped a hand over his eyes. He hadn't slept during the night. Visions and guilt from his past and anxiety over Angel wandering around alone as well as the possibility a warrior could kill him before he found the Indians had kept him wide awake. But the apparition in front of him had to be a dream. Cavalry troopers learned how to sleep in their saddles, and he was pretty sure he'd fallen asleep. It was the only way to explain Angel standing fifty yards ahead, smiling.

He didn't pull back on the reins, but his horse stopped, its nose touching Angel's shoulder.

"Wade? Are you sick?" She hurried to the side of his horse and tugged on his arm.

Wade shook his head and stared down at the concerned eyes of Angel, in person, not a dream. "W-what? I thought I was dreaming

81

when I saw you standing there." He dismounted and gathered her in his arms.

"Is that why you tried to walk your horse over me?" She pushed back, staring into his face.

"Yes, no. Hell." He let her go and tugged his hat off, running a hand over his burning, gritty eyes. "I didn't sleep all night worrying about you, thinking about my past, and wondering if a warrior would find me."

Her arms wrapped around his waist, and her head rested on his chest. "Do not worry for me. I am safe. But do worry about the warriors. Come." She slipped her hand into his and grasped his mount's reins. She led him to the edge of the trail and into a small area concealed by rock outcroppings.

"I will stay with you now so you may sleep and not fear being found." She pulled his blanket off the back of his saddle.

"No. I have to keep moving. I've lost time by sitting all night by that dang tree, when I should have been moving." He grabbed the blanket.

She tugged. "Your horse needed rest as did you."

He tugged. "My horse is rested. I can sleep on him as he walks."

She nearly sent Wade to the ground, ripping the blanket from his hands. "You will not be aware of warriors sneaking up on you if you are sleeping on the horse." Angel spread the blanket. "Lie down."

He had to smile at her pushiness and her forcefulness. She grabbed his arm and yanked him down onto the wool covering. His hat landed at his feet, and she gently pressed his shoulders to the ground. His body relaxed at her touch, and his eyelids grew heavy. He fought to stay awake, to enjoy the time he had with her, but drowsiness claimed his senses, and he dreamed of Angel in his arms.

《》《》《》

Her touch had put him to sleep. He needed rest and she could provide it as she provided his healing. Sa-qan trailed a hand over his wide chest. His clothing did not stop the memories of gliding her hands over his skin and muscle when she healed him. She shook her head and stood, walking to the horse. The animal could use more to eat. She led it to a small patch of grass, loosened the strap holding the saddle, and allowed it freedom to graze.

Sa-qan knelt beside Wade. The small barricade of rock provided safety. No one would find him. She should leave. Her fingers trailed over his mustache. His wonderful lips formed a smile. He had good dreams this time and not bad. She lay down, her head resting on his chest, and listened to his heart beat. The even rhythm strong and true. He wanted her people safe. Just like she did.

Sa-qan remained, inhaling his scent and listening to his heart until the sun poured warm golden beams straight into the rock enclosure.

Something shaded the warm sun from her head. The hair on her arms tingled, and she felt his presence before she looked up.

Shifting her head, she peered up into the angry red eyes of her brother.

You were to meet us at the Nimiipuu camp this morning. His quivering elk form shook with wrath.

I was on my way when I saw how tired he was. I stopped him and helped him sleep. She stood, keeping her movements fluid and quick to avoid waking Wade. She strode on silent feet out of the enclosed area to find a place where she could keep an eye on Wade and continue her conversation with her brother.

She peered down at Wade, narrowed her eyes, and faced her brother, crossing her arms. "You do not have to come looking for me all the time."

"Do you fear I will find you mating with the soldier?" The scorn in her brother's voice stung as much as his shameful statement.

"I will not mate with a mortal. I cannot give myself to anything other than the Nimiipuu." She poked a finger between the elk's eyes. "I have more self-control than you and Himiin. I care for the soldier because he cares for our people. He is a voice among the soldiers."

"That is why I caught you resting your head upon him?" Wewukiye walked to the edge of the outcropping and stared down. "You do not help yourself by continually making contact with this man. You may be denying your feelings but they show. If I see them, so does the so·yá·po."

Sa-qan watched Wade sleeping. Did he see her feelings? She did care for him in a way she did not understand. She glanced at her brother. He knew the love of another. Should she ask him what if felt like? *No.* She could not love anyone other than the Nimiipuu. The emotions she had for this soldier had to do with his need to help her people. Nothing more.

"I only see him as an ally to our people. I harbor the same emotions for him as I do the Nimiipuu. Do not make more of what you see."

Wewukiye stared into her eyes. "You are the only one who believes your untruths, sister." He walked away, stopped, and faced her. "Come with me now, if your only concern with this man is for our people."

"I cannot. He fell asleep before I could point him in the direction of the soldiers moving toward the Nimiipuu from the north."

"Why must he go to these soldiers?"

"They will cross paths with the Nimiipuu next. I wish for Wade to talk the soldiers into finding a way to stop the killing."

Wewukiye snorted. "The so·yá·po will not stop until they have killed all the warriors." He narrowed his eyes. "You are only helping them."

"You speak like a Nimiipuu warrior. Wade has the sense to know there must be a way to stop the killing. He would make a good leader." She pivoted away from her brother and scurried down the cliff toward Wade.

Sa-qan stopped beside a rock and watched Wade awaken. He stretched his arms over his head. His long legs extended, and his hips rose slightly when his boot heels dug into the ground and his back arched. Her mouth became dry at the sight. She swallowed and a ball of fire rolled down her throat, swirling around inside her body and catching her on fire.

An ache unlike any she had ever experienced began at the core of that fire and pulsed out to her fingers and toes. She licked her lips and tried to deny her brother's words but at this moment she did want to mate with this man. The urge hit her as hard and fast as a blast of winter air off the Lake Nimiipuu's beloved mountains.

Wade sat up. "Angel?"

"I am here." She walked out from the shadow of the rock. The smile ruffling his mustache and lighting his eyes licked her flames of desire even hotter.

He held up a hand. She took it, and he tugged her down beside him.

"I don't know how you did it but that's the best sleep I've had since you healed me." He kissed the tip of her nose. "Thank you."

She fisted her hands in his hair. "You are welcome." Their lips met, and she poured her affection for him into the connection.

Pú-timt wax ná-qt
(11)

Wade didn't know what had come over Angel, but he wasn't about to shove her away. Not when he could drown in her kiss and experience life as a whole man if only for this brief moment. He slid his hands up her sides, inching around and cupping her breasts. She gasped and his tongue touched hers. The sweetness and sensation brought him completely to attention.

He changed the angle of the kiss when her hands squeezed his shoulders. Her fingers kneaded his shoulders and arms, taking away the tightness bunched in his muscles from hours in the saddle. Her sweet lips matched his, kiss for kiss, filling his lonely heart with hope. Hope that he could give his heart to someone again.

Desire grew as the sweetness spun into urgency. One hand slid up her leg while the other cupped the back of her head, holding her hostage in a deep seductive kiss. He wanted to taste Angel everywhere. To give her something in return for all she'd done for him. He released her mouth and dropped wet open-mouthed kisses down her neck and chest to the vee of the neckline of her dress. Kissing the soft swell of her breasts at the opening.

A soft moan of appreciation whispered across her lips.

"Angel, you give me hope I could be a whole man again." Wade pressed his lips to her skin, enjoying the silkiness and heat. "After so many years of loneliness and following orders, I didn't think I could ever be anything but a puppet being manipulated by strings." He glanced up into her face. She shuttered her eyes with her eyelashes but not before he caught a glimpse of an emotion he'd lost all hope of seeing when someone looked at him.

Wade captured her lips once more, kissing her with the tenderness she deserved. He drew out of the kiss. "Let me take you back to your brother."

She shook her head and parted her sweet lips to say something, but he placed a brief kiss on her mouth.

"You have given me something today I thought I'd never find. Now let me give you something. Let me escort you back to your brother and make sure you're safe. Then I'll go see if I can get a higher ranking officer to listen to reason."

Tears glistened in Angel's eye. "I told my brother you were good for the Nimiipuu." She touched her lips with her fingers. "And good for me." Lips, puffy from their kisses, curved into a bright smile, lighting her eyes.

Wade held her shoulders. "I think we are good for one another. But until the army stops chasing the Nez Perce, I can't promise you anything other than moments like this should we meet." His gut squeezed with fear, knowing he had to let her go and hope no harm came to her until this campaign ended. Then he'd resign and find her.

She nodded. "I will find you when you are alone."

The conviction in her words brought back the questions of how she always found him and never feared the danger. "How do you find me?"

Her small round shoulders rose and fell. "You and I cross paths." She placed a palm against his cheek and leaned in kissing his lips chastely. Her breath whispered warm across his lips. "And I like the way you make my body warm while in your arms."

His arms crushed her against his body. He kissed her deep and long until they both grew weak from lack of air. Wade rested his forehead on Angel's. "You'd best keep your distance from me for a while."

"Why?"

He gazed into her eyes and nearly groaned witnessing the same desire swimming in their depths. "Because, there are more things I want to do with you than just kiss you."

A giggle mingled in the air between them.

"Do you find my desires for you funny?"

"No. It makes me happy. I wish to experience the coming together of our bodies, but..." She hiccupped. A glistening tear trailed down her cheek.

He caught the tear on his finger. "What is this? Why are you sad?" He tipped her face up, peering into her eyes.

"I cannot. We cannot become one. I have a duty to my people. I cannot put pleasure before that duty." She pushed away and stood. "There are other soldiers coming from the north. They will find my people before Cut Arm. Go that way"—she pointed northeast—"and you will find them. Talk with them and see if they will make peace with my people."

"Wait. How do you know there are more soldiers? Angel. Don't leave. I know we are on different sides now, but after— "

"We cannot be. Not now, not ever. It is the way it is."

The sadness dulling her eyes—eyes that moments before had shone with so much love and desire—ripped at his insides.

She spun about, ran through the rocks, and disappeared.

"Angel!" It was useless to call. She wouldn't come back, and he could give away his secluded location. No matter what she said, he wouldn't give up on her. He'd found his salvation in her arms, and he'd damn well do everything in his power to see they were together when this campaign ended

He didn't understand how she knew so much about the army movements, but he believed she knew a troop came from the northeast. Most likely Sturgis from Fort Ellis. General Howard would pull in troops from every direction to try and overtake the Nez Perce.

Wade rolled up his blanket, tightened the cinch on his horse, and mounted. He didn't know when or if he'd see Angel again before this was all over, but he'd find her when it was and see if she still held so strong to her conviction she couldn't be with him and still help her people.

«»«»«»

Sa-qan stumbled away from the rock formation. A good distance from the area, she shifted into a bald eagle and leaped into the sky. She circled and spotted Wade headed the direction she told him to go. Her heart throbbed. Sharing kisses and being held by him surpassed anything she had encountered as a spirit. The exhilaration and heat of his touch could not be bad.

Why have you brought this man into my life right now? Is it because he will help the Nimiipuu or is it to test my loyalty to my people? She waited, but the Creator did not respond. *Why have you stopped speaking to me? Especially, now, when I need your guidance the most.*

She gazed one last time at Wade and caught an updraft, floating on it toward the Nimiipuu camp. Her wings faltered at the sight of a group of warriors escorting a wagon and several horses with so·yá·po. She flew lower and discovered two women in the group.

Where are you, brother?

Watching the warriors with their captives.

Sa-qan scanned the area around the incoming group and found her brother and sister. She landed in a tree near them. "How did these so·yá·po become captured?"

"They insisted on meeting with Joseph." Wewukiye shook his head, swaying his antlers precariously. "All would be well if Yellow Wolf had brought them, but he was pushed aside by this hostile group."

She peered at the Nimiipuu warrior in the lead. "Yes. He believes blood on his hands makes him stronger." Sa-qan faced her brother. "You must enter that warrior and keep him from hurting the so·yá·po. These are not soldiers. They should not die. It will only bring more anger upon the Nimiipuu if these people are killed."

Wewukiye nodded and shifted to smoke.

"What are we to do?" Dove asked.

"We will wait to see what the chiefs do. If they talk about killing the so·yá·po then we will enter them." Sa-qan shifted to smoke and drifted toward the camp in search of White Bird. The most volatile chief.

The warriors led the so·yá·po to the chiefs.

Joseph, Looking Glass, and White Bird, with Sa-qan as his conscience, told the warriors not to harm the captives and to separate the women from the men.

Convinced White Bird would remain loyal to his words, Sa-qan slipped from his body and watched the Nimiipuu from a tree. The camp began preparations to move on.

Once the Nimiipuu started moving, shots rang out. Sa-qan leaped from the limb and soared toward the sound. A group of the hotheaded warriors had shot three of the so·yá·po men who tried to escape. She spotted one hiding in the trees and another running as fast as he could through the forest. If he made his way to the soldiers, he would tell them of the killings. Her chest ached knowing these few bad-tempered warriors could have them all killed.

Sa-qan shifted to smoke and re-entered White Bird. If he insisted the rest of the so·yá·po be let loose, the hot headed warriors would heed his advice. She hoped by showing good intentions with these, perhaps the captives would tell the soldiers the Nimiipuu were not all bad.

That evening in a drizzling rain, the chiefs ordered the young man and two women to be set free. The women received horses and the man left afoot with food. They did not want them to travel too fast and get to the soldiers with their location.

Sa-qan stayed with the Nimiipuu for ten suns while watching the soldiers from the north steadily draw near. She wanted to see Wade, but knew in her heart he must keep traveling and catch up to the soldiers. If he could convince their leader to talk with the Nimiipuu she would do her part to make the chiefs talk with him.

At night, huddled on a limb she thought of his kisses and gentle touch. What would she have to give up to be wrapped in his arms every night? She would need to become mortal. Until the Nimiipuu found safety, she could not think of such a thing.

This night she took flight, unable to remain still. The wind carried the scent of the army drawing near.

«»«»«»

Wade paced back and forth. He'd caught up with Sturgis the evening before. Fury consumed him learning Colonel Miles had sent word to Sturgis to "strike the Nez Perce a severe blow if possible before sending any word to them of surrender." Wade pivoted from the path he'd paced the last thirty minutes. If he couldn't stop the army he had to warn Angel. He'd promised her he'd do what he could to get the army to make good, but the higher ranking officers remained determined to make a precedence with the Nez Perce. He found it ironic the Nez Perce had killed fewer civilians and military than any other tribe, yet the army had made the peace loving group the scapegoats.

He strode to his horse and began saddling the animal.

"Where're you goin'?" a civilian guide asked.

"Out to check things." Wade held the bridle up to his mount's mouth.

"I heard you tryin' to convince Sturgis to give the Injuns a chance to surrender. You ain't goin' out there and powwowing with them are ya?" The man equaled his height but had twenty more pounds on him.

Wade faced his accuser. "I've been riding in this army a lot longer than you've been scouting. I wouldn't be tossing around insinuations you have no grounds to know."

Wade swung up into the saddle and tapped his heels into the horse's sides. He took off at a lope out of the camp and down the side of the river. He hadn't a clue how to get in contact with Angel, but he hoped by riding toward the Nez Perce, she would somehow know to look for him. He wasn't sure how she did it, but he had the feeling she would sense his nearness.

The sun had set and the cold fall night began to settle around him. Sensations of being watched started nagging him the last hour. If it wasn't Angel, he feared it could be Nez Perce warriors. A lone soldier would be a satisfying target for any warrior.

He wound his way through the trees and walked a distance in a small stream, hopefully hiding his tracks. An area against the side of a small cliff where he wouldn't have to watch his back loomed in front of him. He dismounted. His horse immediately began eating the tall dying grass along the base of the cliff. He gave the horse ample rope to graze and unhooked the cinch, tossing the saddle along with his bags and blanket on the ground.

The gray of dusk blurred the trees and bushes. A fire would be nice, but he couldn't risk giving away his location to the Indians. He sat down with a canteen, hunk of hardtack, his rifle, and a blanket wrapped around his shoulders warding off the cold mist that started falling. His mind wandered to Angel. What had she been doing since he last saw her? Would he find her and relay the information before the soldiers caught the Nez Perce?

His stomach soured at the thought of telling her he couldn't stop the army's vendetta. Would she blame him? His mind so occupied with his thoughts, he didn't register the eerie quiet until his horse nickered and shuffled its feet.

He raised his rifle to his shoulder at the same moment a large, light-colored creature dropped out of the sky and landed on his horse.

Pú-timt wax lepít
(12)

His horse screamed.

Wade shot his rifle in the air, afraid he'd hit his horse if he aimed at the cougar clinging to the animal's back. The blast didn't dislodge the big cat. He grabbed the barrel of his gun and swung it like a club at the animal. The butt of the weapon cracked across the cougar's back but the cat didn't relinquish its hold.

The terrified screams of his horse filled the area and bounced off the cliff, doubling the horror. Wade's heart raced at his helplessness to save the animal and reminded him once again of the countless times he'd failed his soldiers, and then his family. He watched unable to approach the crazed gelding and reluctant to try to shoot the cougar. The horse reared back, snapping the rope. In one leap, it set off through the trees with the large cat on its back.

"Hell!" The horse would be dead shortly if it didn't dislodge the cat, and he'd be without a mount, again. Repercussions of the one shot he'd fired pushed him into action. If a warrior heard, he could be found at any moment. He had to move. Get away from here and not leave a trail. The mist changed to a good downpour. That would help hide his tracks but make traveling even slower without a mount. Wade slung his saddlebags over one shoulder, his saddle over the other, and clutched his rifle in his free hand. He tilted his hat back to allow the rain to run off the back brim and started jogging the direction his horse ran. Nearly toppling nose first in to the wet slippery yellow clay, he slowed to a frustrating walk. Thirty minutes later, he heard scuffling noises to his right.

He parted the bushes with the barrel of his rifle and stared into the growing darkness. The dark outlines of his horse on the ground being fought over by a cougar and coyotes filled the small clearing. Snarls and growls accosted his ears, metallic smell of blood and stench of gut twitched his nose. Nature once again completing a cycle.

Wade ducked his head and backed away, sloshing rainwater down the front of his jacket from his hat. He'd heard and smelled worse on battlefields. The visual mimicked the fear he had for the Nez Perce. Troops converging on the camp, tearing families apart, and killing the chiefs. The vision spun in his head like a bad dream.

He had to keep moving. Warn them. Thankful for his long legs and Angel's healing, he set off in a southerly route. He had food for three days, if his luck held and his legs didn't give out before he found the Nez Perce. From all accounts of the Crow scouts the Nez Perce traveled only a day ahead of Sturgis's group. He should catch up to them by morning if a Nez Perce scout didn't kill him first.

«»«»«»

Sa-qan heard a horse scream and a rifle shot. The sounds came somewhere midway between the Nimiipuu and the soldiers' camp where she'd been searching for Wade. Had Wade set out to find her or had a scout found trouble? She soared through the dark night, her keen sight scanning the earth's floor. She found a cougar and coyotes eating a horse. That could account for the scream.

She continued to scan the area and spotted a man on foot. Catching a lower wind current, she drifted closer. *Wade*. Her heart fluttered. He looks for me. He carried his saddle as he slogged through the slick ground and pouring rain. The horse being eaten must have been his. Was he hurt? Fear he was injured, jarred her landing.

Her feathers barely settled before she shifted into her woman form and struck out through the valley to catch up to Wade. She pushed through two bushes and came nose to barrel with his rifle. He squinted in the dark.

"Who are you?" His voice held menace.

"Sa-qan," she replied, holding out a hand. She had to remember mortals could not see as well in the dark.

"Angel! I thought you were…Never mind." He dropped everything and gathered her into his arms, kissing the top of her head.

She wrapped her arms around his familiar body, breathing in the earthy scent of horse, wet wool, and his own tantalizing musk. "Your horse…"

"A cougar jumped him when I stopped for the night." His arms tightened around her, and his heart quickened beneath her ear.

"Why are you heading to the Nimiipuu?"

His body stiffened, and he kissed her head before leaning back.

"I can't persuade the officer in charge of this group of soldiers to visit with the chiefs." He swallowed and his eyes glistened. "Angel, he received an order from the highest commanding officer to kill as many Nez Perce as he can before even trying to negotiate. They want to set an example with your people."

"Kill our people?" Her stomach squeezed, nearly doubling her over. She backed away from Wade. No. If her people were gone…She clutched her middle and stared at the man in front of her. "Why? We did not kill the so·yá·po unless they killed first."

"The warriors have left a trail of bodies. All those ranchers and miners haven't tried to kill them." He reached out to her, but she backed away, shaking her head.

"My people cannot be taken from this earth. I will have failed." She would be no better than her father. Had her encounters with Wade been a test of the Creator to see if she were like her father? Would the Creator allow the Nimiipuu to perish if she sided with this so·yá·po? Her head hurt from all the thoughts colliding inside. Did consorting with this so·yá·po soldier sway her purpose to her people?

"Angel, I came to warn you so you can tell the others. I don't know how to stop them. But I'll keep trying. I promise."

She glared into his eyes. "Do not call me Angel. My name is Sa-qan, Bald Eagle. I am Nimiipuu, not so·yá·po. I will not allow you to keep me from helping my people." She could not let her starved emotions sway her from her duty. "I will not be disloyal and greedy like my father. My people will prosper, and I will see it happens."

"An—Sa-qan." His hands moved soothingly up and down her arms. "I would never come between you and your people. I want to help."

The concern in his voice and warm, gentle touch tugged at her heart inducing a war within her mind and her body. "Do not touch me. I cannot think." She stepped back, forcing space between them. How could the comfort and warmth he instilled in her be so wrong? She rubbed at the pain in the middle of her forehead.

Wade stooped, picking up his things. "I'll head back to the troop and see if I can do anything from there."

The sadness in his voice and his dark gaze probing her face pricked her heart with sadness. She wanted his arms back around her. She had told Wewukiye this man would help her save the Nimiipuu. Did she now believe otherwise? Her heart said he would help her but her head…Her pride wanted to conquer this battle against her people alone. She believed she had to finish this alone, yet she had Wewukiye and Dove. They could not help her with the soldiers. They needed Wade inside the enemy lines.

"I…do not go." She stepped forward, taking the bag from his shoulder. "I need to know everything the soldiers have planned to prepare my people."

He peered at her in the darkness. "You're sure?"

She managed a smile, enjoying his insecurity and obvious desire to stay. "Yes. I am sorry I said mean things."

"The news I gave you wasn't very friendly." He glanced around. "We need to find a place to talk that isn't here getting soaked."

She grasped his hand. "Come, I know a place." She led him to an indention in the white stone forming a nearby cliff. It offered just enough room for them to sit and stay dry.

Wade stepped out of the rain and dropped his saddle, leaning his rifle against the stone. He took off his wet coat and opened his arms. "Come here."

She captured one of his hands in hers and sat, drawing him down beside her. "I wish to think clearly. I cannot do that in your arms."

A glint of satisfaction sparkled in his eyes before his face grew somber. "Are your people very far from here? The soldiers are only a day away. I'm surprised a scout didn't arrive to see about the shot I fired trying to scare the cougar."

"They have been checking the back trail. I find it curious as well." She sent out a mental call to Wewukiye, hoping he roamed the area within her power. *Where are the scouts?*

Your soldier is safe. I followed him and have kept the scouts away. Wewukiye's strong thoughts meant he was near. Sa-qan held her position even though her first inclination nudged her to peer through the night and find her brother. This new information meant she must remain aloof to Wade's attentions this night. She did not want her brother seeing her lose control.

"We must talk fast and send you back before the scouts do find us." She gazed deep into Wade's eyes and saw his weariness. "You are not sleeping." Her hand reached out to him, but she pulled back remembering Wewukiye watched.

"I'm used to not sleeping much. Started with the war and then the campaigns." Wade pulled a blanket out of his bag and placed it around her shoulders. "How are you? For all the walking you must do, you always look rested."

His concern filled her chest with warm moist air like stepping into a sweat lodge. "I am used to traveling great distances. Tell me more about the soldiers." She needed to keep the conversation on a subject that did not conjure up pleasurable thoughts.

"They should approach from there." He pointed the direction she had flown and pulled a stick from his leather pouch. "This is called a spyglass. It will help you see them before they are close." He scooted next to her, and pulled on the ends of the stick. It grew longer. He held the smaller end of the stick to his eye and looked through it in the direction the soldiers traveled.

His closeness warmed her skin and tickled her insides. She wanted to lean over and kiss him. Instead, she shook her head. "I do not need such a thing."

A smile much like she remembered her mother bestowing upon her when she tried to best her older brothers flickered under Wade's mustache.

"This spyglass allows you to see the soldiers from a great distance." He held the stick in front of her face.

She leaned forward.

"Keep your eye open and look through the glass." His warm breath fluttered across her cheek. His nearness started her heart racing and her tongue dried as if coated with moss.

Sa-qan peered down the length of the stick and saw the world cut into pieces. She leaned back. "I see only a jumble of things."

His arm reached around her. His fingers stroked her left cheek. "Close this eye and leave the one looking through the glass open." A soft warm kiss on her temple stirred heat in her center.

She breathed in deep, held her breath, and peered through the object. "Oh your finger is large!" The stick held magic. Sa-qan took the object from Wade and inspected it. First she pushed the ends together making the stick shorter, then pulled it out again. She held the stick to her eye, again, and then the other. Spinning the stick around, she peered through the larger end and discovered everything had grown smaller.

"What magic is this?"

Wade's grin spread across his face. His eyes twinkled. "It isn't magic. It's called science."

"Science?" The word hissed from her tongue like a snake. "This is so·yá·po magic?"

"Some people might call science magic. It's a way to discover how things in this world work, and then use what is learned to make more things using what nature has already created."

His arm drew her closer to his body as he talked. The rumbling of his words in his chest comforted like thunder on a summer day.

"Men discovered refraction from glass by seeing how sunlight is changed when it goes through glass or water. They used this knowledge and made this spy glass. The glass on either end is a different thickness and cut to make it bring the object you look at closer which makes it appear larger."

He held the magic stick up in front of her. "I want you to use this to keep an eye on the soldiers and warn your people."

"You will need it." To tell him she could see great distances while in eagle form and flew above the soldiers would only confuse him.

"No. I can always get another one. I'd rather know you were safe by keeping your distance from the soldiers." He set the stick in her lap and drew her face toward his. "I want to be sure you're around when this is all over."

The fear in his eyes snared her heart. "I will be where the Nimiipuu are. It is my duty to never leave them."

"Duty? I don't want you to come to harm. I couldn't…" He swallowed, his gaze dipping to her mouth. "Hell, An—Sa-qan, I can't sleep thinking you'll get killed. It's been so long since I had a real reason to live… If something happened—"

She cradled his head in her hands and poured her own pent-up emotions into a long, heated kiss. He drew back first.

"I need you in my life. You don't know how empty I've been until you came along." He clasped her head, kissing her, again.

Sa-qan eased back. "You have brought new hope to my loneliness."

Wade leaned his forehead against hers and chuckled. "We make quite a pair. Two lonely people who picked a hell of a time to find one another."

She could not deny his words. Had their loneliness brought them together or was it the will of the Creator? Whatever the reason, she could no longer see her future without Wade in it. Following the soldiers to help him remain safe and keeping the Nimiipuu ahead of the soldiers would be the hardest task she had encountered as a spirit.

Pú-timt wax mita-t
(13)

Wade wished he'd allowed Ang—Sa-qan, the name was pretty but he couldn't think of her as a bald eagle, only as his angel—to keep him company on his walk back to the camp. They'd kissed and talked in the little concave in the sandstone cliff until the rain let up and the sun rising turned the world the light gray before dawn.

He checked his compass and veered more to his left. Chasing his horse last night had put him off his course traveling back to the troops. He thought about just sitting down and waiting for the advancing troops—if they rode this direction, for all he knew they could have changed course after receiving new information. He had no doubt a scout would come along eventually, but he didn't trust the Bannock scouts or his chances if a Nez Perce scout found him. Plus, he wanted to be with the officers when they planned their attack.

Though the problem between the army and the Nez Perce could make even a stalwart officer cringe, having voiced his loneliness and finding Sa-qan accepting of their friendship, a weight had lifted. They had a hard task ahead to get the two factions to come together and talk, but he believed it could be done. Especially having someone inside the Nez Perce camp.

His feet stalled. What had Sa-qan said? She couldn't show herself to the tribe. That didn't make sense. Her adamant desire to help the

Nez Perce had intensified, yet she said she couldn't go among them. How could she bring the chiefs together and tell them about the troops advancing if she didn't go to the camp and talk to them?

This circled his thoughts to the fact she always found him when he looked for her, and she never ate or showed tiredness. How could that be? And getting him up on that ledge? Did her brother help? Who was he, and why hadn't he joined the fleeing Nez Perce? His head ached from all his unanswered questions.

The sun shimmered off the yellow leaved birch trees on the hills to his right when he spotted black smoke rising to the east. The volume of the black cloud could only mean one thing. Nez Perce scouts had once again torched a homestead. Anger boiled in his chest. If they continued to kill civilians the army would soon have every citizen behind them to destroy the Indians.

The plume of smoke would draw the troops. He set off in a straight line, a knot forming in his gut at what he might find.

An hour later, he dropped his saddle and took a sip of water from his canteen, staring at the black timbers smoldering on the pile of charcoals where a cabin had once stood. Two bodies sprawled on the ground a distance from the ashes. This kind of action by the Nez Perce would not be tolerated. His head hurt adding this to the list of bodies the fleeing Indians had left in their wake.

The next time he saw Sa-qan, she would have to listen to him and tell her people to stop this senseless killing. It damaged their plight.

He walked to the closest body. A middle aged man stared up at him, a large seeping wound in his midsection. The image brought back scene after scene of the war. Bile rose in his throat at the memories. Wade swallowed the burning sensation and walked to the other body. He fought more bile and hurried back to his belongings.

Once Sturgis saw this, he feared there would be more bloodshed on both sides. He hated battles, but he couldn't walk away. He'd contemplated leaving the cavalry at the start of this campaign, then his orders came and he couldn't shirk his duty. The urge to leave the army grew each day along with his desire to save the Nez Perce.

He stared at the dead bodies and smoldering building. Why he desired to help the Indians when he witnessed this kind of disregard for life troubled him. Yet, he knew before this ill-wagered campaign the Nez Perce lived as peaceful people. The loss of their home had pushed them to drastic measures. He understood this. Hadn't he joined the cavalry after losing his home? He shook his head at some of the unsavory things he'd done in the name of the U.S. Army. This campaign was one of them.

The only way to help the Nez Perce and right the wrong the government enforced on them was to stay informed of the troops and slip away to relay what he knew to Sa-qan. They wouldn't be able to save all the Indians, but hopefully they could spare most of them.

Two lone riders, Crow army scouts, rode up on him. Their rifle barrels pointed at his chest as their horses stopped a good six feet back. The fact they treated him like a hostile stirred his anger. They worked for the army. For him.

"Where is Sturgis?" he asked, ignoring the round end of the weapon leveled on him.

"Why are you a horse soldier without horse?" The one who spoke grinned at the other one.

"A cougar jumped my mount, and they took off. I've been walking all night to get back to camp." He didn't need to justify anything to the scouts, but knew saying nothing would only aggravate.

"Did you see the cowardly Nez Perce who did this?"

"No. You're the ones following them, why didn't you?" Wade meant to upset the men but wasn't ready for the ferocity of their contempt.

The other scout kneed his horse forward, nearly running Wade over. The one holding the rifle glared down at him. "We find the cowardly Nez Perce, and you soldiers, fight like children." He pressed the barrel of the rifle into Wade's chest. The scout's eyes narrowed, watching, waiting.

Wade stood his ground. To show fear now would not only give the Indian the upper hand, it would also lower his authority with all the scouts. He stared boldly back at the Indian, ignoring the gun rammed into his breast bone. "I'd think your time would be better spent searching for the Nez Perce and not harassing me."

The rumble of many hooves and jingle of metal slowly grew in volume. The scout tipped his head and shoved the barrel one last time into Wade's chest before whirling his horse away and loping south.

Wade relaxed, rubbing the area where the barrel had surely left a bruise. He waited for the column of riders to come into view. Sturgis rode in the front of the seventh cavalry with his officers.

This reoccurring scene of him without a mount while troops rode up had become old.

Sturgis raised his hand, halting the formation. "Lieutenant Watts, I didn't expect to find you here." The colonel's eyes strayed to the saddle on the ground at his feet. "And without a mount."

"I rode south to check the word of the scouts and lost my horse to a cougar." He picked up his saddle and belongings.

The colonel surveyed the destruction and bodies. "Did you see the renegades who did this?"

"No sir, I came upon it only moments before you."

Sturgis's gaze remained fixed on Wade. The calculating going on behind those eyes worried him.

He didn't need Sturgis or anyone else watching him to see where his loyalties lay. If they even had an inkling he talked with Sa-qan, he'd be escorted back to a fort and watched. This campaign had become a passion of the highest military officials.

Sturgis motioned for a sergeant to ride forward. "Murphy, go to the ramada and bring Lieutenant Watts a horse and detach men to bury these two."

The sergeant saluted and whirled his horse to the rear of the troops and trotted off.

"I'll wait here for Murphy to bring my mount and help with the burial detail." Wade phrased his comment to indicate they could continue.

Sturgis shifted in his saddle. "We'll wait. You can ride in the front with the other officers."

Wade saw the slight nods of agreement bob between the men in the front. They would watch him. This quiet distrust would challenge his ability to talk with Sturgis about seeking a peaceful end to this campaign next to impossible.

Murphy arrived with a black gelding and a group of four men with shovels. Sturgis gave the command for the troop to dismount. The trumpeter sounded the order. The formation dismounted while the men with shovels began digging holes.

Sergeant Murphy held the black as Wade outfitted the animal. He paused to find Sturgis and the other officers conferring in a small huddle. Wade thanked Murphy and walked over to the shallow graves now being covered. No one said any words over the bodies but the hushed voices and furtive glances at the newly dug dirt told Wade it weighed on every mind.

Colonel Sturgis remounted, signaled the trumpeter who blew "to mount," and the group made ready to move out. Wade swung up onto his horse and fell into formation beside another lieutenant.

Sturgis moved them out, and they advanced along the path Wade had walked the day before. No one asked his whereabouts, but the scrutiny of the men riding alongside him sobered the air around him. They wouldn't sneak up on the Nez Perce, not if Sa-qan warned her people. Being in the front of the line made him a solid target.

《》《》《》

Sa-qan shifted to smoke and entered a Nez Perce warrior scouting the back trail. She maneuvered him to a position to witness the approaching soldiers. Her heart lurched at the sight of Wade in the front of the long line of soldiers. He would be the first into the attack by the Nimiipuu. The warrior she had entered fought her intrusion. By allowing her feelings for Wade to overtake her, she'd disoriented the warrior. She swirled out of the warrior's body, allowing him to make his own observations and decisions about the soldiers.

His horse spun around and took off at a lope back toward the Nimiipuu camp. The people would be warned.

She shifted to eagle form and circled high up in the sky. How could she keep Wade from harm? Wewukiye had helped the night before. Even after talking with him she did not understand why he had helped when he strongly believed Wade was not good for her or the Nimiipuu. She tried questioning him, but her brother had only said he must get back to Dove.

From her vantage high in the sky, she saw the warrior ride into the camp. A smoke signal warning of the soldiers puffed in the air, calling the warriors away scouting back to help. The Nimiipuu moved out, herding the horses into a canyon with the camp following. Warriors spread out along the rims in front of the canyon's entrance. They would hold the soldiers off and give their families time to keep moving away from the fighting.

The Nimiipuu had readied themselves for the soldiers; now she must find a way to keep Wade from harm.

She caught an air current and rode it down toward the advancing soldiers. The soldiers numbered more than previous skirmishes. Not as many as the Nez Perce warriors but they could harm the women and children should they get through the warriors.

Her keen sight found Wade. His eyes moved, searching for an attack. He knew the Nimiipuu had warning.

She swirled to smoke and entered the horse next to Wade's. The poor animal used every bit of its being to keep up with the forced trot. She moved into the officer. He was hungry, tired, and suspicious of Wade.

Sa-qan held her sympathy for the two at bay so the soldier would not experience her presence in his body. She probed to find out more. Sturgis had told them all to watch Wade. Suspicions filled their minds as to how he traveled about from troop to troop. They believed he held Nez Perce sympathies.

She slipped back into the horse and allowed her fear for Wade to surface. To help him stay out of the attack could make this Sturgis even more suspicious. Her plan to enter his horse and make the animal unruly when the attack started could confirm their suspicions of Wade.

Unable to reason out a good plan, she slipped from the horse, floated into the air, and shifted into an eagle high above the soldiers as the men in the lead trotted between ridges lined with Nimiipuu warriors.

Several rows of soldiers passed before the Nimiipuu fired into the group. Horses nickered and shouts rang out as the bullets hit their targets and soldiers fled to the yellow, red, and gray cliff walls, ducking behind the bushes.

Sa-qan kept her eyes trained on Wade. He dodged the bullets, dove from his horse, and scrambled to the cliff side like the others. She flew closer to the canyon, searching the side for a hiding place. An area large enough for two bodies to huddle in a formation of rocks to hide them. She landed halfway between the spot and Wade. She shifted into her mortal form and climbed down the canyon wall.

Wade hunched behind a bush his attention on the far ridge. She placed a hand on his shoulder.

He pivoted, gun in hand, pointed at her. His eyes widened in surprise and the weapon quickly fell to his side.

"Sa-qan, you shouldn't be here. You could be hurt." He wrapped an arm around her, pulling her down behind the bush.

"I have found a place we can wait for the fighting to end." She placed a hand on his cheek.

His jaw tightened and his eyes peered at her. "I want you safe, but I can't walk away from my duty as an officer." He nodded toward the commotion.

"I wish you safe as well."

"Watts? Lieutenant Watts? Are you hit?" A voice called from not far away.

"They can't find you," Wade whispered and moved to the other side of the bush. "I'm fine, sergeant. Carry on checking for wounded."

A bullet buzzed past Sa-qan, causing her to flinch. The deadly slug landed in the ground next to Wade. He had to come with her. She could heal him once more, but she did not want him to suffer again.

Wade dropped to the ground and crawled to her. "You have to go back with your people. It isn't safe. You could get hit by a bullet from either side."

"I will not leave unless you come with me. You can hide until the warriors return to their families. They are only holding the soldiers back to give the women and children time to get away." Sa-qan held out her hand. "Come with me."

He placed his hand in hers, but his eyes held regret. "I can't run away. I'm an officer. I won't shoot back, but I can't desert my men."

"Someone, please. Aghhh..." The plaintive plea of a man came from not far away.

Wade released her hand and crouched, moving toward the voice. She started to follow.

"Sa-qan! Go!"

She sucked in air at his harsh tone, but the sadness in his eyes gripped her heart. He sent her away for her sake. He did not know she could not be killed by bullets. But to tell him the truth she would also have to tell him she was not a mortal. He had overlooked her being a Nimiipuu but could he understand her being a spirit?

Pú-timt wax pí-lept
(14)

Wade's heart tore when he peered into the fearful eyes of Sa-qan. He hated being gruff with her, but she had to get out of the battle zone. He'd never forgive himself if she suffered a wound or died. As much as he loathed this campaign, he'd sworn to do his duty and as an officer that meant to serve his men and country, not his own needs.

He continued toward the sound of moaning and found a private with a large hole in his leg and blood pooling beside his body. Wade removed the man's belt and tightened it around the bleeding leg above the wound. The private wouldn't make it if he didn't find a doctor.

Shots exploded thirty feet down the ridge. The troops didn't have a chance against the sharp-shooting Indians. Greasewood and sage made poor hiding spots. Warriors hidden along the ridges picked off the soldiers like ducks on a pond.

The troopers stood a better chance if they separated. Harder targets to pick off. He couldn't sit here and nurse the man. He had to check on the others. Wade grabbed hold of the private's infantry strap and dragged the wounded man. The diagonal placement of the strap across the man's chest provided the perfect handle to move the body without picking him up and exposing them as easy targets.

He towed the man toward the sporadic blasts of smoke puffing up from bushes thirty feet away. The stench of gunpowder hung in the air, tickling his nostrils.

"Don't shoot. It's Lieutenant Watts with wounded!" he yelled, fearing the men would hear his approach and start shooting. Two privates sprang forward and helped him pull the wounded man into the small naturally formed trench the men had hunkered into.

He locked eyes with Sergeant Murphy. "Do we know if a doctor was in the front lines?"

"No, sir," Murphy said, shaking his head. The man's eyes grew as big around as a silver dollar.

"We aren't going to die like Custer's men are we, sir?" a private asked.

Wade shook his head. "They aren't out to kill us, just detain us so their women and children can get away."

Murphy tugged on his sleeve. "How do you know that, sir?"

"Because the Nez Perce were, until the government took their land away, a peaceful tribe. They just want left alone." Wade ran a hand over his mustache and scanned the ridge where he'd left Sa-qan. Did she scurry away? Would she return to her brother safely?

"How do you know so much about these Injuns?" a private asked.

"It's my duty to know about all the Indians in my territory." Wade scanned the rims. Puffs of smoke dotted the plateau as the warriors shot into the area. "Murphy, where's Colonel Sturgis?"

"I believe he took the majority of the troops back to try and flank the Injuns."

Wade nodded. "Good counter maneuver. Stay put and low. It'll take them some time to get around behind the ridges. Save the ammunition and don't fire unless the Indians start coming down the sides. I'm going to see if there's anyone else out there wounded."

The Nez Perce had proved time after time they had excellent diversion tactics. By holding the army off here at the ridges it gave their women and children more time to escape. It could also put Sa-qan in danger. He hadn't given her time to tell him how she planned to get away. She could get caught in the crossfire. His chest squeezed. She'd come to save him, yet she could be the one injured.

Wade leaped out of the trench and headed up the canyon slope toward the spot where Sa-qan had found him. If she'd listened, he wouldn't find her, but if her stubbornness had kept her there waiting, believing he'd return, he had to see her. Crouching low, he worked his way up the slope. He didn't want the Indians or the soldiers to see his ascent.

Wade found the spot she'd surprised him and searched the ground for tracks to reveal which direction she'd gone. His boot tracks stood out in the mud, but he couldn't find moccasin prints. His heart raced in his chest. Sa-qan was a little thing, but her prints would still indent in the mud. Even a child or small animal would leave impressions in the wet ground.

Where are you? Wade scanned the cliff and then peered down the side, searching for a sign of her. A bullet buzzed past his head. He dropped to the ground, his heart pounding with fear for Sa-qan and adrenaline from the bullet. Either he regrouped with his men or he hunted the woman whose footprints vanished.

Until he took the uniform off, he'd better remember his duty as a cavalry officer and act accordingly.

The warriors swarmed over the rims and down into the flat. The rest of the troops must have reached the plateaus and pushed the Indians from their perches. He clutched his rifle, waiting. A cold wind blew through the canyon, and he crawled up the cliff wall to press his body behind an outcropping to ward off the wind and hide from the approaching warriors.

Only a fool wouldn't hide. He'd be one against many. Hiding gave him the upper hand as the retreating Indians would think all their enemies chased them. It he shot one warrior there would be little doubt he would be shot.

Brush crackled above him. Wade glanced toward the crest of the plateau. A warrior crept along the cliff wall fifteen feet above him. Blood pumped, whooshing in his head. Fear and survival spun in his head. He didn't want to die today, but he also didn't want to kill. Sa-qan understood killing to survive. If the warrior spotted him, he'd have only one option.

Not wanting the warrior to read his thoughts or feel his gaze, he turned his head slowly and watched from the corner of his eye, raising his rifle in cautious increments. Relief drained him of strength when the warrior moved out of sight. He slumped against the rock wall, listening and waiting.

Twenty anxious minutes passed before he spotted troopers creeping through the bushes above and below him. He fell into the span of soldiers sweeping up and over the ridge.

Three miles ahead across the prairie, the tail end of the Nez Perce disappeared into a canyon. Wade watched as one of the mounted companies surged toward the gap in the ridges. The belch of smoke and crack of rifles firing rallied from those ridges and many troopers fell from their saddles. Another wave of warriors stood guard on the ridges along the canyon opening, pinning the troops down.

Wade snatched a spyglass from the sergeant closest to him and studied the area. Had Sa-qan made it to the group before they disappeared? Or was she out there somewhere hiding from the troops?

"We need to keep moving, Lieutenant."

The sergeant held his hand out for his spyglass as the others wearily started toward the edge of the plateau. Wade's worn out body cried for rest like everyone in this group.

"We'll be no good to them after that climb and walking across that expanse of prairie." Wade waved his arms gathering the odd assortment of men around. "Take time to drink and eat. Then we'll follow."

The cold wind on the top of the plateau blew through his wool coat, chilling his weary limbs. "Let's move just over the top and out of the wind." They all dropped over the rim and sat to take a rest.

The sergeant stole glances at the fighting going on. "Shouldn't we hurry on over there?"

"How well do you shoot when you're tired, Sergeant?" Wade asked and took a drink from his canteen.

The man hung his head.

"We'll rest for fifteen minutes then follow. Refreshed troops are more help than weary ones." He surveyed the twenty or so men mostly cavalry who weren't used to this much walking. "Where are the horses?"

Murphy shrugged. "We bailed off and I haven't seen them since."

He didn't want to voice his opinion the Indians had probably captured the horses by now. It offered the only logical explanation why the handlers hadn't brought them once the Indians retreated. He was damn tired of losing his mount.

Staring across the prairie to the canyon entrance, he watched the puffs of smoke from the rifles. Proof the warriors still kept the army at bay.

"Move out!" he ordered and stood, ignoring the throbbing and stinging in his feet.

The group shuffled along as one unit down the back of the ridge in a direct line toward the fighting. Which he surmised to be a stand-off. Or would be until the Indians decided their families had traveled well ahead of the army.

«»«»«»

Sa-qan soared in the air above Wade and his small band of soldiers. He had survived. She had entered the warrior who walked close to Wade's hiding spot and gave him a blind eye to the soldier. Now Wade led soldiers toward the ones shooting at the warriors. There would be no danger for him until he arrived at the fighting. The warriors remained on the ridges protecting the canyon or helping move their people and scouting ahead for more soldiers.

Wewukiye and Dove followed the people. She would know if they needed her. Her thoughts as usual filled with Wade and how together they could help the Nimiipuu. She pondered this every moment. There had to be a way to save the people but she had not yet discovered one. To allow the soldiers to kill and force the survivors on a reservation would be to have failed. She could not fail.

Creator, what must I do to help my people? Her heart cried out again to the Creator. *Why have you left me when your wisdom is greatly needed?* Once more she tried to understand why he chose to ignore her. His silence worried her as much as failing.

She still believed it necessary to show herself to save Girl of Many Hearts. *If that is your reason for ignoring me, you are wrong.* Her gaze traveled across the land below. She spotted a wounded warrior in the path of Wade's soldiers. Her heart raced. The threat on his life would force him to shoot at the soldiers and be killed.

The soldiers must change their direction. She dove, falling to the earth near the soldiers. She flapped and squawked hoping to draw the soldiers' attention and redirect their course.

"What is that?"

"I don't know. It fell from the sky."

The fragrance of sage filled the air as she continued to flop and beat her wings against the bush.

"It's an eagle!"

"Stay back." Wade's authority rang in his voice.

She wanted to stop flapping to peer into his eyes but chopped that idea short.

"Is it hurt?"

"I don't know but it's best to leave it be. Move out." Wade's tone held a note of awe.

Sa-qan stopped fluttering and stared up into his eyes. The others had retreated; only Wade remained watching. She wanted to speak to him but knew it would only confuse him. The wonder and sympathy in his eyes sent her heart pounding like the ceremonial drums.

Stay to the right. She sent the message to him as she would her brother.

Wade's eyes widened and he spun away abruptly, taking long strides to catch up to the others.

By his reaction, he had heard her words. The knowledge thrilled her. She leaped into the air and flapped her wings, pushing her body higher and higher. Why did knowing he could hear her build this elation? She cared not the reason, only that she could help him make the right decisions without having to—

She glanced down. He was not veering right but taking a straight course. Had she been mistaken about his hearing her? They would pass near the wounded warrior. Her heart rose into her throat. Wade was in the lead. He would be the one the warrior shot.

Pú-timt wax pá-xat
(15)

Wade shook his head. Where had the voice come from? It had sounded like Sa-qan. He glanced over his shoulder at the area where the eagle had flopped around. Enthralled by the beauty of the bird and knowing Sa-qan meant bald eagle he'd been even more entranced. The white head had rivaled Sa-qan's hair in color, and the bird's yellow eyes peering at him had reminded him of Sa-qan. Strongest of all the voice… Had he imagined the warm soft tone so like Sa-qan's?

Why had the voice said, "Stay to the right?" He scanned the area ahead of him. Nothing moved. Had his own instincts told him to veer right, or had he truly heard a warning? He stopped.

His gut twisted, and his body tightened. The hair on his arms tingled. Did danger lie ahead?

"What's wrong, Lieutenant?" Murphy stopped beside him.

"Nothing." He couldn't tell the man he'd heard voices. He decided to take heed of either his own premonitions or the voice and changed his course to the right.

They still had two miles of uneven prairie to cross before they would enter the fighting. He wasn't in a hurry to get there, but if he didn't keep a forced pace the men would get suspicious. They wouldn't understand his need to keep them safe. He'd lost the mental battle needed to be an effective cavalry leader. His new goal was to get through this campaign and keep as many soldiers, civilians, and Indians alive as he could. How meeting one woman had changed his belief about life and duty, he couldn't fathom. He no longer lusted for the next adventure, the empty room at night, or the authority. He just wanted to spend the rest of his life with one person and perhaps a few children.

The thought of sharing the rest of his life with Sa-qan tipped his lips into a smile and warmed the cold that had taken up residence in his chest sixteen years ago. He couldn't voice his intentions until they settled the Nez Perce on a reservation, but it gave him a new goal. Halting this campaign and marrying Sa-qan.

The acrid gunpowder in the air interrupted his musings and brought them up behind the forces volleying with the Indians on the ridges. Vapors rose on the cold air from the guns, the troop's breath, and the nervous, sweating bodies of their horses.

"Watts, where are your horses?" Captain Benteen asked.

"We were wondering the same thing, Captain." Wade halted his men beside the mounted officer. "We believed hiking over here was more important than backtracking and finding our mounts."

"I agree. Fall in and shoot at anything that moves on the ridge." He whirled his horse around and gathered his men.

"You heard the captain," Wade said, watching the Indian's bullets fall short of their intended targets. He doubted their return fire would do any damage either. It was a waste of ammunition to fire at the ridge. But the captain outranked him.

He watched two mounted troops move to flank the ridges similar to the maneuvers on the last plateau. From the lack of targets hit and the slow ascent of the troops on the ridges, they'd be exchanging fire with the warriors for most of the day.

《》《》《》

Sa-qan landed on the cliffs. After watching Wade nearly get shot and finally heeding her warning and avoiding trouble she needed time to allow her senses to calm. She watched from a perch on a rock as the larger group of soldiers circled the ridges at the canyon entrance. It would take them the better part of the day to get within striking distance of the warriors holding the others off. Plenty of time to check on her people.

She leaped off her perch and stretched her wings. If not for her entering the warrior and showing him the approaching soldiers more lives could have been lost this day. She wished to see if the Nimiipuu had traveled a good distance from the fighting. Within minutes, she spotted the long line of horses both loose and pulling travois and hauling people. To hide such a large number of people and animals was impossible. They left large paths of disturbed earth to follow.

Brother, I am here. She continued her course toward the group.

We are near the front on the side of the sleeping sun.

Sa-qan scanned the area and found her brother and his wife trudging along to the side and out of sight of the group. She landed in a tree in front of them.

"How are our people?" she asked.

"They are short on food and tired." Dove said, worry trembling her voice.

"The soldiers are also weary as well as their horses, but they do not stop." Sa-qan remembered the weary and weakening horse and soldier she had entered.

"The warriors are grumbling. Those that kill so·yá·po are bringing more trouble to The People. There are also many who are losing trust in the leaders." Wewukiye stomped his hoof. "If they do not stop bickering, the arguing among the bands will get them all killed." He shook his massive antlers. "I cannot enter all that cause trouble."

"We can only help where we can." Wewukiye's defeat could not take hold in her.

"Your soldier. Can he not do something?" Dove tipped her wide muzzle and large brown eyes to Sa-qan.

Her chest warmed with the thought Wade belonged to her. Not in the sense they had mated and become one, but he held a special place in her heart. One she knew no other could fill. "He is not my soldier, and he is as helpless to change the soldiers as we are to keep the Nimiipuu safe. He is one. There are many so·yá·po who wish to hurt the Nimiipuu."

"We cannot continue to only follow along. There must be action we can take." Wewukiye carried little patience.

"Brother, we can only guide where we can and believe the Creator will not let the Nimiipuu perish."

The People had journeyed on by while they spoke. "Stay with them and do your best to keep peace among them. If they fight among themselves they will be weaker against the enemy."

"We will do our best." Dove nudged Wewukiye's shoulder with her muzzle, and the two walked side by side in the direction the Nimiipuu traveled.

If the Nimiipuu began rejecting the orders of their leaders they would surely perish. Strength could only come from a united group against the soldiers. Her fear for her people drove her into the air and back toward the fighting. She needed Wade's strong arms around her right now. His strength gave her confidence the Nimiipuu would survive.

She circled above the entrance of the canyon. Tents stood as large white mounds and the injured had been gathered. More soldiers had arrived along with large guns on wagons. She watched warriors creep down the ridge headed back toward their families. They slowly retreated leaving enough behind to keep the soldiers busy.

Her gaze sought Wade. Finally, at the edge of the growing camp, she spotted him. How would she find a way to speak to him? Did she dare put words in his head or would that only confuse him? To show herself to him could also prove a problem should someone else see her. Impatience fluttered in her mind. She could see him, yet she could not go to him and speak with him. Could not gain solace in his arms and words.

She continued to circle, watching as he walked through the tethered horses, checking their legs, and moving farther from the assembled soldiers. He was trying to find a way to get to her. Happiness blossomed in her chest. His direction curved toward the side of the ridge. She flew ahead, scouting the cliff side, and found a hidden area they could meet. The obstacle would be finding a way to direct him toward the spot.

Did she dare change to woman and attract his attention? Would others see her and come as well? Wade continued toward the ridge putting more distance between him and the soldiers' camp than the ridge. He would see her before anyone else staring this direction.

Her urgency to talk with him pushed all reason from her mind. She shifted to smoke, rising above the tallest sage, hoping it caught Wade's eye, before shifting to her woman form. The need to see him pricked at her mind. Her heart hastened its beating and her breathing quickened. Yet, her head held her feet in place. In mortal form she was the enemy to the soldiers camped at the entrance to the canyon. To show herself to anyone other than Wade could not only hurt him for consorting with her, but the Nimiipuu.

She held this thought tight in her mind and her heart. Her friendship with Wade would end once the Nimiipuu reached safety. A knot formed in her mid-section. She stiffened her back. Showing herself in mortal form had been her only option to save Girl of Many Hearts and helping the wounded she'd found. She did not regret saving Wade. His friendship toward the Nimiipuu offered them hope. She believed this with all her heart, yet she should have healed him and not allowed him to see or speak with her. Or kiss her.

The memory of his kisses and the way he held her heated her cheeks and scorched a path down her neck to settle in her chest. Eagerness to see him once again took hold. She shook her head. Why did her body overrule her head when it came to Wade?

The sound of brush scraping and labored breathing carried to her on the crisp evening air. She ducked behind the bushes and crept toward the sound. If she did not find Wade, she would leave and not return. His scent drifted to her, and her heart quickened.

"Over here," she said in a loud whisper.

Movement stopped. "Sa-qan?"

The question and eagerness in his voice tripled the delight filling her chest.

"Yes." She stepped toward his voice and he walked into view.

Wade's arms wrapped around her, drawing her against his solid chest and giving her the security she expected.

"I was so worried you'd been caught in the fire between the troops and the Indians." His warm breath heated her scalp before he kissed her head.

"You do not need to fear for me. Watch only that nothing happens to you." She raised her chin and kissed his neck. His skin tasted salty and gritty. He had endured so much as had all the mortals in this endless chase the so·yá·po started.

He held her head in his hands and stared into her eyes. "You keep repeating not to worry about you, but unless you can turn invisible, you're going to be in danger."

The worry pooled in his brown eyes tugged at her conscience. "Come, I have found a place where we can talk and no one will find us." She linked her fingers with his and led him to the hidden spot. The ground dipped in like the hand of the creator had reached down and scooped a handful of earth to use elsewhere. Ringed around the area stood large boulders like the walls around forts she had flown over.

Sa-qan ducked through the opening between two rocks, pulling Wade in behind her. The indention and rocks held out the worst of the wind.

Wade straightened and turned a slow circle, studying the enclosure. "How did you find this?" His gaze settled on her.

"I was looking for a spot to meet you." Her gaze dipped to his chest. She found it harder and harder to not tell him the truth. He thought of her as a mortal. After the Nimiipuu were safe and she no longer needed her woman form, he would be deeply hurt. Perhaps hate her. The thought stabbed like knives in her stomach. He had to know the truth. She did not want him hating her or thinking he caused her to leave.

She opened her mouth to tell him.

His arms wrapped her, and he kissed her.

Her good intentions flew out of her head. Her arms wound around his neck as her body pressed against his. She wished to become one with him. Rather than the admission jarring her senses, it filled her with happiness.

His kiss deepened. His tongue skimmed her lips. She gasped at the softness and he entered. The sensation of his body joining hers so intimately sent a bolt of lightning shooting from her head to her feet.

She pulled back and stared into his eyes. The surprise on his face meant he experienced the lightning as well.

"Did you feel…?" He licked his lips and skimmed a hand over his mustache.

She nodded and gulped. Now would be a good time to tell him. Dove had told her of the lightning when she and Wewukiye kissed before she became a spirit. Did it represent a sign from the Creator? Did a spark such as this with a mortal mean she had found her mate? The idea of Wade beside her always brought pleasant thoughts. Very pleasant.

"There are things—"

Wade pulled her back in his arms. "We'll talk later." His head tipped, and she met his lips.

Lightning or not, she couldn't ignore her need for this man. He nibbled her lips and tasted her thoroughly, weakening her legs. She sagged against Wade. He scooped her into his arms and carried her to a level spot with grass. He placed her on the ground and lowered beside her.

"You're all I think about. Are you safe? Will I see you again?" He dropped kisses over her face and down her neck.

Sa-qan placed a hand on his cheek, riffling the end of his mustache with her thumb. "I think of you more than I should."

His gaze met hers. "Why more than you should?"

"We are different in many ways. Ways—"

He placed a kiss on her lips. "The only way we are different is you are a woman and I am a man. Nothing else matters."

If only that were true. Her heart ached to tell him the truth, but her head once again took control. "We are of different people."

"I'm sure there have been marriages between your people and mine that have worked?" He kissed her neck as his hand skimmed up her side, resting just below her breast.

Heat pooled under his hand. The woman parts between her legs warmed and pulsed. She stared into his eyes. Did he see what he did to her body? His eyes sparked, and his hand moved to her breast, holding it, coveting the mound like a treasure.

Pú-timt wax `oylá-qc
(16)

Wade swallowed the desire bubbling in his throat. His hand holding Sa-qan's breast burned, sending need straight through his body to his throbbing shaft. He hadn't bedded a woman in over a year. The fort prostitutes no longer appealed. He'd thought he'd become too old to have his body react to a female, but the woman peering up at him jolted him alive in every way.

He leaned down to savor her taste once more. This time as he kissed, his hand kneaded her breast. A moan vibrated her chest and intensified his desire. Her hands gripped his head, holding his lips to hers as her body arched, pressing her hips against his and giving him more room to pleasure her breast.

Cupping her backside, he rubbed his desire against her belly. His need to be a part of her life—because making love to her would commit him to her; heart, mind, and body—surpassed any other obligation he'd ever accepted.

"Sa-qan, I want to be part of your life." His husky voice whispering against her lips didn't sound like his.

She stiffened and her hands slowly released their grip on his hair.

"I cannot be a part of your life." The gleam of passion in her eyes dulled to pain.

"I know there are differences. Once this campaign has ended, I want to marry you." He nuzzled her neck. "No woman has ever haunted my thoughts like you, nor made my body crave to be near." He kissed the pulsing vein in her neck. Surely she could see neither would be happy unless they remained in each others lives.

She sighed and her body relaxed under his caressing hands. He wanted her. But not here like this. He'd not take her like some randy buck. He wanted their communion to be long, satisfying for them both, and a bond that would never separate them.

Wade peered into her half-closed eyes. "When this is over, say you'll marry me."

She hid her inner thoughts shuttered behind her pale lashes. Her body tensed in his arms once again. Why did asking her to marry him cool her ardor? Was she using him for folly to learn of the troops movements? The image of her worry when healing his wounds, her excitement when they met, said she cared for him. Yet, where was this brother she spoke of, and how did she always find him and remain unharmed through all of this when she clearly traveled through the middle of the skirmishes?

He grasped her arms and held her away from him to peer into her golden eyes in the growing moonlight. He blinked at the blinding light shimmering in their depths. Her skin heated under his hands.

Her soft lips opened to speak, and his randy body jerked to attention.

"I am not—" She licked her lips, her gaze dropped to below his face.

"You're not what?" he asked it softly, willing her to look at him.

"I am not what you think." Her eyes dimmed, and her body slipped from his hands.

"What do I think?" He didn't like the distance in her voice, her attitude, or the space she forced between them. Wade drew her back into his arms. The wholeness she built in him when he held her couldn't be wrong.

"You believe me to be a Nimiipuu maiden."

"No, you said you were a Nimiipuu, I believed you were a child captive."

She pushed against his chest. The strength in her small arms surprised him. She shoved away and stood, her arms wrapped around her small frame.

He stood.

"You do not know me. I am not a captive. I am Nimiipuu. I will always be Nimiipuu." Her fist pounded on her chest. "My heart belongs to my people. If I give it to anyone or thing other than The People I will no longer exist. I am here to serve only the Nimiipuu. Not my own desires."

Wade stretched his hands toward her, but she remained out of reach. He rubbed a hand over his mustache, watching her. Why would someone so young carry such a strong conviction for her people? And ignore her own happiness?

"One of the great things about people is we have the capacity to love more than one thing at a time."

Her head slowly lifted, her chin pointed his direction, and the flames in her eyes shifted his feet backwards.

"The Creator put me upon this earth to watch the Lake Nimiipuu. I have spent many seasons watching the people and helping them prosper. Now your people wish to kill the reason I exist. I cannot allow this. And I cannot allow my emotions for you to get in the way. I will not put my greed before my people. I will not be like my father." Smoke engulfed her body and she vanished.

Wade stared at the empty spot. What the hell? He rubbed his eyes and walked to the spot, waving his arms. The growing darkness had to have played tricks with his vision. What had she done to make the smoke? He searched behind him. The only way out. How did she get past him without him seeing her? His logical mind worked to sort out what he'd witnessed. Somewhere in his heart, an ache began and whispered Sa-qan had disappeared from his life. And damn if that didn't hurt like hell.

«»«»«»

Sa-qan perched on a rock above the enclosure where she had shared wonderful moments with Wade. Pain grew in her chest, knowing she must keep her distance.

Wade stalked around and around inside the enclosure before slowly trudging back across the dark expanse between the ridge and the soldier camp.

His reaction when she shifted to smoke surprised her. He had stood there watching as if he expected her to walk through the smoke and into his arms. Did he believe in his love for her so thoroughly nothing would shake him? The thought warmed her. Then her good sense slapped her. There could never be anything between them. He was mortal and she a spirit.

Her mind wandered to the kisses they shared and his hands caressing her body into a raging storm. Her body craved his with such intensity she now understood her brothers' motivations for taking mortals as wives. But did she crave the closeness of mating with Wade because they belonged together? Could her maiden body only wish for this because it had been denied for so long?

She had not been around other mortal males in her woman form. Would she react the same to any man?

The speeding rhythm of her heart when her gaze landed on Wade nearing the soldier camp gave her doubts any other man would cause her body to yearn for them. Her heart beat for one, yet it could never be.

Sadness drove her to the air and through the night sky toward the Nimiipuu camp. She wished to be with her brother and sister this night. Loneliness had never bothered her before, but tonight, she did not wish to be alone. Her biggest problem…though she flew toward her family, centered on Wade, the man in the soldiers' camp she wished to keep company.

Sa-qan found Wewukiye and Dove standing guard on the ridge above the Nimiipuu camp. All remained quiet as the moon started slipping toward the earth.

"Are you not feeling well, sister?" Wewukiye peered into her eyes.

Did her sadness and loss of Wade show? "I am only worried for our people. The soldiers continue to push and the people are growing tired."

"It is true." Dove nodded, her large eyes filled with sadness. "I listened to the women as they made camp. Many fear they will lose children to the cold and lack of food. The pace the leaders set each day is hard for the old and the young."

"It is necessary to keep them from the soldiers' bullets." Wewukiye stomped his hoof.

"But they will die from other things if the pace continues." Dove's dark brown eyes stared at Sa-qan. "You must talk to your soldier. He must be urged to stop the killing."

Sa-qan's heart squeezed. She did not want to talk with Wade again. She feared his questions about her changing to smoke, and she feared her ability to not seek the security of his arms and heat of his kisses. "He is not my soldier. I will not see him anymore."

Wewukiye stretched his neck and studied her. "Did he harm you?"

"No. It is my decision." She tried to continue the gaze with her brother but could not hold the exchange.

"What has he done that you no longer wish to see him?" Dove stepped next to her.

"Nothing that requires your concern. I still believe helping him was best for the Nimiipuu, but I should not have allowed our time together to have lingered." Her chest still ached, standing firm on her decision, yet grieving her loss.

"You are in love with him." Dove's eyes twinkled. She nudged Sa-qan's body with her muzzle.

"No!"

Wewukiye raised an eyebrow and stared closer. "I think my sister is fooling only herself and not doing a very good job."

"I am not in love. I cannot be. My heart is for my people and no one else." Sa-qan's heart raced. Panic squeezed her throat. To love Wade would put her people in peril.

"Love for your soldier will not steal what you hold in your heart for your people." Dove nudged Sa-qan with her muzzle. "You have been alone too long. It is not good for even a spirit to be so alone."

Sa-qan peered into her sister's sympathetic eyes. She was lonely. And Wade had filled the hollow spaces in her heart created from her loneliness. But love? She shook her head. The only love she remembered other than the joy the Nimiipuu brought to her was at the hands of her family. The heat and yearnings Wade ignited in her body were nothing like the emotions she held for her family.

"It must be the same for him. Being alone too long. He…he asked me to marry him when this is over." She stared into the eyes of her family. "He does not know I am a spirit. He still believes I am a captive and not Nimiipuu because of my hair and eyes. I-I shifted to smoke in front of him tonight to…I don't know why except he said he wanted to marry me. Be with me. It could never be. I wanted to shock him, have him see me with disfavor. Only he watched without surprise or fear."

"Did you tell him you were a spirit?" Dove watched Wewukiye with adoring eyes. "I was not scared when Wewukiye told me he was a spirit. It only answered my many questions."

"No. I changed to smoke and left him standing alone."

"That is good. He will ask questions you can answer when you meet again." Wewukiye nodded, his massive antlers bobbed.

Sa-qan stared open-beaked at her brother. "Why are you suddenly wanting me to tell him the truth? You told me showing myself to the soldier was a bad idea."

"The Nimiipuu need someone in the soldiers to speak for them. You have opened this so·yá·po's heart to you. He will help your people to make you happy." Wewukiye held her gaze. "Love is strong between two hearts. Differences do not matter if the emotion is pure."

Flames of desire licked through her body, remembering Wade's kisses and caresses. Was that love? "How do I know this is love and not my maiden body reacting?"

Dove leveled her eyes with Sa-qan's. "From your first encounter your eyes have sparkled each time you speak of him. Now your body wants to be his. Forever."

"But I cannot. How can I give my heart and body to this man and still hold the Nimiipuu strong in my heart? They have held my heart for season upon season. I cannot allow my obsession for this man to come between my duty."

"Your love for him will only strengthen your duty to the Nimiipuu." Dove winked. "You will see."

Sa-qan flew up into a tree. If her brother and sister spoke the truth, she must find Wade and tell him the truth also. If he still wished to be with her after the Nimiipuu found freedom—her chest filled with hope—they would find a way.

«»«»«»

Wade woke the next morning wishing he could climb on a horse and ride away from this campaign and straight into Sa-qan's arms. He dreamed of farming and raising a family. All the children gathered around him had blonde hair and golden eyes. He woke in the middle of the night aching with need, having dreamt he and Sa-qan were making love.

He no longer wished to participate in the slaughter of the Nez Perce. That's what it had become to the U.S. government. They'd decided to use the Nez Perce as an example to the other tribes who had yet to go to a reservation.

The trumpeter blew first call. Wade wandered to the fire where several officers' attendants boiled coffee. He held his tin cup out to an attendant. The dark liquid accosted his nostrils and shriveled his tongue, but he drank it. The bitterness only added to the queasiness in his gut. What if he didn't see Sa-qan again?

"Watts!" Sturgis strode with purpose toward Wade.

"Yes, sir." Wade saluted and stood at attention.

"Take ten men and strike out after the Indians. Send reports every evening. I want to know their whereabouts at all times." Sturgis studied him.

Inside he cheered. He could continue at a rapid pace to keep up with Sa-qan. Perhaps run into her again and clear up any misunderstandings they had.

"Yes, sir." Wade pivoted and searched among the troops for men he trusted. "You there." He motioned to three men who served under him since the beginning. "Pull your gear together and saddle up." Sergeant Murphy stepped out from behind a supply wagon. "Sergeant. Round up six more of my men and meet me at the entrance to the canyon in twenty minutes."

Wade didn't wait for the man to acknowledge. He set out toward the ramada to saddle a horse and toss his saddlebag on the animal. With men who knew of his eccentric walks and disappearances he could wander from camp at night and hope to encounter Sa-qan. He walked back through the encampment and frowned. Sturgis was regaling Murphy. No doubt telling him to keep an eye on the wandering lieutenant.

Wade mounted his horse and waited near the entrance. The men arrived, and they headed off at a trot following the well-trodden path of the Nez Perce. The last shots fired from the ridgeline died out the following evening, but Wade still rode with one eye tracking the shadows and swells of the ridge for movement. Had Sturgis sent him ahead in hopes to draw the Indians' hiding spots out? If so, wouldn't the major have handpicked the worst of the troopers to go with him? That would have been his strategy.

They rode all through the day, stopping briefly twice to allow the horses rest and water, before continuing on with the distance-covering trot/walk pace. He pushed the group till dark, traveling past the point the Nez Perce camped the night before. This pace would catch them up in three days if the Indians continued at their current speed.

Two privates built a fire and started coffee brewing. Wade unsaddled and cared for his horse before sampling the coffee. "You should take over for the officers' attendants—this is better than the kerosene prepared this morning." His comment received two grateful smiles from the men.

"Sir, do you wish sentries assigned?" Murphy had said little all day.

"Yes. Three men in shifts of three hours." He sank down next to his saddle and watched Murphy select the trio for first, second, and third watch. The hardtack dried his mouth more than usual. He tossed the bread back in his saddlebag and chewed on a slab of dried meat. His mind wandered to a time as a child when hardtack and dried meat were a treat, not a staple to his existence. Brief snippets of that carefree boy came out in Sa-qan's presence.

Wade conjured up her vision in his mind. Moonlight hair, golden eyes, full, soft lips, and fascinating body. *Where are you?* When would he get a chance to speak to her again? He craved her presence. He wished to soak in her tranquility and wisdom. She made him believe life beyond the military would fulfill him.

I wish you were beside me right now. He closed his eyes and leaned against the boulder behind him.

Come to me.

Pú-timt wax `uyné-pt
(17)

Wade jerked his eyes open and stared around the camp. He heard Sa-qan's voice. Her beckoning warmed his body, but how had he heard her? Where was she?

Murphy watched him with curiosity.

Wade slowed his breathing and ran a hand over his mustache. Relaxing back against the boulder, he pulled his hat over his face to shield his expressions from the man. *How is it I heard her voice?*

There is much I need to explain. Meet me when the moon is high at the base of the cliff where the sun rises.

Her voice floated through his head, again. This time he remained reclined. Only the heavy pounding of his heart and rapid breathing gave away his uncertainty and fear. Fear he'd finally lost his mind. Did he wish so strongly to be with Sa-qan he imagined her voice? He willed his body to relax, regulating his breathing and heartbeats to normal. Eventually, he dropped off to sleep and awoke with a start and the strong urge he needed to be somewhere.

He stretched and remembered Sa-qan's words. The moon had climbed to its zenith. He glanced to the east. A shadow of a cliff stood out in the moonlight. Stretching one more time, he stood and sauntered toward the east, hoping he staged the scene of a man out to relieve himself.

Once he walked through the perimeter of the sentries, he strode with conviction toward the cliff. If he didn't find Sa-qan waiting for him at the base of the cliff he'd know for certain he'd gone crazy.

«»«»«»

Sa-qan watched Wade's approach. She had taken a chance he would ignore her voice in his head or believe himself crazy. But he responded to her request. Did he fully realize she spoke to him? She doubted he believed the voice in his head belonged to her. But his curiosity brought him here, to her.

She shifted to smoke, swirled into her woman form, and walked down the cliff toward him. Wade's hurried footsteps sped her heart. He wished to see her. The last ten steps her breathing quickened and heat curled low in her belly. Memories of their last meeting excited and worried her mind. How did she tell him why she opposed his marriage request? How could she make him understand everything about her?

"Sa-qan?" Wade stopped a short distance from her. His eyes flickered from excited to surprised to puzzled. "How? I couldn't…"

"I asked you to meet me." She held his gaze and stretched a hand out to him. He shook his head before his gaze traveled to her outstretched hand.

"I don't understand." His uncertainty pricked her skin. Had fear vibrated from him, she would have worried about continuing the conversation. Uncertainty could be challenged with fact. Determination gripped her with deeper talons.

She took a step closer and grasped his large hand in hers. "We have much to talk about. Come with me."

He fell into step beside her, his gaze traveling over her face as he walked. "Where are we going?"

"Up where we can keep an eye on the camp, in case the other soldiers come searching for you." She stopped on a small outcropping a third of the way up the cliff. The small glow of the campfire below and the few who slept could be seen from this vantage point.

Wade stared down at the camp. She touched his arm and sat. "Sit with me."

He nodded and sat on the ground beside her. "Explain how I heard your voice in my head telling me to meet you here."

She clasped his hand. His fingers curled around hers and warmth spread up her arm and into her body. His aloofness had sprung doubts. But his accepting her touch dissolved them.

"I tried to tell you the last time we met. I am not what you think." She cleared her throat pushing the trepidation bobbing there back down.

"You've convinced me you're not a captive, you're Nez Perce." He placed a palm against her cheek. "If I felt half the conviction toward the military that you do for the Nez Perce, I'd be a general by now."

Sunshine, warm and friendly, glowed in her chest at his acceptance of her origins. Now, if he could grasp her other knowledge as well. She kissed his palm and stared into his eyes. Taking a deep breath she let her words flow. "I am not just a Nimiipuu maiden. I am a Nimiipuu spirit who can change forms."

His eyes widened, and he leaned back even as his hand remained cupped to her cheek. "What does that mean?"

The tingle of his nerves vibrated on her cheek. She clasped his hand and held it to her pounding heart. He had to understand. "Many seasons ago my father's greed led him to listen to the coyote. Because of his selfish actions, many warriors were killed by our enemies. Our band became inconsolable with grief and turned on his children—my brothers and I. The Creator saved us. He made us spirits to watch over the Lake Nimiipuu. They are the band of my mother's family—the band of Chief Joseph. This happened many seasons before the time of his father, old Chief Joseph. My brothers and I watched the people grow and prosper and helped them survive. Himiin, Wolf, roamed the mountain as a white wolf. Wewukiye, the brother I have told you about, is a bull elk who lives in the lake and his wife, Dove. She is a cow elk. I, Sa-qan, am a bald eagle. From the sky, I guide and protect my people."

His eyes narrowed then opened wide. "You're the bald eagle I saw on the ledge when you tended my bullet holes and then the one…" His eyes narrowed, and he stared through the moonlight at her. "Are you the one that flopped around on the ground? How…Why?" His voice grew shriller, and his hand gripped tighter as he thought about all she said.

He stared at their clasped hands. "I don't understand. You're solid yet soft in all the right places." His gaze lowered to her breasts before slowly returning to her gaze. "How could you be a spirit? I've heard of ghosts but they…" He shook his head. His hand grew limp.

She refused to allow him to disconnect with her. Not now. "I know this is hard to understand. But if you wish to make me your wife, we have to talk."

He stared at her. The hot, passionate gaze that melted her insides no longer pulsed in his eyes. Could they get back what they had? She needed him to believe in her and not be unsure.

"Do you wish to ask me something?"

"The other night. The smoke. Was that a trick?" He rubbed his mustache and stared into her eyes.

"No trick." She drew her hand from his and dissolved into smoke, hovered a moment, then returned to the human form. "I shift to smoke before I take another form."

His head shook slowly as if trying to clear away what he had witnessed.

"You change shapes?"

She shifted to smoke, her eagle form, smoke, and back to her maiden form. "Yes."

He reached out and grasped her hand, turning it over, peering at each finger, and testing their weight and firmness. "Do you change into other forms?"

"I prefer not to, but I can enter other animals or people and manipulate them."

His eyebrows arched and his gaze drilled into her. "Is that how I heard your voice? Were you inside me?" He started to toss her hand away.

She clutched his hand between hers. "No. I did not enter you. You would have felt my presence. We know each other too intimately for me to take over your vessel."

His eyes softened, and his fingers twined with hers. "How did you speak to me?"

"I was not sure you would listen or understand. Wewukiye could speak with Dove before she became a spirit, but she had strong txiẏak, powers. I hoped our power was strong and you would hear me." She smiled shyly at him. "I have never cared to speak with any other mortal male. You make my body sing and my heart light."

He pulled her into his arms and kissed her. An act she had hoped for from the moment she saw him following her summons.

She reveled in his tasting and probing lips. His exploration proved as heady as his previous kisses. Sa-qan fell into the intimacy with abandon. Excitement and yearning vibrated in her. She told him the truth about her so he would know she wished to be his in all ways.

Wade didn't want to think about Sa-qan being anything other than the woman in his arms. The woman he'd pinned his future on. Her fevered kisses, hands stroking his hair, and body pressing against his— meshing her womanly curves to his need—blocked his questions and doubts of sanity from forming in his head.

He ran his hands down her sides and up to cup her breasts. The weight and texture of them proved she was a woman. His woman. Smoke swirled in his mind, and a bald eagle flashed in his memory.

He jerked back. His hands remained on the fullness of her breasts. Sa-qan peered at him, her golden eyes so like the eagle; he shook his head. What was he doing kissing a spirit? Or someone who thought she was a spirit. Had he lost reality and become feeble from this campaign and his wounds? He raised a hand and placed it over the now almost vanished wound in his shoulder. He'd healed faster than anything he'd ever witnessed. Could it be? He stared at the woman in front of him. Sa-qan. A spirit?

Sa-qan placed a hand on top of his. "Does it still pain you?" Her hand grew hazy, and his shoulder warmed just as when she nursed him.

"No, there isn't any pain." He grasped her hand. Her cold fingers wrapped around his. She knelt in front of him, her gaze searching his face.

"I still don't understand." He ran a finger down her cheek. Her inviting lips opened slightly, and her eyes drifted shut. His body leaned in for a kiss, but he checked the motion inches from her lips.

"I want you more than anything I've ever wanted in my life. But I don't understand. How can you be a desirable woman and yet turn to smoke and an eagle before my eyes?" He'd heard stories of medicine men that would disappear and reappear. Were they also spirits?

"Do not think with your mind, think with your heart." She placed her hand on his chest. "Have I healed and cared for you? I am good for you."

"You've given me a desire for a future outside the military. But how can that happen if you're a spirit?"

She leaned in the last few inches and touched his lips with hers, a chaste kiss, before retreating to peer into his eyes. "The Creator will show us. He made Himiin mortal so he could be with Wren, the mortal he loved, and Dove became a spirit to be with Wewukiye. We will help my people and the Creator will reward us."

Wade stared into the eyes of the woman who had completely stolen his heart and possibly his mind. He wanted to help the Nez Perce not only to fulfill her wish but to save her people. How did one go about making a future with a spirit?

He sighed and gave up trying to figure it all out. Sa-qan cuddled against him, willing to fill his arms and relieve his loneliness. Wade wrapped his arms around her, drawing her body tight to his. "I guess knowing all this about you means you won't run off on me."

Her eyes lost their shimmer. "I do not understand."

"Every time I talked about a future with you, you'd disappear. Now that I know who you are, will you hang around and tell me more about being a spirit and perhaps discuss our future?"

Sa-qan's eyelids lowered, veiling her eyes a moment before she returned his gaze. "I will do my best to not run away." She pressed her lips to his.

He didn't want to talk anymore.

Wade took command of the kiss as his hands caressed her back and hips. Sparks snapped between their lips and he reared back. "What…"

"Our spirits have become one." Her eyes glowed like the early morning sun.

"How do you know this?"

"The light and heat of our lips touching."

Wade wasn't sure he liked the idea of sparks snapping when they kissed. "Will it happen every time?"

Her eyes shimmered with amusement. "No." Sa-qan wrapped her arms around his neck and pressed her lips to his. His body hummed with life and desire. Wade returned the kiss, easing her lips open and drinking in the exhilaration she poured forth. Warmth continued to flow through their embrace and intimate contact.

His hands slid under the hem of her dress, caressing the smooth skin on her thighs. She wiggled, settling her bare backside in the palms of his hands. The firm roundness triggered his need and pulsed his shaft.

Wade groaned and broke the kiss, his hands burned from the contact of her body. "Sa-qan, I want you so bad my body is tied in knots, but I won't make love to you here in the open where it has to be quick and on the hard ground." He eased his hands from her body.

She leaned in, her mouth inches from his. "It is my wish to become one with you tonight." Her warm, sweet breath flowed across his face and tickled his mustache.

"You aren't making this easy. I'd like nothing more than to fulfill your wish, but not here." He pulled her head against his chest to hide the passion glowing in her eyes. His control was only so strong. The desire burning in the depths of her eyes scorched his body and weakened his resolve.

Her arms wrapped around his body, and she pressed her soft curves against him, again.

"You're a vixen." He drew her face up and kissed her, wishing for a soft bed and privacy to show her his desire raged as strong as hers.

Sa-qan drew out of the kiss. "I only wish to become yours." She placed a hand on his cheek. "Tomorrow. I will show myself to you in the sky, and you will stop your soldiers for the night. I will tell you where to find me, and we will have cover and blankets."

Her words conjured up a night he'd dreamed of since meeting her. "I like your idea. But how will you—"

She placed a finger upon his lips. "My brother and sister will help. They have given their blessing for us to be one."

"Will I meet them then?" His curiosity about this brother and his wife needed to be resolved.

She turned her head. The heat of her cheeks brushed his. "I have not been kind to my brothers when they fell in love with mortals…I-I did not see how they could throw away all that the Creator gave us for a mortal." Her guilt-ridden eyes gazed into his. "Now, I have walked in their footsteps, and I see I was too harsh. It humbles me that Wewukiye has not rubbed my nose in my past attitude."

"So you aren't ready for him to see us together?" He could picture this woman lecturing her brothers on consorting with a mortal. Hell, it's what he was doing. Consorting with the enemy. But it didn't sit sour in his belly. It warmed his heart and his soul.

"Lt. Watts!"

Pú-timt wax `oymátat
(18)

Wade peered down the cliff. Sergeant Murphy and two others searched the lower ground headed toward the ridge where he and Sa-qan sat. The early morning gray grew lighter with each step they took.

"I will see you tonight." Sa-qan feathered a kiss across his lips and shifted to smoke, disappearing into the sky.

He stood and descended the cliff. Even though he hadn't slept, his body belied the fact, ready for a long day on a horse.

"Sergeant, I'm right here. Why are you looking for me?"

A call from an eagle rang through the light of dawn. How often had Sa-qan watched him from the sky?

Murphy strode forward. "When you didn't return during the night I thought something happened."

"The noises of the others sleeping annoys me. That's why I leave the camp. To sleep." Wade kept on walking. The three men fell in behind him, but Murphy strode beside him. The man's gaze flitted his direction, assessing him.

The sun cloaked the camp in yellow when they arrived. The other troopers had their horses saddled and ready to go. His mount stood saddled as well. He pulled hardtack out of his saddlebag and took the reins from a private.

"Thank you, Private." He mounted his horse and ordered, "Mount up."

They moved out at a trot. It didn't surprise Wade when Murphy rode up beside him.

"Sir, we didn't send someone back to Colonel Sturgis with a report."

"We'll know more tonight and send someone with a report then." He glanced at the sergeant's dirty uniform and weariness sagging his face. The same exhaustion clung to the other men riding with him. "Did you take a sentry shift last night?"

"Yes, sir." The man straightened in his saddle.

"Well, don't tonight. I need you rested. And only have two men a shift with two men getting a full night's sleep every night. We need to have part of the group sharp and rested."

"Yes, sir."

Wade couldn't handle any more conversation. He had too many things about his meeting with Sa-qan to think about.

"Sir?" Murphy's voice broke into his thoughts.

"Sergeant?"

"Do you think these Indians are going to make it to Sitting Bull?"

Wade shifted his attention on the trooper. The man squirmed in his saddle.

"I mean, why are we chasing them? Why don't we let them go? Everyone knows Sitting Bull took to living where no one else wants to."

Wade shook his head. "The Nez Perce have raised our government's anger, and they aren't going to let them get by that easy. And as servants to the government, it's our duty to do what we're told."

Murphy nodded and reined his horse back with the other men.

Wade continued on, wishing for a way to make the government see the waste of lives this campaign had left in its wake. Not only the troops and Indians but the civilians.

«»«»«»

Sa-qan watched the procession of soldiers continue in the path of the Nimiipuu. She knew Wade had to follow the orders of his leaders, but she also knew he would not let his soldiers harm innocent

Nimiipuu. Her heart filled her chest. Tonight they would become one.

She flew straight to the Nimiipuu camp in search of Wewukiye and Dove. The Nimiipuu had traveled a good distance from the camp location by the time she caught up. On the way, she had scouted the area between Wade and the Nimiipuu and found a hastily abandoned earth dwelling she and her brother and sister could clean and ready for the night.

Sister, did you talk with your soldier?

Yes, where are you?

Following the stragglers.

Sa-qan spotted the regal elk and landed on a rock near them. She had witnessed the slow pace of the women, children, and old before drifting to the ground.

"They are weakening," Dove said, staring at the slow progress of those in the back of the group.

"With the soldiers always finding them, they have not had time to rest and hunt for proper food. The warriors are always scouting and running off the Crow and Bannack trying to steal their horses." Wewukiye snorted his anger.

Sa-qan did not like the weariness and loss of hope drifting on the wind. "They need rest, but there is nothing we can do to stall so many soldiers or keep the enemy tribes from harassing." For the first time as a spirit, helplessness emerged. She saw little the three spirits could do to help their people. Too many enemies came after the Nimiipuu at once. She swallowed the fear bubbling in her throat. What would they do if the soldiers captured The People? How would they help them then?

"Joseph has spoken. He has promised they will find Sitting Bull and live in peace." The confidence in Dove's voice brought little comfort to Sa-qan.

"Then it will be so." Wewukiye stomped his hoof.

Sa-qan peered at the procession. How could Joseph have this conviction when she, a spirit with powers, had lost hope?

"Why did you seek us?" Dove broke into Sa-qan's fearful thoughts.

She shook, ruffling her feathers and trying to clear her mind of the failure residing in her chest. "I had..." How could she ask for something so selfish while her people struggled in turmoil?

"Does it have to do with your soldier?" The sparkle in Dove's eyes lightened Sa-qan's mood.

"Yes. I had planned to seek your help in cleaning an abandoned dwelling I found for us to use to become one." Heat sizzled up her neck and made her head warm like flying close to the sun.

"Why do you need a lodge? What is wrong with using mother earth's cushion and the Creator's stars?" Wewukiye narrowed his eyes, watching her.

"I was willing last night with such a bed. Wade said he would not become one without a soft bed and lodging." Her rapid heart beats nearly choked her as her brother continued to study her.

He snorted. "What kind of a man must have such to show his woman he loves her?"

Dove nudged Wewukiye with her muzzle. "Remember when I spoke with Agent William at the fort? His lodge had soft places to sit. Perhaps the so·yá·po cannot sit and sleep on hard surfaces?"

"But he sits on a hard saddle all day and sleeps on the ground at night." Sa-qan insisted, now also curious about Wade's demand.

"He made this up, knowing it could not be done," Wewukiye said, bobbing his head and antlers.

Sa-qan wrinkled her brow in thought. Was this true? Did he not want to become one? Heat scorched from her belly out to her hands and feet. His kisses and roaming hands as well as his manhood had wanted her. That he could not hide. She shook her head. "He wants to be one with me. This I am sure."

Dove peered at the disappearing Nimiipuu. "Then we must make this lodge ready and bring blankets. Once you have become one, he will help your people."

Sa-qan leapt into the air. "Follow me." Her brother and sister loped across the valley, following her to the earth shelter in the side of a hill. A prairie squirrel ran out the opening as Sa-qan landed. Squares of stacked sod and dirt made a small dwelling in the rise. The front wall had an opening and two short walls on the sides extended the space. A small rock fireplace stood in one of the short walls. Wood containers, two chairs, a table, and so·yá·po cooking pots scattered across the floor. A wood structure with rope laced back and forth stood in the corner. The occupants had made a hasty retreat. Perhaps they fled, learning of the Nez Perce traveling in the area. Sa-qan did not blame them. Many of the warriors had taken revenge to their hearts.

Wewukiye and Dove changed to human form and entered the dwelling behind Sa-qan.

"Only when you are dead do you live in mother earth," Wewukiye scoffed.

"This will be perfect," Dove said. "We will clean. You fly and find blankets." She pointed to the opening. "Bring an extra one to hang on the opening."

"Thank you both." Sa-qan hugged her brother and sister and shifted to her eagle form. Where would she find blankets? Soaring in the air, she spotted an altercation between Nimiipuu scouts and a group of so·yá·po. Her heart cringed when they raised their guns and shot at the Nimiipuu. Within minutes the so·yá·po no longer moved, and the Nimiipuu loaded all the food onto the horses.

She circled in the air, fearful of landing and finding a so·yá·po still alive. If she found a wounded man, her instincts would push her to heal. But to help the Nimiipuu prosper, her heart would not allow her to help men out to harm her people.

Sa-qan landed on a rock and studied the men. The tang of blood tainted the crisp air. Not a man moved. Only the sound of mother earth rustled in the breeze. She hopped down and crossed to the supplies the warriors flung about searching for food and weapons. Four blankets lay scattered about. She piled them together and clutched them in her talons.

Leaping into the air, she carried the blankets back to the earth dwelling with a heavy heart. She wished to be one with Wade, but the circumstance that allowed her to find blankets dulled her excitement.

Sa-qan shifted to woman form and stepped into the dwelling. Her sad thoughts vanished at the magic her brother and sister had performed. Animal droppings no longer sprinkled the floor. Pine scent filled the air from the boughs piled near the wooden thing in the corner. She carried the blankets to the structure.

"Why did you not spread the boughs on the ropes?"

"We needed a blanket to keep the pine from falling through." Dove placed a blanket over the frame and spread the pine boughs, placing two more blankets on top. "This is how so·yá·po sleep. When I lived at the mission as a young girl we were told to sleep on them, but we usually put our blankets on the floor."

Wewukiye took the last blanket from Sa-qan and stretched it across the opening using two sticks, one at each corner, to shove the blanket corners into the dirt wall and hold the covering in place.

"You will not be able to have a fire. The so·yá·po fire pit is not safe. Birds use it for a home." Wewukiye crossed his arms over his chest. Disapproval wrinkled his brow.

"We will be warm enough, I am sure." Sa-qan's face heated thinking of Wade's kisses and wondering what his unclothed body would look like.

Dove placed an arm around her shoulders. "Sister, I wish you the same happiness your brother has brought to me."

Wewukiye wrapped his arms around both of them. "This night will bring a new brother to our family." He grasped Sa-qan's hands. "If he is not worthy of you and our people, you will know tonight."

His gaze shivered doubt across her shoulders. If her body craved his, how would she know if he was not worthy?

"Come, my husband, we must return to the people." Dove captured Wewukiye's hand. The two exchanged a heated gaze and stepped to the opening.

"We wish to see you tomorrow," Dove said over her shoulder as the two shifted to smoke and then into elk.

Sa-qan watched the two lope into the distance. Their bond was special. Did she and Wade have the same bond? Would tonight bind them or prove she was meant to be alone—forever?

She shifted to her eagle form and leapt into the air. Time to find Wade and follow until she signaled him to stop.

《》《》《》

The sun's warming rays weakened as the day drew to an end. The troopers no longer sat straight and tall. Several slumped asleep in their saddles. If a scouting party came upon them they would all be dead within minutes. Wade didn't like the idea of his men coming to such an end. He'd noticed several of the men watching him with quizzical expressions. No doubt they wondered how he could be so refreshed. They hadn't spent the previous night in the arms of a spirit.

A screech drew his attention to the sky. A large bald eagle circled overhead. He scanned the area and spotted a small creek and a grove of aspen trees.

"Sergeant, we'll camp there tonight." He pointed to the trees and reined his horse around. Everyone dismounted, falling into the nightly routine of caring for their animals before themselves.

Wade unsaddled his mount, led it to water, and staked it out to eat the tan-colored fall grass. He plopped his saddle and belongings on the ground a distance from the others and waited for a private to get coffee brewing. A quick scan of the weary troopers told him he didn't have the heart to send one racing back to Sturgis with a report. They all needed rest. And there wasn't a rested horse in the bunch. The animals couldn't make a grueling ride either.

Murphy approached. "Sir, who are you sending with the report to Colonel Sturgis?"

"No one. There isn't a horse in the bunch who could go another mile let alone the twenty it would take to report to Sturgis. Until we come across fresh horses, he'll have to wait for our report."

"But—"

"I'll not risk a man's life on a worn out horse to send back that we haven't found anything. When we have a sighting of the Nez Perce, we'll worry about getting word to Sturgis."

The anxiety on the sergeant's young face ate at Wade's conscience. "This is my decision not yours. I'm the commanding officer of this excursion." He waved toward the others sprawled on their blankets. "Get some sleep. We all need it."

The trooper raised his eyebrows at the last statement but slowly returned to his blanket and lay down without eating. Most of the exhausted men didn't pull hardtack out of their knapsacks. They were all too tired to chew the dry, dense bread.

Wade's body buzzed with anticipation. Would he and Sa-qan make love tonight? He'd witnessed her disappointment last night when he refused to make her his on that dirty, stone cliff side. But what would be any different tonight? When he'd commented on the need for privacy and a soft bed he wanted to show her she meant more to him than taking her in the wild like an animal.

I am here. Follow the stream down past the trees. I will meet you there.

Sa-qan's soft voice triggered desire. He glanced at the men. Only the two on guard were awake and barely. Would his men be safe if he left? He didn't like the idea of leaving exhausted soldiers vulnerable.

Are there warriors close by?

All have settled for the night. Sa-qan replied

His men could sleep unhampered tonight. *I'll be there shortly.*

Wade rose, grabbed his saddlebag, and wandered to the creek. He followed it for a distance and stopped. Dropping the bags and kneeling next to the stream, he unbuttoned his shirt and washed his upper body before mixing shave soap. Using a small mirror he carried for this purpose, he scrapped the whiskers from his face and trimmed his mustache with small scissors. His hands shook as he wiped his face with his old shirt. What would the men think if someone stumbled upon him getting shined up? He slipped on his clean shirt, tossed his saddlebag over his shoulder, and continued along the creek.

When he spotted Sa-qan, he placed the saddlebag at the base of a tree and strode toward her. The moonbeams intensified the shine of her hair and sparkled in her eyes. She held her hands out to him. Her smile of invitation stopped his heart before jump-starting it into double time.

He pulled her into his arms, capturing her lips in a long, thirsty kiss. He leaned back, gasping for air and starving for more.

"Come. I found a place for us." Sa-qan twined her fingers with his and led him over a rise. They walked in silence. He enjoyed the grip of her hand and the confidence in her steps as she led him away from his sleeping troop and toward what he hoped to be heaven on earth. The anticipation of running his hands over her curves and sharing their desire for one another sizzled heat along his limbs and blazed like the stump fires he and his brother built helping their father clear the land.

His footsteps stumbled. That marked the first time he'd recalled a memory without guilt or shame attached. Only a melancholy sadness of missing his family invaded his senses. He stared at the woman striding beside him across the buffalo-shorn prairie grass over yet another rise. Had opening his heart to her also opened his heart to himself?

Before he had time to ponder the thought, a soddy came into view. A blanket hung over the open doorway. He pulled back on Sa-qan's hand.

"What are you doing? We can't invade on someone."

Her sparkling eyes and smile settled the jitters bouncing across his skin. "I found it empty. Wewukiye and Dove helped me ready it for this night."

A different kind of nervous griped his gut. "Your brother helped you ready a place for a man to…" he couldn't get the rest out. Would he have helped his sister prepare a place for a man of her choosing to take her innocence? Hell no. Not before they married.

Her gaze locked with his. "He has learned when I want something he cannot stop me."

"B-but to allow you to…with a man…we aren't married. My desire for you has stomped all over my clear thinking." He grasped her upper arms. "Sa-qan, Angel, my body burns to make love to you but I can't…that's something two people who are married should do. Not like this."

She placed a finger on his lips. Her eyes blazed hot with desire. "When we have become one, we will be married. It is the way of my people." She moved the blanket aside and drew him into the house.

The freshly swept dirt floor and an Indian water pouch hanging from a stick in the wall exuded welcome. Blankets on a bed frame in the far corner captured his attention. Pine scent filled his nostrils moments before Sa-qan slipped into his arms and pressed her lips to his. He'd entered heaven or as close as he'd ever come to heaven on earth. He breathed in her fresh outdoor and herb scent. Their seclusion and love making tonight would bind them. At least in the eyes of her people; for now that was all that mattered to him. He'd deal with making her his wife in his world later.

Her fingers worked the buttons of his shirt open. He moaned when she splayed her hands across his flannel undershirt.

"Sa-qan, slow down. We have all night." He captured her hands, holding them between their chests. Gazing into her eyes, he grappled with his control. This would be her first coupling, and he wanted to make it special.

He traced her cheek with a finger pad, dropping soft kisses in the wake of its path. She shivered and sighed. A smile quivered on his lips. He planned to elicit those reactions from her for hours.

Pú-timt wax kúyc
(19)

Sa-qan's skin quivered, and her body ached for something she knew only Wade could give her. His gentle caress and searing kisses took her to heights beyond anything she had experienced as an eagle soaring through the sky. The heat his touch lit in her belly blazed hot and needy.

She shoved his shirt to the floor and worked on the fastenings on the white, softer shirt underneath. Her hands skimmed across his hot skin and through the sprinkling of dark curls on his chest. Desire struck her full force. She could not touch him enough or inhale enough of his scent.

Dropping soft open-mouthed kisses across his skin, she tasted his earthy mix of soap, salt, and Wade.

He groaned and drew her mouth to his. His tongue slipped between her lips and touched hers. Dizziness weakened her legs, and she sagged against his hard body, wondering at the power of his kiss to weaken her so. He released her mouth and ventured down her jaw and neck licking, nipping, and kissing. An ache started in her chest and moved lower, pulsing her woman parts. Her body had never felt so alive.

Wade stepped back.

She moaned and reached for him.

"I want to touch your skin." He grasped the bottom of her deer skin dress and drew it up over her head, revealing her body to him.

No one had ever seen her in this state. But she knew from witnessing the Nimiipuu women when they bathed, her form would be appealing. The desire that flashed and burned in Wade's eyes also told her.

"You are so beautiful." He reached out, weighing her breasts in his hands. His palms caressed the sides of her breasts and skimmed down her sides to rest on the curve of her hips. "So beautiful." He pulled her snug against him and captured her lips once more.

Sa-qan dove into the kiss. His hot, hard muscles pressed against her breasts made her nipples tingle and the ache in her woman parts start all over again. She moaned and ground her hips against his deerskin leggings. Her hands pressed between their bodies, working the string on his breeches loose.

Wade held her away from him. "Wait for me on the bed." He turned her to the corner and swatted her playfully on the bottom.

She scurried to the corner and sat on the bed watching him. He slipped his boots off, then his socks, and last he lowered his underclothes at the same time as his leggings, revealing his enlarged manhood. Sa-qan inhaled sharply. She had never witnessed mortals mating, only animals. She had watched the Nimiipuu men take baths. Were so·yá·po men different than the Nimiipuu men? Seeing the naked warriors had never made her curious to take their man parts into her hands, but right now, her palms itched to caress and hold Wade.

He walked to the bed.

She reached out, grasping the hot, firm appendage. The softness reminded her of a well-tanned deer hide.

"Sa-qan, you keep caressing me like that and I'll be spent before you find pleasure."

"It pleases me to hold you this way." She glanced up. His eyes were half closed, his lips slightly parted, and pleasure relaxed his features.

"It pleases me to make love to you." He placed his hand on her shoulder and nudged her onto her back. His body covered hers. His hard manhood pressed between them, nestling against her maiden curls, sending more exciting sensations sparking through her body.

Wade's mouth covered hers and sent her mind spiraling as her body arched to press ever closer to his. She wanted closer, to feel him within her.

She pulled out of the kiss. "I want you."

He rose up, gathering air between them. She started to protest, then his hand rubbed a spot that jerked her body, and his finger slipped into her body. His entry and retreat motions made her body wiggle and push toward his hand. The actions filled her with pleasure, but she instinctively knew there was more. Much more.

"Please. I want you, all of you," she pleaded, grasping his head and seducing his mouth with a deep kiss.

Strong arms banded around her, his knee spread her legs more, and he pressed at her entry. Slow, tentative progress teased her senses.

"I need you now." She thrust her hips, pushing him deeper.

"I have to go slow—this is your first time, it could hurt." The worry in his voice did little to ease her need.

"The pain will be worth the pleasure. I cannot take any more of this slowness." She grabbed his backside and pulled him to her at the same time she thrust her hips. He seated all the way, and they met pelvis to pelvis. A slash of pain struck before the fullness of him expanded her heart.

He stroked her center in the primal rhythm she knew well from the ceremonial drums of the Nimiipuu. Her body responded movement for movement. Pressure built at their linked bodies.

He moved faster.

She drew him deeper.

Her body sparked from a bolt of lightning that scorched through her body, numbed her mind and her limbs, and sealed her heart to Wade's.

"Sa-qan!" he called and his seed spilled with force inside her. Making her his and binding them in the eyes of her people and the Creator.

Wade hugged Sa-qan tight, kissing her face and finally sealing their lips in a long, tender kiss. He loved this woman with every inch of his flesh and soul. Even if their love making hadn't been explosive he would have felt the same. She had entered his heart before he entered her body and made her his.

He lifted his head and peered into her eyes. "That was even better than my dreams." The love and acceptance glistening in her golden gaze filled his chest with pride. She was his.

"I have thought of this night many times since our paths crossed. Now I know why this ceremony binds two hearts." She trailed her fingers down his cheek. "You are the only mortal who could ever bring me this happiness and contentment."

The word mortal hauled all the questions and problems before them back into his mind. He shifted to his side, drawing her with him. "I'd rather forget about our differences and the obvious influences that could cause us problems, but we can't ignore what is happening. Not unless you'd run away with me." He knew she wouldn't, but he'd dreamed of the two of them heading west and never looking back.

Her eyes dulled. She shook her head slowly. "I cannot abandon my people. They need me more now than all the seasons I have watched over them."

He sighed. "I knew you'd say that, but I had to ask." He hugged her tight. Her convictions to her people were one to the many things he loved about the woman. "We aren't going to be able to spend time like this every night until the Nez Perce surrender and go to a reservation." Her body stiffened. He caressed her back and nibbled on her ear. "I know that's not what you or the rest want but I'm afraid it will come to that or your people will be killed."

She shoved against his chest, and he let her put space between them.

"I have seen the people on the reservations. They are treated worse than cattle. We would be better off to leave this earth than live like that."

"I agree. The reservations are horrific if the agents are greedy and have other agendas. But isn't carrying on the Nez Perce ways more important than dying to avoid living on a reservation?" He skimmed a finger down her cheek and rubbed his thumb across her kissable bottom lip. "I'll do all I can to help, but I can't promise I can save the Nez Perce." He cupped the back of her head and drew her into a kiss.

Her body relaxed.

He used his other hand to fondle her full, lush breasts, hardening the nipples. He lowered his head and suckled the raspberry nubbins. She moaned, wound her hands in his hair, and pressed his face into her luscious mounds.

He'd make love to her one more time. He'd make sure his angel floated to heaven more than once, then he had to get back to camp. He couldn't chance someone looking for him and stumbling upon their love nest.

«»«»«»

The crescent moon hung low in the dark sky, awaiting the arrival of the sun to push it out of sight as Wade walked back to the grove of trees, holding Sa-qan's hand. The second round of love making had weakened both of them. He slept with the weight of Sa-qan's head resting on his shoulder. She'd divulged more about herself. She didn't eat or sleep. Both daily necessities he needed to survive. When he asked if she could become with child from their joining, she didn't know. He wanted children with her, but wasn't sure what would happen given their different worlds. He wouldn't trade their love making or his love for her, but their future hung on so many things. One being how they would bridge their differences. How did one live with a spirit? While she was flesh and blood in his hands right now what would prevent her from changing shapes and disappearing from his life?

Sa-qan squeezed his hand. He stopped and gazed into her eyes. Uncertainty swirled.

"Are you regretting our coming together?"

Tugging Sa-qan into his arms, he kissed her luscious lips. "No, I'll never regret making you mine. I'm just trying to figure out how to make it all work."

She snuggled her head into his shoulder. "I will think on this as well."

He chuckled. "Two heads are always better than one." He kissed her and joined their hands.

"I have to get back before they come looking for me." He glanced at her glowing face. "Can we still talk in our minds?"

Her smile lit her whole face. "Yes."

"Then I'll try to let you know what is happening and if I can slip away to see you again." He stopped at the tree where he'd left his saddlebags. "When this is over we'll be together. I promise."

She stood on her tiptoes and kissed his lips. "I will look forward to that day with all my heart." She shifted to smoke, and he remained in a trance relishing the tingle on his lips.

The shrill call of an eagle shook him back to reality. He picked up his saddlebag and headed to the camp. If anyone saw his approach they'd see he'd cleaned up to start the day.

He yearned to be back at the soddy with Sa-qan in his arms. They may have become husband and wife by her people's laws, but he couldn't breathe a word about her to anyone until this campaign ended and he'd married her in a church. He knew his mother would have understood had she been alive and able to talk this out with him. But in the eyes of the government, they weren't married. He wouldn't bring shame to Sa-qan by trying to pass her off as his wife without the paperwork to prove it.

Besides, he still had to get through this campaign alive and help keep the Nez Perce from getting annihilated by the U.S. government. When this battle started he'd been ready to help pressure the Indians into moving to the reservation and allowing more civilians to homestead on their land. Now he just wanted the bloodshed to stop and the Indians peacefully settled anywhere they wanted. If that meant figuring out a way to keep the army from catching the Nez Perce before they joined Sitting Bull, then that's what he'd do. His love for Sa-qan now extended to her people and helping her fulfill her commitments.

Le'éptit
(20)

Sa-qan flew above the Nimiipuu camp tucked out of sight of the river her people had crossed that morning. The crossing took place both upstream and downstream from the landing for boats and supplies belonging to the so·yá·po. The Nimiipuu and horses were allowed passage without incident. She had circled in the air watching as the small group of soldiers held their weapons, but did not stop the Nimiipuu from crossing.

Now Joseph and another approached the landing unarmed. She wished Wade were here to help the soldier understand hunger plagued her people. Since she and Wade had become one, they had only visited once and it had been cut short by the soldiers seeking his guidance. Not nearly long enough for either one, but they both honored their duties. His horses and men fared worse than the Nimiipuu. He remained close to keep them from harm, much the same as she remained close to the Nimiipuu.

A so·yá·po met Joseph and another Nimiipuu warrior. The so·yá·po left, and a soldier talked with Joseph before the soldier returned to the buildings and came back carrying supplies. Joseph accepted the bundles. The bundles could not hold enough food to feed the Lake Nimiipuu band which only made up a quarter of the people at the camp waiting for food.

Joseph returned to the camp and a heated discussion began. She watched the anger build in the warriors. Small groups left the discussion, heading back to the river. The warriors set a building on fire, and as the so·yá·po tried to stop the blaze, the warriors looted the other buildings, bringing back food for their families. The People needed food, but she could not condone the behavior of the warriors.

It heartened her to see the children eating, but the way the warriors stole the food would only make the soldiers angrier. Only a handful of soldiers watched the burning fires. She leaped into the air and started circling the area. If such a small force were sentinels for the river there must be more somewhere.

«»«»«»

Wade saw smoke billowing in the distance. His heart sickened. On the trail of the Nimiipuu he'd found too many homes destroyed. Sa-qan told him the Indians asked for food first and when they were refused took drastic matters. Their actions didn't help their cause. The more Whites they killed and plundered, the less sympathy he could muster from the government.

He rubbed a hand over his unshaven face and stared at the smoke. His troops might reach the spot by nightfall. Wade twisted in his saddle and scanned his weary troops. He couldn't push his men or their mounts that hard.

They were a good day's ride behind the Nimiipuu. He wanted to leave the men for Howard to pick up and head out on his own. He missed Sa-qan. Memories of their discussions and heated kisses were all that kept him from falling victim to the fatigue of his troops. He rested well, dreaming of his angel.

An eagle's shrill cry invaded his thoughts. He glanced up, catching sight of Sa-qan. Her magnificence as a woman and as an eagle enthralled him. How his logical mind could accept her forms and the reality he could speak to her and love her when she wasn't a mortal intrigued him.

Follow me. We must talk. Her words slipping into his thoughts he didn't understand, but he didn't question, only listened and obeyed.

"Sergeant Murphy, halt the troops and rest the horses. I'll scout ahead." Wade didn't wait for a response. The sergeant had grown accustomed to this type of command from his lieutenant.

Wade urged his tired horse into a trot and followed the soaring eagle north. Once he'd put two miles between he and his men, he reined his mount toward a clump of aspen trees and dismounted.

Sa-qan walked out from behind a tree and straight into his outstretched arms. Enfolding her to his chest, he drank in her scent and savored her soft curves pressed against him.

"I've missed you." He tipped her face up, kissing the lips he dreamed about every night and day.

She returned the kiss, breath for breath and tongue to tongue. Her bold exchange heated his blood and surged his desire beyond the limits of his buckskin breeches.

He drew out of the kiss, clutching her to his throbbing body. He'd never wanted a woman as fiercely as he wanted this one. His physical needs burned and ached to the point of pushing past desire to agony.

"My need to be one with you makes my body ache," he whispered against her ear.

"I feel the same." Her hands worked at the buttons on his jacket.

"This is hardly the pla—"

She stilled his words with a searing kiss.

Propriety and chivalry be damned. If he didn't make love to her soon… Her hands slipped through his three layers of upper clothing and slid across his skin. The brisk autumn air couldn't cool his fever for Sa-qan.

He pulled out of the kiss, spread his jacket and coat on the ground, and lowered her upon them. "I can't wait for the appropriate place, but I can supply a barrier between your skin and the cold ground." As he spoke she pulled her dress over her head, displaying her womanly attributes for his heated gaze. "You really know how to knock a man off his game."

An alluring smile tipped her luscious lips, and he groaned when her fingers dipped along the waistband of his breeches.

"You must take off your clothes. I wish to feel your skin to mine."

Her breathy command plopped him on his backside, and he

yanked his boots off.

Standing, he shucked his breeches. His shaft sprang out, aching and throbbing. He bit his mustache as Sa-qan reached out, taking him into her delicate hands. The soft touch nearly had him spilling his seed. He quickly knelt, cradling her head in his hands.

"I want you to know, there has never been another woman who stirred my desires or claimed my heart." He kissed her lips, her jaw, her neck, and worked his way down to her beautiful breasts. He licked and nibbled the raspberry nipples, enjoying her intake of breath and gasps of pleasure. His ache subsided as he brought her bliss.

All he ever wanted was to bring her happiness. He eased her to her back, covered her body with his, and slipped into Sa-qan. Awareness of her body, hot, wet, and welcoming sent his heart galloping. Her hips tipped, giving him a deeper thrust. Tears welled in his eyes at the pleasure her body gave him. He captured her lips in a long, wet kiss, injecting all his passion and love for her into the mating of their tongues.

Her fingers dug into his backside, pulling him deeper, moving him in a rhythm that played in his head. Her body came up to meet his with each thrust and grind. Wade placed his hands beside her head and pushed up. His gaze locked on her glowing eyes as he continued the rhythm she'd established. Stars glittered in her eyes and the glowing lights resembled twin suns, blinding him. Her body vibrated and clenched his. One last thrust spilled his soul deep within her shimmering body.

He collapsed, drawing her to him and rolling to his back, bringing her body over him like a blanket. He kissed her and dropped his head to the hard earth. "I thought the first time we made love was earth rattling."

Sa-qan rose up, her forearms planted on his chest, her lovely nipples brushing against him. "When we come together it feels as though a lightning spear rips through my body, giving me light and life. It is both frightening and very pleasurable." She leaned down, kissing his chin. "I find much about you makes me happy."

Her words triggered another squeeze of his heart. "You make me very happy. Happier than I've been in years." He rolled, slipping her desirable body under him. Her soft curves, lush breasts, and kissable lips had his body springing to life once again. "I only regret we aren't in our home where I could pamper you and love you until dawn." He lowered to kiss her and saw wariness flicker in her eyes.

"Did I say something wrong?" He grieved the idea of leaving her warm body, but couldn't ignore the brief hesitation in her eyes. Wade rolled off and sat, drawing her up onto his lap. "Why do you look and feel like you're going to disappear?"

The sorrow in her eyes when she looked at him, struck as sharp and blunt as an axe in his back.

"How will we be together? We are of two worlds." Her softly spoken words didn't put fear in his heart it challenged him to work to find a way.

"We'll worry about that once the Nez Perce are settled. Right now, I want to enjoy the few moments I get with you. No thoughts of later." He held her chin in his hand, drawing her lips to his. He brushed them softly, eliciting a soft moan from her before seducing her mouth. His hands roamed her body at will, following the curves and dips, memorizing the places that caused her to squirm and the ones that filled his mouth with her gasps. His hands grazed the golden hair at the juncture of her legs. Her hips moved toward his hand.

He smiled against her lips, delved into her sweet mouth with his tongue, and his fingers into her hot moist center. She rocked against his hand and moaned. Her movements rubbed the length of his alert shaft, flaming his desire. Not releasing her from his kiss, he turned her body and settled her over his throbbing need. She drew him in inch by agonizing inch. He pulled out of the kiss, expelling a hiss of barely held restraint.

Fully seated deep in her body, she moved up and down, bobbing her breasts in his face. He grasped a nipple between his lips. She moaned and moved faster. He grasped her backside, helping her move up and down. He nipped her rosy nubbin. Her body contracted around him, she gasped his name, and dropped into his lap as he lost control, once again giving every essence of him to her in his release.

He clutched her body to his as she remained seated in his lap, their bodies and hearts fused. The steady thrum of her heart to his and her breath combining with his—he did believe they had become one. He knew to have her out of his life he would feel only half a man.

Wade pushed her shimmery white hair out of her face and kissed her nose. He'd never seen her so lethargic. "Did I hurt you?" fear gripped him that he'd been too rough this last time.

She opened her eyes. Their golden depths glittered. Her kiss-swollen lips tilted into a devastating smile that flipped his heart. "You lifted me to the clouds and beyond. My body will always thirst for you, and my heart will hold you forever."

"I take it that means I didn't hurt you?" His heart hummed with delight from her words.

"No, you could never hurt me. But you have drained my powers." Her forehead wrinkled in a frown. "It is curious that you weaken my powers when we make love just as I am drained when I heal."

"I don't find it curious, because you have healed my heart." He kissed her forehead until the wrinkles disappeared.

She tipped her face, skimming her lips across his. "Was your heart injured?"

"In a way. Until I met you I'd hidden behind my duties as a cavalry officer to keep from confronting my sorrows from the past. Losing my family, the war, and all the things that had slowly eaten away at my desire to live." He peered into her intelligent loving eyes. "Meeting and loving you has made me realize there is a life outside of the military, and I want to try it, again. With you." He stopped her from dipping her head and stared into her eyes. "We will be together when this is over. We'll find a way. I promise." He sealed his promise with a tender kiss.

Sa-qan melted in his arms. He believed in his words. She must, too. Her heart would only beat if she had Wade in her life. This she realized when her body shattered in waves of unbridled ecstasy and her heart soaked in his essence. They were one and would always be one.

She wound her arms around his neck, pressed her tingling breasts to his chest, and wiggled in his lap, bringing his maleness to life inside her once more.

«»«»«»

Sa-qan stood beside Wade. The sun had begun to set.

"I've been gone too long from my troops. I need to get back or they're going to come looking for me." Wade squeezed her hand.

"I have witnessed soldiers coming from the fort beyond the river. They will catch up to the Nimiipuu before Cut Arm. You must get to them and ask them to let the Nimiipuu escape."

"I can't ask them to allow the Nez Perce to escape, but I can try and stall them. My horse, however, will never make it." He patted his horse.

"I will bring you a horse this night. You can go to the soldiers." She put a hand on his prickly cheek. She had enjoyed the roughness and the softness of him as they became one. She liked many things about Wade. She could not stop the curving of her lips.

His eyes lit with merriment as he placed a hand over hers. "Why are you smiling?"

"I see a man who honors his duties and a man who will hold my heart with gentleness." She raised onto her toes and kissed his lips. "I will see you soon." She shifted to smoke, drifted toward the darkening sky, and swirled into an eagle. She must find a rested horse for Wade to ride to catch the soldiers headed toward the Nimiipuu. He had to talk to the soldiers. Between them they had to stop the killing.

Le'éptit wax ná-qt
(21)

Wade rode into camp. Three rabbit carcasses proved the men had more than hardtack in their bellies. He waved Murphy over to him out of earshot from the rest of the men.

"Sergeant, the Indians are moving farther ahead of us every day due to our tired mounts and low rations. I didn't see any sign of a back guard. I want you and the men to wait here for supplies and Sturgis to catch up. I'm going to go on ahead and see if I can't figure out their intentions on the direction they're heading." Wade chewed on hardtack, swallowed hard, and eyed the pile of rabbit bones.

"Sir, do you think it's wise for you to continue chasing them Indians?" Murphy ran a hand through his red curls. "Your horse isn't any stronger than the rest of ours."

"When I come across a farm, I'll purchase a new mount." Hopefully Sa-qan could find him a horse. Did spirits steal? He hoped not, but it would be best if he didn't ask her how she acquired a mount for him.

The sergeant shook his head. "Every homestead we've come across has been wiped out by the Indians."

"I'll travel off the Nez Perce's path and see what I can find." He didn't like telling fibs to his own troops. Sa-qan said the other troops approached from a different direction.

"Go to sleep, Sergeant. I'll leave in the morning." Wade took the offered coffee a private brought him and sank to his blanket. After three rounds of love making with Sa-qan he was weary but not tired. He closed his eyes, thought about his angel, and drifted off, hatching a plan to catch the troops coming from the north.

«»«»«»

Sa-qan found a so·yá·po dwelling with cattle and horses. She landed on the fence and watched the horses, deciding which would be the strongest to carry Wade a great distance the fastest. Her legs grew tired as she studied the horses. Wade must have been right about her healing his heart. That would explain why she fought weakness. She had yet to rest since their giving of their bodies to one another.

The dark horse with white socks gave off the aura of spirit and strength. She drifted to smoke and entered the horse. He had a strong heart but also a quest for freedom. This made directing the animal to jump the fence and run away easy.

When the horse tired, she walked to the spot where she and Wade became one and waited. He would arrive shortly after the sun came up. She drifted out of the animal. The bounty of grass would fill his belly while she waited and rested. Weariness wrapped around her like a warm wool blanket.

«»«»«»

Sunshine warmed her face and the snort of a horse shook her awake. Sa-qan stretched and watched the horse. She had not fallen asleep before as a spirit. Did Wade's injured heart require that much healing that it drained her txiẏak more than physical healing?

The horse raised its head and nickered. She rose, wrapping an arm around the animal's neck, calming the creature so it did not run.

Wade rode up. The animal under him hung his weary head and walked tenderly. Wade stopped, slipped from the animal, and walked up to her, looping a rope around the spirited horse's neck.

"This is a fine animal. I'm not going to ask where you acquired it." Disapproval and wariness dulled the initial welcome in his eyes. He kissed her cheek and placed the rope in her hand.

He knew she took a so·yá·po horse. He kissed her, but he did not approve of her taking the horse even for the good of the Nimiipuu.

"Would it help to know this animal did not wish to pull a wagon?" she asked, watching him take the saddle from his horse.

He faced her, the riding gear in his arms. "I don't want to hear how you stole someone's horse. They hang White men for that offense."

She stood with her back to Wade as he saddled the horse. He took the rope from her and slid the bridle onto the animal's head. Why had he hurt her with his sharp tongue and unkind words? If he held a strong belief in riding a stolen horse why did he saddle the animal?

Sa-qan grabbed Wade's arm. "If you look down on me for taking this horse, why do you accept to ride him?"

His eyes softened, and his free arm wrapped around her shoulders. "Because I have fallen for a woman, and I will do anything short of killing to help her." His eyes shown with love as his head dipped and his lips pressed to hers.

Her heart raced with the knowledge he could forgive her actions even if he did not agree with them. And Wewukiye had known this truth. Because Wade loved her he would help her people.

She curled her arms around his neck, returning the kiss.

Wade drew out of her arms. "Show me the direction I must ride to catch up with the troops."

Where had her mind gone? They must hurry. She had flown the direction of the soldiers before getting the horse. The troops steadily gained on the Nimiipuu.

"I will fly ahead of you." She concentrated on shifting. Smoke swirled around her; the eagle form did not come as easily as usual. She had to concentrate harder before the transformation began.

The effort needed to change left her shaking. To ward off the tremors, she ruffled her feathers and stared up at Wade. He mounted the horse and waited for her to take to the air.

What was happening? First she slept and now changing forms trembled her body.

Wade smiled at her and motioned. "I'm ready, let's go."

She leaped into the air and flapped her wings, soaring toward the sun. Her mind worked on the puzzle of the weaknesses she had experienced as her eyes scanned the ground. Wade and the horse trotted along behind her. She soared higher and spotted the Nimipuu in the distance.

The Nimiipuu now spent longer time each day in camp and traveled slower. They believed with Cut Arm far behind they were safe. Once she lured Wade toward the soldiers, she would return to the camp and find a way to make them aware of the troops growing closer.

Sa-qan dropped back down to where Wade could see her easily and circled. She continued circling and soaring until the sun hovered directly over the earth. Wade moved at a direct pace toward the soldiers. Her wings grew heavy, forcing her to find air currents to carry her along. This had never happened to her before. She had always flown for days never taking a break.

Sa-qan landed on a rock not far from Wade. He pulled his horse up beside the rock as she slipped into her woman form. The change, again, taking longer and more concentration than usual.

"Continue this direction and you will catch up to the soldiers by this time tomorrow." Her body quivered from fatigue. How could this be? She fought the urge to ask him to hold her.

"Sa-qan, angel, you don't look well." Wade started to dismount.

"Stay on the horse. Go to the soldiers. Help my people." It took all her strength to wave her hand. She did not wish him to see her in her weak condition.

He ignored her plea and dismounted, pulling her into his arms. "What's wrong? You're shaking."

"I-I do not know. I am…weak." She stared into his caring eyes. A new strength built in her chest and seeped to her limbs. "Go on. I will be fine. Once I have rested I will return to the Nimiipuu. You must go. These soldiers must have compassion in their hearts for my people."

"I can't leave you the way you are." Concern radiated from him.

She kissed his cheek. "Go. Carry your love for me and my people with you."

"I don't like leaving you alone like this." The worry etched on his brow added to her growing strength.

"Wewukiye will be here soon. Go." She pushed on his chest,

standing on her own, and forcing her lips to smile. "Go."

He watched her a moment. "You're sure your brother is coming?"

She nodded. He would come when she called to him. "Yes. Go. You are wasting time."

Wade mounted his horse, scanned her from her head to her feet, and said, "I love you and do this for you."

Tears burned in her eyes. She sniffed and nodded. "You have my heart."

He spun the horse on its haunches and loped the direction of the soldiers.

Sa-qan collapsed to the ground when only a billow of dust registered Wade's departure. What was wrong with her? In all her seasons as a spirit she had never grown so weak or confused.

Wewukiye, I need you. Come fast.

Thoughts bounced around in her head. Did the Creator weaken her body to show his disapproval of her becoming one with a mortal? She thought of the magical moments with Wade. The love and hope he filled her with and the wonderful sensations of becoming one with him. How could that harm the Nimiipuu and her duty? He held the Nimiipuu in his heart as he held her. Wade, as a soldier, could help them work toward a common ground with the so·yá·po. This she believed with all her heart.

"Sister, what is the matter?" Wewukiye and Dove skidded to a stop in front of her.

The sight of her family trickled tears down her cheeks. Family cared for and protected one another. She stared at the two through tear-blurred vision. Dove shifted to woman form and sank to the ground beside her, embracing her.

"Shhh, did you and Wade quarrel?" she asked.

"No. He is headed to talk to the soldiers coming from the fort." She sniffed and peered up at her brother. His eyes softened as he changed to a man and crouched beside her.

"Why are you crying? What is wrong?" He put a hand on her shoulder.

"I fell asleep. I have never had a need for sleep since becoming a spirit. And when I flew to show Wade where the soldiers are I became tired and now…" She swallowed the lump of fear lodged in her throat.

"This vessel is weak and I cannot turn to smoke to change."

Wewukiye glanced at Dove. He cleared his throat. "Sister, may I place my hand on your belly?"

Sa-qan nodded but wondered what he could learn by such an action.

His large, warm hand rested low on her torso. He closed his eyes and chanted. His words sought answers to her body. She studied his face as he sang. His expression remained unchanged. His eyes opened. The light blue orbs peered into hers.

"Sister, you are growing a mortal seed. As it grows your spirit powers lessen and you will become mortal." His even tone and uncensored words struck her as soundly as a tree falling on her.

A seed. Wade's child grew within her. Warmth wrapped around her heart. She would be mortal and have Wade's child. They could be together.

She would become mortal. What about the Nimiipuu? They needed her. How could she help them if she no longer flew above seeing their enemies before they arrived?

Dove wrapped her arms around her. "Congratulations, sister. You will remain with your soldier and have children."

"But what about our people? How can I help them if I am mortal?"

"It will come to you just as you have found the way to be with your mate." Wewukiye took her hand. "If you rest, can you still shift into an eagle?"

"I do not know. Why did I not feel the child within me?" It bothered her that she could be losing her powers so quickly.

"It is a part of you. You cannot detect yourself." Wewukiye said.

"But how will I survive as a mortal?" She would require food, shelter, and rest.

"Your soldier will care for you." Dove pat her arm.

"He cannot help me until the soldiers leave the Nimiipuu alone." Fear gripped her, crushing her chest, making it hard to breathe.

"You can wait here. I will bring your soldier to you." Wewukiye nodded his head as if he had given her a good choice.

"No, I must remain with our people. I must help them." Sa-qan clutched her brother's arm. "You must take me to the Lake Nimiipuu. I will live with Silent Doe and Girl of Many Hearts. They will remember me as the one who saved them. They will help."

"How will your soldier find you?" Worry trembled Dove's voice.

Sa-qan peered into her brother and sister's eyes. "You will go to him and tell him where I am. When all is well he will come for me."

"I could leave right now and catch him. Bring him back to you." Wewukiye shifted into his elk form.

"No. He must meet with the soldiers and talk with them. He is needed to help the Nimiipuu. I will be fine with Silent Doe." Confident words did not soothe the ache in her heart and longing to be in Wade's strong arms. How selfish. Even as a mortal, protecting the Nimiipuu came first. She would not disfavor herself in the eyes of her people or the Creator. The child growing within her would be welcomed by her people.

Dove shifted to an elk.

Wewukiye knelt down. "Climb on. We will take you to the Nimiipuu camp."

Sa-qan climbed onto Wewukiye's broad back and held onto the hair at the base of his massive neck. Fear of her future washed a shiver across her skin. What did she tell the Nimiipuu when she arrived in their camp? How did she explain being alone? They would be wary of her moonbeam hair and sunshine eyes.

When would she see Wade again? There would be no more meetings. She had no way to reach him. What would he think when she did not run into him or speak to him? Would he listen with his heart and search for her?

Wewukiye set off at a smooth lope, covering the distance quickly. He stopped where they could see the camp but not be seen.

Her heart lodged in her throat. Since becoming a spirit this would be her first vulnerable moment. Her life hung on the Nimiipuu accepting her into their camp. Her only other option would be to ride Wewukiye to the soldiers and search for Wade. That would put her in more peril and hinder Wade's ability to persuade the soldiers to talk with the Nimiipuu.

She slid from her brother's back. Her legs wobbled, but she straightened and took a step forward. "I will speak to you when I am settled."

"What will you tell them?" Dove's wide, caring eyes warmed Sa-qan.

"I became separated from my Nimiipuu family and have been following them. It is what I told the old woman when I helped heal her family and two warriors." She hugged Dove and Wewukiye. "I will continue to use whatever powers I still have to help the Nimiipuu and talk with you."

"I will tell your soldier what has happened." Wewukiye nodded.

"No. If he learns of the child and my change, he will stop working toward the good of the Nimiipuu and come to me. He cannot learn of this until our people are no longer troubled by the soldiers."

"This is wrong—"

She cut Dove off. "I know Wade. He would come to my aid. The people need him more than I do." She wanted Wewukiye to tell Wade. Wanted it with every breath she took, but she would not be selfish. Never would she put her needs before The People.

She inhaled deeply, let the air out slowly, and faced the camp. Keeping her gaze locked on the dwellings of the Lake Nimiipuu, she set out across the dying grass of the meadow.

Halfway across the open area, a warrior on a horse raced toward her. Beyond him people formed a line at the edge of the camp. He rode his horse around her.

"What is a White woman doing wearing a Nimiipuu buckskin dress?" he asked, continuing to circle her.

"I am Nimiipuu. I have become lost from my family and wish to speak with the family of Lightning Wolf and Silent Doe." She walked with determination toward the camp.

The warrior stuck out his foot, stopping her forward motion. "You have the hair and eyes of a so·yá·po. You may not enter the camp."

She glared at him. "Then bring Lightning Wolf and Silent Doe to me. I will wait." She crossed her arms and stood firmly in place.

The man called out and a young boy ran toward them. The warrior met the boy halfway, leaned down to speak to him, and then rode back, keeping his horse between Sa-qan and the camp.

Arms crossed, her glare never leaving the warrior's face, she waited for Silent Doe. The sound of voices nearing the warrior on horseback could be heard. She sucked in air spotting Lightning Wolf,

Silent Doe, and Joseph stepping around the horse.

Le'éptit wax lepít
(22)

Sa-qan nodded to Lightning Wolf and Joseph before gazing into Silent Doe's eyes. The woman studied her then smiled, grabbing her husband's arm.

"This is the woman who saved Girl of Many Hearts and myself at Big Hole." Silent Doe stepped forward, reaching out a hand.

Sa-qan gripped the offered hand. "Thank you for remembering. I am in need of your help."

Joseph watched her with bright intelligent eyes then scanned the area behind her. "You have hair the color of a warrior who showed himself to us when Girl of Many Hearts came to this earth. Do you know this man?"

Did Joseph know Wewukiye was a spirit? Sa-qan returned the chief's gaze. "He is my brother."

Joseph nodded.

"She will stay with us." Silent Doe wrapped an arm around Sa-qan's shoulders and led her toward the camp.

"She could be a spy," the warrior on the horse said, pushing between them and the camp.

"I have welcomed this woman. She is not a spy." Joseph shoved on the neck of the horse, moving it aside for them to walk.

Sa-qan wished to warn Joseph of the approaching soldiers but did not want to talk of it in front of the distrusting warrior. She would wait for a moment alone with the chief to tell him all she knew.

The Nimiipuu gathered around, watching her entry into their camp. She would be required to help with the chores. Now that she was mortal she would have to deal with all the everyday tasks of living. Much knowledge she should know due to her age she did not. Having been plucked from mortal life at a young age and living as a spirit who required nothing of the mortal world she would be less educated than Girl of Many Hearts. How would she cover her lack of knowledge of the Nimiipuu way of life?

Silent Doe stopped at a dwelling of green poles, blankets, and hides. The lodge was more than most families had for shelter. The woman ducked through the blanket opening, holding it aside for Sa-qan.

Girl of Many Hearts rose from where she sat weaving a basket and hugged her about the waist. The small dwelling barely offered enough room for the three inhabitants to sleep. She hadn't noticed a lodge for the unmarried women. Where did they dwell? Where would she sleep?

"Sit, my sister." Silent Doe folded her legs and sat on a blanket.

Sa-qan sat across from her. Girl of Many Hearts settled beside her.

"Girl of Many Hearts told me of your great bravery and skill." Silent Doe's gaze remained friendly.

"It was my duty to save both you and Girl of Many Hearts." Sa-qan squeezed her shaking hands together.

"Daughter, fetch our guest nourishment." Silent Doe smiled at her daughter.

Girl of Many Hearts rose and exited the dwelling.

"She knows the mother who brought her to this earth was special." Silent Doe's voice dropped to a near whisper. "She does not know the man who loved her mother held special txiẏak." She nodded. "I witnessed their love and great power when they came together. You have his look. And knowing you saved my life, I believe you hold his txiẏak."

Sa-qan shook her head. "I once held his power. It no longer flows through me. That is why I must join this band. I need…" She hated to ask for help. Having been a spirit for so long and needing no one, the notion sat as prickly as using berry bushes for a bed.

"You need your people." Silent Doe placed a hand on her knee.

She also needed Wade, but she could not tell this woman she loved the enemy.

"Yes. I need my people." *And they need me.*

Girl of Many Hearts returned with a bowl of broth. She handed it to Sa-qan and sat.

The meaty scent of the broth made Sa-qan's mouth water. How many season had it been since food had passed her lips? Too many to count. She sighed, raised the bowl to her lips, and drank the filling liquid. The warmth settled in her stomach and her eyelids became heavy.

"You are tired. Rest." Silent Doe gestured for her to lie down were she sat.

Her weary body accepted the offer. She tipped to her side and closed her eyes. Girl of Many Hearts covered her with a blanket, and she slipped into dreams of Wade and happiness.

《》《》《》

Wade caught sight of the troop mid-morning the following day. He'd battled over turning around or continuing the whole distance. Worry for Sa-qan weighed heavy in his heart and his mind. He'd never seen her tired or fearful. She'd been both when he left her. What had happened to steal her strength? Not their love making. Afterwards she had glowed and professed her love for him. Once this campaign ended he would make her his wife, and they would find a place to live where no one knew their pasts.

A group of five troopers charged out of the line toward him. They slid to a stop in front of his horse.

"State your name and your business," ordered a sergeant.

"Lieutenant Wade Watts, seventh cavalry, Troop H, requesting a meeting with your commanding officer." He sat straight in his saddle, waiting for the men to escort him to the head of the platoon.

They fell in around him, the horses and troops were weary but not as worn out as the men and mounts under Sturgis.

He recognized the commanding officer. Colonel Miles from Fort

171

Keogh. He had nearly four hundred cavalry and infantry men along with a large contingent of Cheyenne and Sioux and a Hotchkiss gun and Napoleon cannon. This group came prepared to wipe out the Nez Perce, and they were within the striking distance to do so.

Wade's heart plummeted and his guts twisted. How could he persuade them to parley with the Nez Perce?

He reined his horse to a stop and saluted. "Colonel Miles."

"Lieutenant Watts. You're a long way from your territory." The colonel's gaze roamed over him, and then his horse.

"I started with General Howard at the onset of this campaign and have been following the Nez Perce constantly since." He wasn't ready to reveal his allegiance with the Indians to the colonel just yet. Rather, he'd listen to the officer and see where he could play on the man's sympathies.

"That's admirable that you've managed to forge ahead and keep the Indians in sight." The colonel motioned for the troops to move out. A trumpet sounded, and Wade fell in beside, Miles.

"Tell me what you've witnessed about this campaign." Miles kept his horse to a walk.

Wade appreciated the slow pace after his night of extended gaits to reach this battalion. "The massacre of women and children at Big Hole was monstrous on our part, and I believe the reason the Nez Perce are leaving a trail of civilian bodies in their wake. They don't believe, even in war, of harming women and children. Our troops crossed that line at Big Hole and the Nez Perce feel even more betrayed by our government."

Miles stared at him. "Are you harboring sympathies for the Nez Perce?"

He wasn't going to lie. Miles was a strong leader and a military strategist, who held strong ethics.

"I'd been immersing myself in the various Indian tribes' cultures while at the fort. The more I follow the Nez Perce and see the way they keep us penned down while their families escape, the more I see they have compassion and are only trying to save their families. You can't fault them for that."

Wade returned Miles's intent stare. "They could have wiped us out twice in confrontations but they didn't. Their fighting techniques are that skilled over ours."

Miles nodded his head and nudged his horse into a trot.

The pace made it hard to continue the discussion. Wade settled in and watched those around him. Let his words sink in and maybe the colonel would come up with an alternative to a battle. It may be a long shot, but Miles had always been open to more than one way.

Wade settled into the bouncing rhythm of the gait and thought about Sa-qan. The vision of her telling him to go hung in his mind. From the very first time he met her, she had exuded strength and life. Yesterday, the dark skin under eyes and the weakness in her motions worried him. She'd told him as a spirit she didn't get tired or sick. Apprehension squeezed his chest. Dread, cold and deep, knotted his stomach. Something was terribly wrong, and she put her life after that of her people by sending him here.

Sa-qan can you hear me? He called to her with his mind, hoping, praying she heard him and responded. He'd continue to work on changing the outcome of the confrontation between this platoon and the Nez Perce, but he would be continually searching for Sa-qan.

Scouts raced back toward them.

Wade listened in. The Nez Perce camped four to six miles ahead with mostly open ground between them. Miles spurred the group into a forced trot, determined to catch the group.

They could be upon the Indians by evening. Frustration throbbed in his temples as he called out to Sa-qan. *The troops will come upon your people today.*

Le'éptit wax mita't
(23)

Sa-qan woke from her nap and found herself alone in the dwelling. The need to find Joseph and warn him of the approaching soldiers pushed her to her feet and out into the camp. Women carved on buffalo the scouts killed brought back to feed the hungry. Others packed horses preparing to continue their journey to freedom. Cold wind, hinting of snow, swirled through the encampment biting at her skin and seeping to her bones. Sa-qan hugged her arms around her body wishing she had wrapped a blanket around her before stepping outside. She had spent so many years as a spirit, needing a wrap for warmth had not entered her thoughts.

Children scurried around the adults playing chase and stick games. She found Silent Doe cooking over a communal fire.

Sa-qan touched the woman's shoulder. "Where is Joseph? I must speak with him."

Silent Doe glanced at her and shook her head. "You will speak with no one if you catch a sickness from the cold. Go back to the dwelling and wrap a blanket around you."

"It is important I speak with him." She did not wish to ignore the woman's wisdom but the need to speak with Joseph pulsed in her head.

"You have saved my life and that of my daughter, but I have yet to learn your name." Silent Doe faced her.

"I am Sa-qan." She pushed her hair over her shoulders and straightened, peering at the woman with the authority her name commanded.

Silent Doe smiled and nodded. "Yes, you have the shimmering white head and piercing golden eyes of a bald eagle. Your family chose your name well."

Sa-qan did not wish to tell the woman she could not remember her birth name before the Creator took her and bestowed Sa-qan on her along with her ability to become an eagle. "Thank you. I must talk with Joseph." Urgency tugged at her heart more than her initial need to talk with the chief.

"Come. I will not allow you to catch the sickness." The woman wrapped an arm around Sa-qan's shoulders, sharing the warmth of her blanket and led her back to the dwelling her husband and another now dismantled. Girl of Many Hearts stood next to their pile of belongings.

"Are we moving?" Sa-qan couldn't hide the hopefulness in her voice.

"Yes. There are those of us who do not wish to linger even though Looking Glass believes we are safe," Lightning Wolf said, taking down the poles.

"You are right to continue. We are not safe. I have seen soldiers coming." Sa-qan pointed the direction she last saw the soldiers. Urgency again stabbed her chest. She spun to Silent Doe. "This is what I must tell Joseph."

Silent Doe picked up a blanket and handed it to Sa-qan. "He and Noise of Running Water are checking the horses. May the wind carry you swiftly." She pointed toward a meadow filled with horses.

"Thank you." Sa-qan wound the blanket around her and crossed the encampment with long strides carrying her toward the area where the Lake Nimiipuu horses grazed. She caught sight of Joseph at the same time a scout rode atop a bluff not far from the camp and shouted, "Enemies right on us! Soon the Attack!"

The rumbling of many hooves vibrated the ground like a buffalo stampede. The soldiers appeared over a rise and spread, wrapping around the camp like embracing arms. Instead of security, the sight speared terror like frozen shafts of ice into her body. Her feet did not move as she frantically sought a familiar face among the soldiers.

"Sa-qan! Hurry!" Silent Doe's voice pulled her as violently as the woman's grip on her arm dragged her back toward the camp. "We must hide."

The blast of rifles, rumble of running horses, and the cries of the women and children seeking cover blurred. Sa-qan followed Silent Doe trying to outrun the panic climbing her limbs and finding a grip on her heart. Fear for herself and the child growing within her pounded in her chest. As a mortal she could now be killed by a bullet, knife, or club. Shivers of dread wracked her body. Wade, where are you? How would she survive this? Now she knew firsthand how the Nimiipuu spent the last moons under terror and uncertainty. She marveled at the stamina and strength of Silent Doe.

Once the warriors formed a barrier between the soldiers and their families, the women cautiously returned to the camp. The blasts of guns, shrieks of horses, and cries of men filled the air. The sounds became background to the chatter of the women preparing for the battle.

"Come. We will provide food and water for the warriors." Silent Doe joined a group of women cooking over a fire pit in the center of the camp.

Others sharpened knives and filled leather straps with bullets. The children gathered the skins of water in one place making it easy for the warriors to get a drink when they came in from fighting. All went about their jobs as if a battle did not rage across the river.

Sa-qan took a deep breath and drew in the strength and resoluteness of her people.

The warriors held off the initial attack of the soldiers, proving to be better shots and well hidden. The soldiers retreated, leaving strewn bodies behind on the cold ground.

Sa-qan fought the urge to sneak away from Silent Doe's watchful eyes and hunt for Wade among the fallen. Several times throughout the day she tried to talk with Wade in her mind. When neither he nor Wewukiye responded, she grew more despondent.

Wounded warriors wandered into camp, needing healing. She

placed her hands on the first man and started to chant before she remembered she could no longer help in that manner. She continued chanting as she cleaned and applied herbs to the wounds.

Dusk gradually hid the men fighting, but the sparks spitting out the ends of the rifles and the clusters of shots reminded them the soldiers had not gone away. The sharp stench of gun smoke hung in the cold air, held down to the earth by the low gray clouds. Blasts of gunfire lessened and the wailing for dead loved ones filled the darkening sky.

More warriors returned to eat, drink, refill with bullets, and tell of the wounded and dead.

Silent Doe handed Sa-qan a wide blade knife. "We must dig holes for hiding. The soldiers could come closer during the night."

Sa-qan grasped the heavy knife and followed Silent Doe and Girl of Many Hearts to a spot in front of a bluff. Other women dug at the earth with knives and digging sticks. Shoulder to shoulder, all through the night, they bent to the task of chopping at the dirt, filling pots, and piling the dirt in front of the holes. Her arms ached from hacking and digging. Girl of Many Hearts had not spoken a word as she scooped up the loosened dirt.

Exhausted, Sa-qan could barely climb out of the waist deep hole wide enough for six or more women to huddle in.

"We will put our things in this hole," Silent Doe said, slowly walking toward her family's belongings still piled near the partly dismantled dwelling.

Her arms refused to work as Sa-qan bent to pick up a basket. Why could she fly all day and night as an eagle and never tire, yet doing work as a mortal had stripped her of strength? "I can do no more. I must sleep." She started to spread a blanket on the ground.

"Not here. In the hole. It is safer." Silent Doe grasped her arm, keeping her on her feet.

Did the woman realize once she lay down she would not have the strength to get up again? Her feet weighed heavy as the granite boulders on the Lake Nimiipuu mountain. Her brother's mountain. Had Himiin become exhausted this easily once he remained a mortal? How she wished he still lived of this earth so she could ask him.

A burst of gunfire close to camp jolted her thoughts and jerked her body, reviving aches. The wailing for dead loved ones and children crying of cold and hunger had become the background noise of her thoughts during the digging. The darkness hid the enemy and her worries. The burst of shots reminded her Wade was out there somewhere. Was he safe? Or had he been in the front of the attack and lay wounded or dying among the soldiers? Her heart ached to find him. She could no longer talk with Wade through their thoughts, but surely her spirit brother would hear her. *Wewukiye, if you hear me, please look after Wade.*

She, Silent Doe, and Girl of Many Hearts lugged their belongings to the trench and climbed in. Silent Doe spread all their blankets and hides over them to ward off the snow and sleet that had begun to fall.

«»«»«»

Wade had managed to drop back during the initial attack. Now, he sat in the dark on guard duty. Miles posted the guards to keep the Indians penned between the troops and the bluff behind their camp. He'd rather be listening in on the strategy meeting of the officers, but he'd volunteered to sit here, hoping Sa-qan would come to him. Ordered to sit in twos, he'd waited until the guard change and made an excuse to go retrieve a knife he'd dropped. Once hidden in the dark, he wandered beyond the guard perimeter and looked for Sa-qan.

Sa-qan, I'm here alone. Come to me.

A volley of rounds exchanged between guards five hundred yards to his left and a spot on a bluff.

He hunkered into his coat hoping the snow and sleet would let up and wiggled his toes to keep the blood circulating. Was Sa-qan warm? Wade stared into the darkness and snorted. She was a spirit. The weather didn't bother her. What he wouldn't give to be wrapped in her warm loving arms at this moment.

A tap on his shoulder spun his body and lodged his heart in his throat.

A hand grabbed his rifle at the same time he witnessed glowing blue eyes.

"It is I, Wewukiye, Sa-qan's brother." The quiet deep melodic voice held a trace of Sa-qan's tone.

"It's good to finally meet you, but where's Sa-qan?" he whispered back. His stomach curdled, worrying something had happened to her.

"She is in the camp of the Lake Nimiipuu."

Panic stabbed his chest. "Why? She should be soaring in the sky, not in danger."

"She wished me not to tell, but I fear for her as you do." He handed the rifle back and placed his hands on Wade's shoulders. "Sit. We have much to talk about."

Wade dropped onto the hard rock. The pain shooting down his cold legs registered slightly less than the panic squeezing his heart. "Is she ill? I didn't want to leave her. She looked ill, not herself. But she insisted her people came first."

"She has a strong sense of duty, my sister."

The pride in Wewukiye's voice bolstered Wade, relieving his initial fear.

"She wished me not to tell, but I have never been able to keep silent. Especially when secrets could harm my family."

"What do you mean? Is she in danger?" Wade had found the slow delivery style of Sa-qan's speech seductive, but when her brother spoke the same it only infuriated him the man didn't get on with what he wanted to say.

"When you and Sa-qan became one, you planted a mortal seed in her."

Wade barely registered the disgruntled tone as the idea he could be a father nudged aside all else. "She's with child? My child?" Elation grew into full blown euphoria. He hadn't thought about children until Sa-qan came into his life and now, knowing she carried their child…he slapped the man next to him on the shoulder. "I'm going to be a father."

"Do not congratulate yourself. With the mortal seed growing in her, she loses her spirit powers. This is why she can no longer speak to you in your head. She can no longer change into an eagle. She has become mortal. And must live as a mortal in the village of the Nimiipuu."

Anger and terror rushed from Wade's head to his toes and back up. The cold vanished as rage burned hot. Why had she sent him away knowing she carried his child? Knowing she could no longer take care of herself?

Did she hate him for stripping her of her powers? Did that mean more to her than his love?

"She is in the village, as vulnerable as the people. You must stop the soldiers to keep her alive." Wewukiye's voice pierced his thoughts.

Visions of the carnage at Big Hole sickened Wade's gut. Sa-qan and their child would be in danger. This had now become more than helping the Nez Perce. He must help his new family.

Wade stood. He had to get back to the camp and talk with Miles. There had to be a way to stop the killing before it was too late.

"Is she alone?" Wade didn't want to think of her all alone with no place to stay and dependent on others for food. That would crush her independent spirit.

"She is living with my daughter's family. She is well and loved."

"Your daughter? Is your daughter mortal?"

"It is a long story. One you can ask my sister. I must go."

"Tell Sa-qan I love her and the baby. We'll be together as soon as I can get the fighting stopped."

"She will know. May you find the strength to follow your words."

Wade knew the spirit had left by the faint scent of smoke lingering in the air. His conviction to stop the fighting now took on a greater importance. The colonel had to listen. The lives of his family depended on him.

At the camp, he sought Miles. He found the colonel walking among the wounded around the hospital tent.

"We took a hard beating. Those Indians are crack shots," the doctor said to Miles.

"Yes. We can't make another run at them or we'll lose even more." The colonel shifted, catching sight of Wade. "Lt. Watts, I see you made it unscathed."

"Yes, sir. Colonel, if I could have a word with you." Wade motioned away from the wounded.

The colonel nodded and followed him to a spot void of other troopers.

"Sir, seeing all the wounded and knowing the Nez Perce hold their freedom with high regard, maybe you should try to talk with them and see if they won't come peaceably. They have women and children to think of. Once the sun comes up and they see there is no way out, they may be willing to surrender." Wade struggled to keep the whine of desperation from his voice. His heart pound with anxiety for Sa-qan.

"We've got them in a good place. We'll keep them penned in and wait for reinforcements." Miles stared at him. "We weren't able to stop some who escaped to the North. My biggest fear is Sitting Bull coming down here with a contingent to save the Nez Perce."

"You're not even positive Sitting Bull will help the Nez Perce. Look at all the other tribes who went against the Nez Perce and helped us track them." Wade had to get the idea of surrender in the man's thinking.

Miles glared at him. "I've been calling to the Nez Perce all day asking them to talk with me."

"Sir, will you talk to them about a surrender and not just call them out to kill them?" Dread sliced through his heart, icing his blood. He'd been witness to just such an injustice once before and didn't want to see it happen again.

Miles shrugged and walked away.

He couldn't be part of a military that killed women and children to make a point. If it looked like that was the goal of this leader, he'd leave and find a way to get into the Nez Perce camp and warn them before taking Sa-qan and fleeing. This campaign had sickened his heart, and he no longer wished to champion this government.

Le'éptit wax pí-lept
(24)

Sa-qan woke cold, stiff, and hungry. Her stomach rumbled as did Girl of Many Hearts's. They huddled in the blankets and hides chewing on the small piece of dried meat Silent Doe offered and sipping water. Many others huddled in the trench to avoid the flying bullets from the rifles and big guns of the soldiers. She had only lived with the threat of the soldiers for one day and her body tensed with apprehension and fear dogged her every thought. How had her people survived the three moons of this terror? Their strength proved stronger than she had believed of mortals.

Her only moment of solace during the night came when Wewukiye entered her dreams and told her Wade was unharmed and worked to bring them together. Security had warmed her cold, tired body at the thought of Wade.

But as the day grew colder and evening brought more bullets and more deaths, she worried for them all. The women took turns telling stories to the children and caring for the warriors arriving with injuries. Rumors of some Nimiipuu escaping filled Sa-qan's heart with hope. They would not all perish at the hands of the soldiers.

On the fourth day of nonstop fighting, a warrior spotted a white flag waving in the brutal cold air. Sa-qan whispered thanks to the

Creator and Wade. Had the two finally worked on the conscience of the soldier's leader? Slowly, the women and children climbed out of the trenches. Warriors began to return, finding their families and fortifying their bodies.

Sa-qan climbed out of the trench, wrapping a blanket around her shoulders to ward off the bitter wind and snow. Chills chased up and down her arms, but the knowledge the soldiers may soon end the killing ignited a flame of anticipation in her heart. With the truce there was a chance she could see Wade.

They gathered around a small fire started from buffalo chips. The heat barely warmed water to make soup for the children, but the silence of the guns and hope in the air did as much as food in their stomachs.

Sa-qan stared across the expanse between the camp and the soldiers. Out of the flurry of snow three unarmed Cheyenne warriors walked toward their camp. She took a step in their direction. Could this be a delegation to end the fighting? Her heart raced. Had Wade persuaded the leaders to end this?

Silent Doe grabbed her arm. "It might be a trick."

She knew the Cheyenne scouted for the soldiers. "Perhaps they are here to stop the fighting." Sa-qan removed Silent Doe's hand. She swallowed the knot of fear in her throat. She had witnessed scouts kill before, but Sa-qan sensed these men were not to be feared.

A warrior of Joseph's family fell into step beside her along with another warrior.

They stopped a short distance from the Cheyenne scouts. The scouts extended their hands. Sa-qan and the Nimiipuu warriors clasped palms with the Cheyenne in greeting and warily watched for a surprise attack.

"You have come to speak with us?" Sa-qan asked.

"The soldier leader Colonel Miles wishes to speak with your chief, Joseph."

She watched the warriors who walked out with her. The words spoken by the Cheyenne etched questions on their weary faces.

"If he will speak with Miles, they will let the women and children go," said one scout while the other Cheyenne nodded their heads.

"How do we know you speak for the White soldier?" the

Nimiipuu warrior asked.

"Your chief can speak with the White soldier. We can make it happen."

Excitement bubbled in Sa-qan. Finally the Nimiipuu would no longer be hunted. She removed her necklace, a bone carved into an eagle head given to her by Girl of Many Hearts. She handed it to the lead warrior, hoping he would show it around and Wade would know she was safe. "Take this to your leader as our good faith gift."

The Nimiipuu nodded their agreement to the offer.

The Cheyenne scouts took the offering and walked back toward the soldiers. Sa-qan waited to turn her back, hoping to catch a glimpse of Wade. She saw nothing other than strewn bodies in the bleakness between the two camps as the scouts disappeared.

Sa-qan returned to the camp and helped Silent Doe hand out food to the children. The wailing continued for the fallen warriors. Her heart ached for the dead. She yearned for the day she could hold Wade in her arms and dispel her worries he had been harmed.

Later that day a truce was called while Joseph and five warriors met with the soldiers. During the truce, the soldiers and Nimiipuu passed one another on the battlefield collecting their dead and wounded. She watched each soldier who came into the area hoping for a glimpse of Wade. Each face that was not his trickled more unease into her heart. Had he been injured in the fighting?

As the women buried their dead, Silent Doe helped prepare Frog, Joseph's brother, who died in this latest skirmish, to go to the Creator. His death weighed heavy on Joseph's heart and conscience. Sa-qan had been near as the chief knelt beside his brother and wept. She believed losing his brother had given Joseph the push to try and prevent more bloodshed.

Sa-qan treated the wounded the best she could with only mortal knowledge and herbs.

Joseph returned. Concern still marred his face. He spoke with the other chiefs, and they loaded weapons on a horse. He and several warriors met the soldier leader between the two camps. Sa-qan watched the gathering. Her heart raced, searching the soldiers for a glimpse of Wade. Disappointment rested heavy in her chest when she did not spot him.

The Nimiipuu headed back toward the camp when an interpreter called out to them. She watched Joseph return to the soldiers. They surrounded the chief, hustling him toward the soldier's camp. Horror at the sight pierced Sa-qan's heart. Joseph held the people together. Betrayal and anger washed through her. Angry words around her proved all felt the betrayal.

The warriors raced back to the camp.

"They have captured our chief! The lying so·yá·po have taken him!"

«»«»«»

Wade couldn't believe his eyes when Miles and his negotiation group raced into the camp with Chief Joseph between them.

"Are you trying to get us all slaughtered?"

Miles was a lunatic if he thought the Nez Perce wouldn't retaliate. From what Sa-qan told him, Joseph was the most level-headed of the chiefs. What would happen to her if the others laid siege on the soldiers? The return fire could kill all the innocents.

"We have something to bargain with now." Miles faced the men standing around staring at the proud Indian still sitting atop his horse. "Put him under arrest."

Compelled to take care of the chief, Wade stepped into the midst. The best way he could see to keep the chief alive was to remain with him.

"Watts, you have other things to attend to." Miles's order was hard to ignore, given the many years Wade had followed orders.

Wade stepped back, keeping his gaze on Joseph. The chief nodded toward him. Wade saw the same pride and commitment in the Indian's eyes as he'd witnessed many times in Sa-qan's.

Wade reluctantly returned to his duties. Once he completed them, he'd check on the prisoner, and then he'd have a few private words with Miles. His kidnapping the chief could end up being the death sentence to every soldier in the camp.

His detail rescued the dead, recorded their names, and buried each deceased soldier. The considerable death toll grieved his heart for the wasted lives on both sides. Wade talked with the sergeant in charge before slipping away to the tent housing Chief Joseph.

"Lieutenant. No one is allowed entry." The guard lowered his rifle across the tent flap.

"I'm here to check on the prisoner." He added an extra inflection of authority in his voice.

"By whose orders, sir?"

Without flinching, Wade said, "Colonel Miles."

The guard raised his rifle, and Wade entered the tent.

Wade's eyes adjusted to the darkness inside the cold structure. The chief was shackled and rolled up in a blanket like a swaddled baby. Anger at the chief's treatment clenched Wade's jaw and added to the throb in his temples.

"I can't believe this." Wade mumble, approaching the man lying on the floor.

Joseph's dark eyes narrowed.

"I'm not going to hurt you." Wade slipped a hand under the large man and together they raised him to his feet.

"I can't do anything about the shackles, but I can unwrap the blanket so you can sit instead of be left on the ground like a log." He walked around the chief, unwrapping the tightly wound blanket and settling it around his shoulders. "I hope you don't consider the treatment of Miles and the men who did this to you as that of all White men."

"There are good and bad men among all people," Joseph said in halting English.

"That's true. I've been trying for days to get Colonel Miles to talk with you, but I didn't think he'd do something this asinine as kidnapping you." Wade ran a hand over his mustache. If left up to him, he'd find the keys to the shackles and help the Indian escape.

Joseph tilted his head. "You do not carry the same hatred toward the Nimiipuu."

Did he tell this man about his future plans with Sa-qan? The sound of shuffling feet beyond the canvas held his tongue. If the wrong person heard and recounted his words to Miles it was a sure thing he'd be on trial for treason. Best to keep that information to himself. Which also made it impossible for him to ask about Sa-qan.

He knew she was alive. The Cheyenne who started the

negotiations had returned from the Nimiipuu camp carrying an eagle necklace, saying a woman with white hair and yellow eyes gave him the trinket. Sa-qan had survived the past days' fighting. The knowledge had untwisted the knot of dread lodged in his gut.

"I'll bring you food on my next visit." He stared into the Indian's eyes. The strength in their depths reminded him of Sa-qan. Their unflappable strength had endeared these people to him.

The man nodded and Wade exited the tent. Miles stood beside a horse and rider. Wade strode over and caught the tail end of the conversation.

"Study the layout and count the people and weapons. I want you to bring back a full reconnaissance report."

Second Lieutenant Lovell Jerome saluted and nudged his horse out of the camp.

"Sir, do you think it's smart to send one man over to the Indians when you captured their chief?" Wade watched the calculating stare of Miles shift from Jerome's vanishing form and light on him.

"Watts, are you questioning my command?" Miles glared at him.

"I question your reasons behind the underhanded way you treat the Nez Perce."

"I plan to have accepted the Nez Perce's surrender before Howard gets here and steals my triumph." He spun away.

"Conceit. That's what got Custer in trouble." Wade mumbled staring at the colonel's back.

«»«»«»

Sa-qan glanced up from the warrior she tended as a soldier rode into camp. Her heart raced with anticipation until she didn't recognize the man. Several warriors immediately grabbed him, dragging him off his horse. A quarrel broke out over killing him or keeping him to trade for Joseph.

The chiefs stepped in allowing the man to live in hopes Joseph was receiving good care. They placed the soldier in a trench guarded by warriors who followed the orders of the leaders to keep the more hostile warriors from harming him.

Sa-qan brought him water. She wished to ask him about Wade but to do so would only throw suspicions on her about her knowledge of the soldiers. The soldier was polite, but his eyes constantly scanned the camp. Not out of concern for himself but more as if imposing the camp upon his memory.

She returned to the small fire, taking in all the conversations. Many voiced contempt for the soldiers and wished to attack. It would take the severe disapproval of the others to keep these hostile warriors under control. Several families made plans to sneak out under the cover of night. They no longer believed the chiefs could protect them. That to stay meant certain death. The devoted Lake Nimiipuu feared for their chief in the hands of the soldiers.

Sa-qan stared across the battlefield, wishing she could contact Wade. He was so close, yet she had no way to contact him or know his movements as she had as a spirit. With all the violent talk about the soldiers she wished to feel the safety of his loving arms, proof he was safe.

Wewukiye can you help Wade and I to meet?

Her brother must hear her speaking to him for he'd told her in her dreams about Wade. Would she have to wait until she slept to learn if a meeting was possible?

"Sa-qan, your help is needed," Silent Doe said, arriving at her side.

Her heart quickened thinking something had happened to Girl of Many Hearts.

Silent Doe led her to the only dwelling still standing. It held the wounded brought in from the battlefield and those that fought their way back to their families. The cold shelter kept the snow and rain off the injured. Families brought blankets to keep their loved ones warm.

Instead of ducking into the shelter, Silent Doe passed the dwelling and continued toward the side of the bluff. Sa-qan slowed her steps. She trusted the woman, but questioned why she led her away from the security of the camp.

Silent Doe stopped and smiled. Her eyes glowed. "Hurry my sister, your brother will take you to meet your soldier." Dove's essence shimmered around Silent Doe, filling Sa-qan with joy.

"You and my brother have made me very happy this day." She hugged Silent Doe's body and Dove's essence and walked around the bluff. Her brother's magnificent elk form stood under a tree.

"My brother, how will you bring me to Wade?" She petted his soft nose.

"Sit upon my back. I will take you to him. He waits for you in a draw the soldiers are not guarding." Wewukiye knelt.

She climbed onto his back and grasped a handful of his mane. "How is it you can speak with Wade, but I cannot hear you speak to me in my mind?"

"Your fear has closed your mind. It happens to mortals. When they are scared they cannot think clearly or hear the voices spoken which could ease their troubles." Wewukiye set out at a jog through the valley and over the ridge to another smaller valley. She clung to his warm body and hid her face in her blanket to fend off the brutal cold air.

He stopped and she peeked out.

Wade walked toward them. A horse tied to a tree snorted and raised its head, its eyes round and frightened.

Wade reached up to lift her off her brother. He had become accustomed to her immortal life. Could she learn to be a mortal as easily? His large warm hands grasped her waist and lowered her to the ground in front of him.

"I will return before the sun becomes tired."

Wewukiye's words registered before she became caught in the happiness shining in Wade's eyes. She nodded and smiled up at Wade.

"I've worried about you." Wade pulled her close.

"As I have you." She tipped her chin up and gazed into his eyes. The happiness in them now battled with concern.

He lowered his head and their lips touched. Heat flashed through her body. She was home. His arms gave her shelter. His embrace filled her with happiness. The kiss deepened as she pressed closer. She wished for warmer weather so they could touch skin to skin. She wound her arms around his neck. Her blanket opened exposing, her body to the cold.

Wade pulled out of the kiss, drew the blanket around her, and opened his coat, enfolding her next to his body under the thick garment. She wrapped her arms around his waist and hugged him, breathing in his scent.

He kissed her head before resting his cheek on her hair. "Sa-qan, angel, I've wanted to hold you like this since our last meeting."

"I have wished the same." She snuggled her face into his shirt and listened to the steady thump of his heart.

"If I didn't feel the need to make sure Colonel Miles treats your chief right, I'd put you on my horse and we'd hightail it out of here."

The wistfulness and conviction in his tone drew her attention. "Is Joseph well?"

"They aren't treating him as well as they should, but he's tough. I've helped him as much as I can without getting myself locked up for treason. I can't help you or anyone if they lock me up."

"Do not become a prisoner. We need you." She kissed the prickly, supple underside of his chin. "I need you." Fear of losing him and joy of being held in his arms fought in her throat clogging the air making it hard for her to whisper her last words.

"I promise to be there for you, and the baby." He leaned down to kiss her.

Sa-qan pulled back. "How do you know about the child in me?"

"Wewukiye told me." His eyes softened. "He said you have become mortal because of my seed." He gently grasped her chin and peered into her eyes. "Will you one day hate me for taking away your spirit powers?"

Le'éptit wax pá-xat
(25)

Wade watched her eyes brighten then fade as if Sa-qan hoped to hide her uncertainty from him. He would never forgive himself his lusty ways if she grew to hate him. The thought of losing her banded his arms around her small body.

She placed a palm on his cheek. Her warm fingers burned against his cold skin.

"I would never hate you for making me one with you and giving me the gift of a child." She frowned. "I only wish it had not happened until the Nimiipuu are no longer chased by the soldiers."

Guilt set like a cannon ball in his gut. "I'm sorry for not thinking of the consequences of our making love. I've never wanted or craved a woman as I do you."

Her eyes shone bright, not as bright as when she was a spirit, but their light let him know his words filled her with happiness.

He dipped his head and captured her sweet lips. There would never come a day he wouldn't want to taste Sa-qan's sweetness and passion. She responded to the kiss, opening, allowing him entry. Their tongues tasted and teased, mating as their bodies wished.

Wade pulled out of the kiss first, gasping for air. "You set my body on fire." His hands worked their way passed the layers of blanket to touch only her supple deerskin dress between his fingers and her body. He pressed her tighter, pushing his arousal against her belly.

"My body and heart wishes to be one with you, again." Her breathless proclamation came as her hands slipped under his shirts and between his buckskin leggings and skin.

Her touch so close to his throbbing manhood rumbled a groan through his tightly clenched teeth.

He grasped her wrists, tugging them up between their bodies. "Sa-qan, your touch…" He cleared his throat and willed his racing heart to slow. "As much as I would love to make your wish come true, here and now isn't a good place. It's too cold and wet. I'd never forgive myself if you became ill and something happened to you or the baby."

Wade led her to a semi-sheltered area under a tree. He pulled her back inside his coat and leaned against the tree, drawing her snug against him.

"We need to determine when the best time would be to live together." Wade watched Sa-qan's content face as she snuggled her cheek against his chest and gazed up at him.

"I cannot leave the Nimiipuu. The Creator put me on this earth to help them. I must fulfill my duty."

"If you're no longer a spirit, doesn't that break your deal with the Creator?" He still wasn't sure who the Creator was and why she remained steadfastly loyal to him.

"As long as I am alive it is my duty to help the Nimiipuu." She pushed on his chest, but he held her firmly in place.

"I'm just wondering is all. Don't get upset." He kissed her head. "As soon as this campaign is over, I'm getting out of the army." He tipped her chin up. "When my papers clear, I'll be on your doorstep expecting you to marry me the way my people do."

Her eyes glittered with unshed tears. "You could lose friends marrying a Nimiipuu."

"If they don't respect who I love then they aren't my friends." He kissed her tenderly. Hot body scorching kisses would have to wait until the conditions allowed them to follow the desires those kisses brought.

The gray sky darkened as the descending moon disappeared behind clouds. Her brother would arrive soon. Wade didn't want to let

Sa-qan go. For the fiftieth time in the last twenty-four hours he wanted to sweep her into his arms, hop on a horse, and head for anywhere but of here. They could start over somewhere where no one knew them and live as husband and wife. Raise a family. His thoughts snapped to a halt. His angel would never be happy far from her people.

"Wewukiye will return soon. Promise me you will stay safe?" Sa-qan touched his chin, drawing his attention away from his thoughts.

"Nothing will keep me from spending the rest of my life with you and our child." He stared into her concerned eyes. "You have to promise me the same. Stay hidden if there is more fighting. Watching the troops shooting at the camp tore at my heart knowing you and other women and children were there. Colonel Miles is hard to persuade. He has his mind set on being the officer who accepts the Nez Perce's surrender. And after the stunt he pulled today, kidnapping the chief, I believe he'll go to any length to make it happen."

"Keep Joseph safe. He thought always of the people while the soldiers chased and killed." Sa-qan snuggled deeper into his arms.

He wished he could take her back to camp and keep her warm in his tent.

"Do you have shelter?" he asked, needing to know she was provided for.

"Lightning Wolf had the dwelling down when the soldiers arrived. I have spent the last nights in a pit Silent Doe, Girl of Many Hearts, and I dug the first night."

His chest squeezed thinking of her and the other women and children huddled in a hole in the ground trying to stay warm. "I'll find you shelter. It's not good for you to live that way when you're with child."

"I am not the only woman carrying a child or nursing a baby." She pushed on him putting distance between them.

"Don't pull away. I'm sure the husbands of the other women would do what they could to keep them safe and warm if they weren't fighting."

"Or dead." Sadness in her voice twisted his heart.

Wade gathered her tighter against him. "I'll do my best to stay alive and come for you. You have to believe me. I'll not let you go through life alone. I'm to blame for you no longer being a spirit, and I plan to help you fulfill your duty however I can." He wouldn't run from this tragedy like he'd done so many years ago when he came upon his family's farm in ruin and no one left to care. Many nights over the past fifteen years he'd chastised his cowardly behavior. At the time running from the ruin and old memories seemed like the best thing. Now, he knew he could never run from bad memories only make new, happier ones.

"I did not discourage you when you became one with me. I wished it as much or stronger than you. You did not change me. It was my selfish need to be with you that took my powers. Because of that I will live and endure all the hardships of my people." Her chin rose, and she stared defiantly into his eyes.

"You weren't selfish. Every woman and man needs to find a mate who makes them whole. You've done that for me." He placed a kiss on her lips. "I've learned a lot from you and your people about family. Something I'd forgotten since losing mine."

His horse's head popped up from grazing and he snorted.

"I think your brother is returning." Wade wrapped the blanket tight around Sa-qan and tucked her against his side as a tall blond warrior walked toward them. The resemblance between the two couldn't be missed. If the hair and bone structure weren't enough, they both held themselves with graceful authority. A Nez Perce woman walked out from behind Wewukiye. Her eyes shone with happiness. She stepped around the warrior and extended her hands to him.

"Welcome to the family. I am Dove, Wewukiye's wife."

Sa-qan did not wish to leave the warmth and security of Wade's arm, but she wanted him to greet her sister so her watchful brother could find nothing wrong with her so·yá·po mate.

Wade extended the arm not wrapped around her and took one of Dove's hands in his. "It's a pleasure to finally meet you. Sa-qan talks about you both kindly."

Wewukiye snorted. "I think you are talking about some other woman. My sister finds much wrong with me."

"I do not. I could never ask for a kinder, funnier brother." Sa-qan's heart squeezed that her brother thought she did not place him in good favor.

"But you have been unhappy with me many times over the

seasons." Wewukiye nodded and stood beside his wife, placing an arm around her waist.

Sa-qan smiled. "Lately, you have been proving me wrong."

The surprise in her brother's eyes blurted a laugh from her happy chest. Wade's arm around her drew her closer.

"Have you made plans?" Dove asked, leaning into her husband.

"I'd like to take Sa-qan away from here now, but she refuses, and I can't help your people if I'm not with the army." The sorrow in Wade's voice pulled Sa-qan's gaze to his face.

She placed a hand on his cheek. "I wish my duty did not make me who I am, but I cannot leave the people to make my life easier."

His warm breath and mustache tickled her palm as he kissed it. "I know. I wouldn't love you if you didn't have that conviction to duty."

Her insides warmed and swirled with happiness.

"We must go," Wewukiye said, extending his hand to her.

Wade squeezed her tight, kissed her head, and slowly released her. "Take care of her. As soon as this is over, I promise, I'll come get you."

The conviction in his eyes sped her heart. "I will be waiting." She kissed his hand before letting it slip from her grasp. Wewukiye grasped her arm, leading her and Dove away. Sa-qan glanced over her shoulder, taking in the sight of Wade standing under the tree weighed down by sadness and helplessness the same as she carried. When would they see one another again? Her heart bled for the separation and the unknown threats to their happiness.

"You will see him again. He has promised." Dove's soft conviction did little to ease the anxiety creeping into Sa-qan's chest.

"If we both survive." She glanced up at her brother's face. His jaw clenched. Did he also fear they would not make it through the fighting?

"You will live a happy life together." Dove said.

"How do you know this?" She wanted to believe her sister, but she had been a mortal long enough to know their bodies could only take so much starvation, fatigue, discouragement, and wounds before they left this earth.

"Your hearts beat strong for one another, and you are both good for our people. The Creator may not be able to stop all obstacles, but he will see that you do not perish before you have fulfilled your duty even as a mortal."

"I hope you are right, my sister." Sa-qan stopped when her brother did.

He and Dove shifted to elk.

She climbed on her brother's back for the return trip to the Nimiipuu stronghold. The Creator could no longer speak to her. But did he still look out for her as he did all people? Would he help her and Wade be together? If she held Dove's conviction in her heart, she could overcome any adversity until they were together again. She rubbed her stomach—as a family.

«»«»«»

Wade rode his horse back into the encampment. He noticed the bustle of tents being raised and Yellowstone Kelly, one of Miles's civilian scouts, had arrived with quartermaster wagons of supplies and a twelve-pounder Napoleon gun. The sight of the gleaming bronze gun froze Wade's heart. If that made direct hits in the Nez Perce camp…he didn't want to think of the damage to the innocent women and children.

Ignoring the panic eating at his gut, he strode to Chief Joseph's containment tent. The guards shook their heads when he approached.

"Privates, allow me entry," he said with the authority he'd learned over the years.

The private on the left recoiled briefly and said, "Colonel Miles said this tent was off limits to anyone other than him or his attendants."

"Why? I entered the tent earlier." He studied the men for signs of weakening.

"He said someone has taken liberties of helping the chief."

So he didn't like Wade making the chief more comfortable. The colonel had a lot to learn about getting what he wanted from the Indians. You didn't beat anything out of them.

"I'm only checking on his condition. If something happens to the chief while in our care, what do you think those already angry warriors will do to us?" He slid his gaze toward the large white tent for the wounded and then toward the area they buried the dead.

He glanced at both privates. Fright blanched their faces and widened their eyes. "We've been lucky so far. Don't you think taking care of our prisoner would help our odds of getting out of here alive?"

The private on the right tucked his rifle against his side. "Yes, sir. We didn't see ya."

"Thank you." Wade ducked into the tent and waited for his eyes to adjust to the darkness.

Chief Joseph sat in the chair, his feet and hands still shackled, his head held high.

"Joseph, it's me, Lt. Watts. I'm the one who unwound the blanket from your body."

"I know. I heard your voice talking with the others."

"How are they treating you? Anything I can bring you that's within my powers?" Wade crossed to the dark shape of the sitting man.

"I am fine. How are my people?" The worry in his voice spoke of his devotion to his people.

"They are as well as can be expected, considering the fighting." Indecision over telling the man about the big gun that had arrived warred in Wade's mind. It would only worry the man more to know about it. Since there was little he could do.

"Why do your words honor my people?"

"I've come to hold your people with high respect. But I am a soldier and I also hold my duty with respect."

The man grunted ascent. "You are a man who holds honor close to your heart."

Wade hadn't thought of his loyalty to the army in that way before. "I'm not so sure I'd go that far, but I appreciate your thinking that highly of me."

Heavy footsteps and voices approached. He didn't want the privates to get in trouble for allowing him entry. "I have to go. But I'll be back and check on you." He couldn't go out the tent flap. Wade walked to the back of the tent, dropped to the floor, and rolled out from under the canvas into the dark of night. Standing quickly, he brushed the worst of the dirt off and walked to the front of the tent.

"Colonel Miles, may I join you in checking on the prisoner?"

In the lantern light of the colonel's attendant, he spotted the privates on guard passing relieved glances.

"Lt. Watts, I don't see where the prisoner's condition is of any interest to you." Miles opened the flap and entered, followed by the light-carrying attendant.

Wade strode across the camp to locate his belonging and find a spot to himself. He needed to reflect on his meeting with Sa-qan and try to send a message to Wewukiye about the new threat to the Nez Perce.

Le'éptit wax `oylá-qc
(26)

Sa-qan returned to the Nimiipuu camp. She walked past the pit holding the soldier. His accommodations were dry and clean and he rested well. She hoped Joseph received the same treatment. Silent Doe and Girl of Many Hearts exited the dwelling for the wounded. She hurried to their sides.

"Is everything well with Lightning Wolf?" Silent Doe's husband stayed inside the camp more than out fighting. His age left him less agile for fighting, but he remained calm and clear headed to keep the women and children together and safe.

"He is well." Silent Doe offered a weak smile and nodded back toward the dwelling of the wounded. "There are many husbands and brothers who are not well and hold anger in their hearts that they cannot be out protecting their families."

Sa-qan knew the anger and futility well. It had taken up in her heart and head since she became mortal. "We can do our best to heal them. That is all." She hated the frustration that assaulted her when she could not use her txiẏak to heal anymore. If she were still a spirit she could have all the wounded back on their feet in a day or two. Instead, they must wait for the slow healing herbs to make their magic.

"This is true. We can only help so much. The rest is up to their bodies and minds." Silent Doe put an arm around Girl of Many hearts. "Come, daughter, we shall sleep and dream of the return of our chief and the end of this fighting."

Sa-qan followed the woman and girl to the trench they had dug. She shivered remembering the cold of the night before. More than ever she wished for the warmth of Wade's strong arms.

Sa-qan lay down in the spot Silent Doe offered. She pulled another blanket around her already blanket-wrapped body and tried to think of happy thoughts. Visions of Wade's lonely stance by the tree when she walked away filed her with sorrow. His promise to be together warmed her heart and dreams came.

She sat on a log as a child dangling her feet into the cold water of a stream. Her father stood in the stream catching trout.

A bee buzzed her face and landed on her hand. She was not worried. She knew to remain calm. If the bee held no fear, it would not poke. Her father approached, carrying a spotted fish. His gaze landed on the bee. He gently blew on the insect, sending its wings into motion and carrying it away.

"Daughter, I will shield you from all trouble," he said, stepping from the stream and walking into the woods.

Security wrapped around her and visions of Wade holding her tight brought peace and home.

An angry crowd with moonbeam hair and blue eyes surged around Sa-qan and her brothers. "Your father killed my husband!"

"My brother."

"My son."

The anger of the people tightened her throat, took her breath, and tore at her heart. Where was her father? He promised to shield her.

"His greed and selfishness has killed our band." The chief glared at Himiin, Wewukiye, and herself. He no longer called them his children.

"Father, you promised. Where are you?"

Crying registered and she woke. Her cold body remained curled in a ball as she listened to the misery of the cold and hungry children whimpering. Her heart ached for them. Anger burned in her belly. Betrayal slithered through her mind like a snake. She peered into the growing light of dawn, staring at the area beyond the fighting. Would

Wade betray her and her people like her father had done? She loved her father, and he had disappointed her. Would Wade do the same? For the Nimiipuu knew you could not trust a so·yá·po soldier. So·yá·po words held no truth, only false hopes for the Nimiipuu.

«»«»«»

The fourth sun brought an exchange of Joseph for the soldier who rode into camp. Hopes grew that the return of Joseph meant a stop to the fighting. Children cried from hunger, and the cold ailed many of the old.

The chiefs and older warriors took the solider prisoner to meet the officers and Joseph. Sa-qan stared intently, but did not find Wade among the officers. That he never joined the other officers started doubts in her mind as to how hard he worked to help her people. Did he speak as her father, promising untruths about always being there for her?

The exchange of prisoners took place between the camps on a spread buffalo robe. The men shook hands and Joseph rode into the camp with the Nimiipuu escort. As Sa-qan watched, the white flag of truce on the soldiers' side came down.

Warriors around her laughed. "Three times the soldiers lie with white flags. We cannot believe them."

Her dream and a sense of betrayal hung in her mind, thinking of all the things Wade had said to her. Words and promises she wanted to hear. Was he like the other soldiers?

Chief Joseph spoke. "I was hobbled in the soldier camp. We must fight more."

His words saddened Sa-qan as the warriors rushed to take up weapons and the sound of rifles and bullets filled the air once more, sending the women and children into their holes. The fighting continued throughout the day, tapering off as the gray clouds and snow evaporated into darkness and the discharge of guns lessened.

Sa-qan huddled in the pit during the night listening to crying children, her hands and feet slowly growing numb from the freezing night air. Snow coated her blankets. She suffered from the cold and hunger like all the Nimiipuu. Shame washed over her for wishing she were still a spirit and able to withstand the poor conditions.

The clatter of teeth jolted her selfish thoughts. She wiggled next to Girl of Many Hearts and added her minimal body heat to the child's hoping to spare her from the bone-chilling night.

«»«»«»

Boom! The loud noise and screams ripped Sa-qan from another torturing dream. Her body was moist with sweat, her heart raced, sadness wrapped around her as tightly as the blanket around her body. Girl of Many Hearts shook in her arms.

Silent Doe grabbed their arms, jerking and frantic. "Get out! Get out!"

A large object landed in the hole next to them, crushing a child's leg.

Sa-qan grabbed her blankets and followed Silent Doe and Girl of Many Hearts to the base of the cliff behind the pits.

"The soldiers use big guns on the women and children!" yelled a warrior as he helped carry a wounded woman out of a hole.

Sa-qan's stomach churned. If it was not empty, the contents would have landed at her feet. Fear quaked her cold numb limbs. If someone did not persuade the soldiers to stop, the Nimiipuu would not survive. What was Wade doing?

We are all going to die. She sent the message hoping either Wewukiye or Wade heard her. Wewukiye told her she could not receive messages if she did not conquer her panic and fear. But watching injured women and children carried out of the pits drained her of the strength to push aside her fears.

«»«»«»

Wade raced to the canon and stared at the target.

"Those are women and children you're targeting!" he said, grabbing Miles by the sleeve to get the man's attention.

The colonel jerked his arm loose and raised a hand. "Sergeant, see that Lt. Watts remains detained until I give orders otherwise."

The sergeant clutched Wade's arm, pulling him away from the

colonel.

"Why are you detaining me? I have a right to know." Wade shook the sergeant's grip loose and faced the colonel.

"For insubordination. Every move I've made to bring the Indians to surrender you've challenged. I'm tired of you questioning my authority in front of the troops." Miles waved his hand. "Sergeant, take him away and don't allow him any visitors."

Rage heated Wade's face and pulsed in his temples. The man was a lunatic. Why didn't he understand targeting the women and children would only make the warriors angrier? And Sa-qan. Dear Lord, she and their baby could be killed.

"You're only making things worse. The Nez Perce won't tolerate you killing their families." Wade struggled and another sergeant jumped in to help.

The two hauled him to the tent Joseph had occupied and shoved him in. Wade paced the interior. He could slide out the back as he'd done when visiting the chief, but what then? If caught they could shackle him and then he'd have no mobility.

He had to think. First he had to make sure Sa-qan was unharmed. *Wewukiye, make sure Sa-qan is safe. They have detained me.*

Believing Sa-qan's brother would look out for her, Wade stood near the tent opening listening for updates.

At dark, rumors ran through the camp that General Howard had arrived. Wade wasn't sure if this meant good news or bad. The general had made it clear he wanted to best the Nez Perce, but he also heard the general had brought two older Nez Perce with him. The two elders wished to reunite their families.

Frustration wore a path inside the tent as Wade paced. He needed to know the full story rather than snippets of conversations from the men passing by. Darkness enveloped the tent, and he slipped out the back. No one had entered the tent since his detainment. With the general's arrival, Miles would be doing his damndest to capture the Nez Perce and gain the recognition over Howard. That would leave him little thought to the lieutenant he'd detained.

Wade kept to the edges of groups and listened in. Two Nez Perce men accompanied the general, both wanting peace. *Good news.* He continued through the main camp, remaining aloof to all but the privates who saluted, in search of the Nez Perce men.

He found Captain John and Old George in a tent being interviewed by a newspaper man. Not wanting to be involved, he listened to the interview. An interpreter also sat in on the discussion. The newspaper man asked questions sympathetic to the Nez Perce plight. When the man exited the tent, Wade walked up to him.

"Sir, I understand you're here doing a story on the flight of the Nez Perce. I've been following Joseph and his band the whole way and may have some insights for you." Wade drew the man away from the heart of the camp to the outer edges.

"I can't write in the dark," the man said, pulling back.

"I'm sorry, I can't be seen talking with you." Wade had to go on his gut hunch this man wouldn't go running to Miles or General Howard. "I can't be seen talking to you. I'm supposed to be detained due to my sympathies with the Nez Perce."

"I see." The excitement in the man's voice shot newfound hope into Wade's mission.

"What would you like to know?" Wade sat in the cold with the man for over an hour telling him the truths he knew about Sa-qan's people he'd learned from her.

"If you ever have more you'd be willing to share, look me up at the Washington Post."

"Will do." Wade shook the man's hand and started formulating a plan. First, he had to get out of the army.

«»«»«»

Sa-qan watched as two older Nimiipuu men walked into camp. White Bull greeted them hostilely. Warriors, loyal to Joseph, took White Bull's weapons and the old men sat and talked with Joseph and the council. Sa-qan and Silent Doe offered water to the newcomers and lingered at the edge of the discussion. The two elders spoke of Cut Arm and Miles wanting peace and allowing the Nimiipuu to return to the reservation near their homes.

The two Nez Perce men returned to the soldiers. Joseph and the others continued to talk. Silent Doe and Sa-qan again offered water and stayed at the edge of the council, listening.

Sa-qan's heart filled with hope for her people. A surrender would mean no more killing and terror. The old men had given hope to those close enough to hear their words. Relief relaxed the people's faces and chased fear into the cold sky.

Joseph mounted his horse and rode to meet the officers of the soldiers. Sa-qan watched huddled with the others, wishing she had kept the magic stick Wade gave her to see objects far away. She wished to see if he helped with negotiations. And yearned for a glimpse of his caring face. Her dreams lately chewed on her mind and planted doubts about Wade. Would he be there when they walked into the soldier camp and surrendered? If so, would he be able to welcome her or would they have to pretend they did not know one another?

She longed for the moment they could be together.

She grew anxious about being held captive. Until they reached the reservation, she would be kept from her family—Wade, Wewukiye, and Dove. Maybe Wade had been right when he offered to take her far from here. They would have been free to find a way to help her people. As a captive she had no way to help. Fear she had failed shook her body.

"You are cold. Come." Silent Doe placed an arm around her, drawing her to the trench where Girl of Many Hearts huddled in blankets and buffalo robes.

"We will wait here for Joseph's return." Silent Doe climbed into the hole as well and they snuggled together.

Sa-qan tried to close her eyes but gnawing in her stomach grew loud.

Silent Doe held out the last of their dried meat. "Eat. Soon we will have food from the soldiers."

Sa-qan glanced at Girl of Many Hearts. "Your daughter needs the food."

Silent Does stared into her eyes. "So does your child."

The woman's words shocked Sa-qan. "How do you know?"

"You rub your belly like other women who carry a child, and you stare dreamily into the sky." She glanced down then back up into Sa-qan's eyes. "I have not asked about the father, believing he was lost in the fighting."

Sa-qan peered into the woman's eyes. Could she keep the secret of Wade? They had grown close the past few days. Would she think less of her for loving a soldier? Fear Silent Doe could not understand faded as the thought of discussing her love for Wade would chase away the doubts that had begun to creep into her thoughts.

"You cannot tell others." Sa-qan peeked over the top of the pit and then into the woman and girl's eyes.

"We have kept the secret of your healing strengths." Silent Doe patted Girl of Many Heart's head.

"This is just as important. My husband is a soldier." She had expected a reaction but not the distrust narrowing the woman's eyes. "He is not shooting at our people. He is working to talk the others into a peaceful end."

Silent Doe shook her head. "I find it hard to believe a soldier cares about our people."

"Wade does. He has been following and talking with the soldier leaders. He holds the Nimiipuu in his heart as strongly as he holds my heart." She grasped Silent Doe's hand. "You must not tell anyone."

"Why are you here if not to tell the soldiers about us?" Silent Doe's body stiffened and pulled away.

"I cannot help my people if I am not among them. As he cannot stop the soldiers if he is not with them." She willed the woman to understand and not tell the Nimiipuu who hated all so·yá·po.

"I knew your brother. He was a strong warrior and held our people in his heart." Silent Doe studied her so long Sa-qan feared the woman would not trust her first instincts.

"I will honor his family and your secret." Silent Doe squeezed her hand.

"Thank you." Sa-qan's stomach growled, again. "I will only eat if you two join me." They shared the meager dried meat and waited for Joseph's return.

Le'éptit wax `uyné-pt
(27)

Wade was grateful Colonel Miles had forgotten Wade's detainment, worrying about Howard taking credit for capturing the Nez Perce. Keeping out of sight of the colonel, Wade stood at the back of the circle of officers as they discussed what to do while Old George and Captain John visited with the Nez Perce a second time, taking with them interpreter Tom Hill, whom Joseph requested and trusted.

Hill and the others returned. Wade couldn't get close enough to hear the discussion, but soon Howard and Miles mounted their horses and rode to the halfway point between the Nez Perce camp and the military camp. They met Joseph and a small contingent of Nez Perce. Howard's adjutant sat beside the officer, writing in a book.

Wade wished he could be a spirit at that moment and enter a horse to hear their discussion. The meeting ended. The Nez Perce rode back to the camp and the officers returned.

Quiet fell over the camp as everyone sat around waiting to see the outcome of the council between the chiefs. Mid-afternoon, Joseph, mounted on a horse, a Winchester across his lap, rode toward the army camp, his head bowed. Five men walking on either side of Joseph's horse held onto his clothing.

Wade's heart raced in his chest. He'd heard Howard say the

Indians would be put on the reservation near their homes. He stared at the camp beyond the battlefield. Soon, he'd hold Sa-qan in his arms. With the campaign over, he'd sign his resignation papers and find a home for the two of them near the reservation.

The chief rode up the incline toward the army camp, his procession impressive and heartbreaking. Pain stabbed Wade's chest with sadness for the strong man who had worked to keep his people safe and free. Joseph dismounted gracefully and walked forward, holding his rifle out to General Howard. The general stepped back and motioned for Joseph to give the weapon to Miles.

"From where the sun stands, forever and ever, I will never fight again." The interpreter said for Joseph. Everyone shook hands and Joseph walked into the encampment with Howard and Miles on either side. When the officers and chief were out of sight, Wade stepped forward, accepting weapons from warriors and chiefs who accompanied Joseph.

Soon men, women, and children emerged from the Indian encampment, crossing the distance between the two camps, and surrendering. The men handed over their weapons as Joseph and the other leaders had done. They straggled in wearing dirty, torn clothing. The women and children were thin, with wide, wary eyes. The warriors rode skinny, lethargic horses. The sight tore at Wade's heart. He searched each group that arrived, searching for his moonbeam-haired Sa-qan.

Finally, a small procession of a warrior, a woman, the child he remembered Sa-qan saving, and Sa-qan wearily entered the camp behind another family. He wanted desperately to take her into his arms and carry her to a warm tent and feed her, but he still had to be careful of his actions. He wasn't out of the army yet. Instead, he'd convey in his words and actions his relief to see her.

He strode to the sergeant logging in all the arrivals.

"Welcome to our camp." His gaze remained on Sa-qan's. Her eyes sparked with hope and longing then dimmed when he didn't advance any closer.

Wade cleared his throat. "We have hot food for you, and we'll help you find shelter." He motioned for the group to follow, but before he spun around he witnessed an exchange between the woman and Sa-qan.

His arms itched to hold Sa-qan, but that would have to wait until under the cover of darkness. Then he could speak to her and tell her of his plan for their future.

He walked toward a group of Nez Perce warming at a fire and eating. A distance from the group he pointed to the ground. "Place your belongings here for now."

He knew Sa-qan understood him, but he didn't know if the others did. The woman beside Sa-qan glared at him as she set her pack down. Sa-qan avoided his gaze. Her pale face and shaking hands twisted his gut.

Be damned what others think. He had to touch her and know she was well. He stepped toward her, taking her cold hands into his. "Are you well?" he asked quietly, unable to keep the concern and love from his voice. He searched her face and willed his heat and energy to aid her.

Hope swelled in Sa-qan's chest. Wade's distance upon their arrival had shattered her belief he still cared and brought forth all the thoughts of betrayal she had dreamt. Now, as his caring brown eyes gazed at her and his warm, strong hands clutched hers, she knew he wished to hold her as much as she wished to be held.

Silent Doe nudged her, and she pulled her hands from Wade's. Surprise and frustration flashed in his eyes.

"Lt. Watts. Your duties do not include mingling with our captives."

She could not tell if the officer walking up behind Wade saw their clenched hands. But the anger flashing in Wade's eyes and the stiffening of his body proved this officer and Wade did not get along.

"Sir, I escorted this group to the holding area."

He continued to hold her eye contact. What did he wish her to know? Was he trying to speak to her as they had when she was a spirit? She opened her heart and her mind but she only captured his frustration.

"If I catch you neglecting your duties, again, I'll have you detained. Again." The man stared with much dislike at Wade's back.

Wade slowly pivoted on his heel.

Sa-qan urged her foot forward to step up behind him and give her support, but one look in the officer's eyes told her he wished her to make another move. Something that would allow him to punish Wade.

Silent Doe touched her arm.

"Colonel Abernathy. I know my duties and am headed to perform them." Wade spun back to her and Lightning Wolf's family. "I'll be around if you have any questions."

The weight of the colonel's stare hit her as she watched Wade walk away. She stared back at the colonel's narrowed perusal of her.

"Who are you?" he asked, stepping forward.

Reflex had her stepping back. She did not like the way he handled Wade, and she did not like the hostility in his glare.

"I am Sa-qan."

"No, what's your birth name?" He continued to watch her, his gaze hovering on her hair and meeting her defiant glare.

She could not remember the name given her as a child, only her spirit name. "Sa-qan."

"You don't have the appearance of a Nez Perce squaw." The man reached out to grasp her chin.

Sa-qan stepped back and glared at him. "I am Nimiipuu. Nez Perce as you call it."

"I've never seen a squaw with white hair." The man took a step toward her.

Lightning Wolf stepped between her and the officer. She did not want Lightning Wolf to get in trouble. Wade should be the one to step in, but he had abandoned her.

The officer glared at Lightning Wolf, then her, before stepping back. He pivoted and strode away.

"Was the first soldier your man?" Silent Doe asked as they all walked toward the soldier handing out food.

Sa-qan nodded. She feared Silent Doe would also think Wade should have stayed and stood up to the officer.

"His feelings for you show in his eyes." Silent Doe stopped, holding them back from the others as Lightning Wolf and Girl of Many Hearts received food. "He wishes to speak to you but worries for your safety if he does."

"How can you see this?" She stared at the woman. How had Silent Doe witnessed this when she, Sa-qan, found his intentions muddled?

"I see him with pure eyes. You see him with emotion." Silent Doe put an arm around her shoulders. "We will find a way for you two to talk."

Sa-qan couldn't shake the trail of betrayal slithering cold across her skin.

"The last soldier did not like your man talking to you. He could cause your man trouble, then how would he help you and your child?"

Sa-qan wrapped her arms around her belly. Wade's distance was to keep her and the child safe. The cold slowly evaporated as she reached out for a steaming plate of meat and broth. She hoped Silent Doe's wisdom was right. Her body warmed thinking of being held in Wade's arms tonight.

«»«»«»

Wade paced back and forth. How could he get a message to Sa-qan to meet him at the far side of the camp? He'd spotted Abernathy several times through the evening wandering by to make sure Wade remained at his post overseeing the supplies.

He had to find a place where no one would see them. Abernathy had been out to get him ever since the attack at Big Hole. The colonel had labeled Wade an Indian sympathizer due to his saving Sa-qan and the girl. The private he'd told to stand down was in Abernathy's platoon. Seeing he and Sa-qan, the white-haired Nez Perce woman, together, had to have Abernathy's mind spinning with conjecture.

Wade paced behind the tents separating the captives from the camp. Sa-qan's brother couldn't help them. He paced and ran scenarios over in his head until two men arguing caught his attention. He followed the raised voices and encountered the newspaper man, Baker, in a heated discussion with Miles.

"There will be no sensationalizing the Nez Perce." Miles slammed his fist into his palm and stalked away.

Wade waited until the officer's back disappeared out of sight and walked toward Baker. "I couldn't help overhearing your conversation."

The man smiled ruefully. "I'm sure the whole camp heard us. It hinders my talking with the Nez Perce when Colonel Miles won't allow me access."

"I can get you access." Wade knew it was risky but would bode better if he walked into the Nez Perce camp with the reporter. He'd introduce the man to the people with Sa-qan and then sneak her away for some private moments.

"You'd go against your superior's orders?" Baker squinted in the growing darkness, staring into Wade's face.

"Both sides of the story should be told." He stepped closer to Baker. "Follow me."

Wade strode with conviction by the men standing guard. The Nez Perce had fashioned makeshift shelters of their belongings and harvested poles from the area. He searched the people huddled around small fires scattered among the shelters.

He noticed Baker falling behind as he scribbled in a book. Wade stopped, waiting for the man to catch up. A tug on his sleeve dropped his gaze to the girl Sa-qan called her niece.

"Sa-qan." The child said and pulled on his sleeve.

Baker had stopped and conversed with a warrior. With his sympathies lying with the Indians, Wade didn't believe Baker faced any danger. He smiled down at the girl and motioned for her to lead the way. She smiled and led him to the far side of the encampment.

Guards stood outside the perimeter of the camp. How could he and Sa-qan slip pass the guards?

They approached a fire in front of a squat buffalo hide covered structure. His heart skipped. Sa-qan sat wrapped in a blanket by the fire. The man and woman she'd arrived with as well as another couple and three children circled the small pit of flames.

The girl spoke and all turned their gazes on him. Sa-qan's eyes brightened and she stood.

He ached to pull her into his arms and warm her. The wary glances from the others at the fire kept him a few steps back. Now that he was near Sa-qan, he was unsure how they would speak. He didn't know who around the fire understood English.

The girl's mother said something to Sa-qan.

Sa-qan nodded her head and walked toward the shelter. "Come inside," she said, ducking into the hide covered tent.

Wade scanned the group. The woman who spoke nodded and smiled. He returned the smile and hurried to the structure. He dropped to his knees to enter the small opening and crawled on his hands and knees into the dark interior.

Blankets and more hides covered the floor. Their softness and warmth padded his hands as he groped in the darkness. Finally, his fingers clutched Sa-qan's small hand. He drew it to his lips, savoring the touch of her flesh.

Her intake of breath sparked his desire like flint to rock. He tugged on her hand drawing her blanket clad body to his.

"I've missed you," he murmured, kissing his way to her lips. He kissed every inch of her face cradled in his palms. "When I saw Miles aiming the cannon at the women and children, I feared for your life and wanted to turn the weapon on him."

She shuddered. He folded her back against him, trying to provide warmth and comfort.

"I have missed your arms." Sa-qan snuggled against him.

"We'll be together soon. I promise. No more of this sneaking around." He kissed the top of her head. He wanted to shout to the world she was his woman, but he had to wait until he formally resigned from the army. A court martial or accusations of treason for fraternizing with the enemy wouldn't get them together, only apart.

"What will happen to my people now?" She leaned back.

The darkness of the structure prevented him from seeing her expressions. "Miles and Howard agreed to keep them at a fort near here through the winter then return them to the reservation near their homes."

"This is good. Many are sick or wounded. They would not survive the return." Her palm rested on his jaw. "Will you be at the fort? Is that where we will be together?"

Her gentle touch and soft words addled his thoughts. He tilted his head and kissed her palm. "I'll meet you there as soon as I can get my letter off to Washington to resign—leave the army." Her body stiffened. "I can't just say I'm done being a soldier and walk away. I have to follow protocol—rules, or I'll end up in prison." He grasped her chin. Touching nose to nose, he tried to see her eyes in the dark. She had to understand. "If I don't watch myself around you, they could toss me in prison for treason. That means I have been friends with the enemy—you. And if I just walk away without writing a letter and being let go, I could go to prison for failure to do my duty."

Sa-qan huffed, her warm breath fluttered over his skin. "So·yá·po have many rules. The Nimiipuu do not need to keep their own people prisoners."

"Believe me. I want to be with you. Now and forever. But I would always be looking over my shoulder should I take off from the army without the proper protocol."

A woman's hushed whisper sounded at the entrance to the structure.

Sa-qan grabbed his face in a talon-like grip. "The angry soldier approaches."

Le'éptit wax `oymátat
(28)

Sa-qan's heart raced. Wade had to leave but not through the opening. Silent Doe had whispered the angry soldier from earlier approached.

"You must go out the back," she whispered, pulling on his hand.

"If I stay here he'll go away." Wade wrapped his arms around her.

If only she could be as confident as he. Her instincts said the soldier came to find Wade. The soldier knew Wade hid in the tent with her.

She pushed at his arms. "No. He has come to find you here." Her harsh whisper loosened his arms.

"What? How do you know?" he whispered back, gripping her arms.

"He does not like you. I saw it in his eyes earlier today when you left. He knows you and I feel much for one another. I cannot always hide my feelings. He watched me as you walked away and he saw."

"Damn."

She knew he rubbed his mustache even if she could not see. His actions were carved in her memory.

If he stayed and stood up to the man, she would stand firmly behind him. Though she no longer had spirit traits, her belief in her convictions still held her solid and strong. She and Wade must be together to benefit the Nimiipuu.

She heard more than one so·yá·po voice outside the dwelling. "Shhh." She led Wade to the opening to listen.

"Where's that white-haired squaw that was with you earlier?" the angry man asked. Wade's grip on her hand tightened. She squeaked and he loosened his hold.

"Sorry," he whispered, his lips touching her ear. "That man has had it in for me since the beginning of the campaign. I don't want to cause you any trouble. If he'd just reprimand me I'd show myself, but he'd take it out on you." He kissed her cheek. "I won't let that happen. I'll find a way to see you tomorrow night."

His hand slipped from hers before she could say or do anything. The dwelling would move when he crawled under the back. She placed her hand on the opening, waiting for the quiver of the hides from his exit before she grasped the blanket covering and shook the structure as she stepped out.

The angry soldier stood between the fire and the dwelling. His fists clenched and unclenched. A gleam in his eyes sent a shiver down her back.

"What were you doing in there?" he asked, taking a step toward her.

"Sleeping until I heard the squawking of an angry black bird."

The soldier brushed her comment away like a fly, but Silent Doe snickered.

"Were you sleeping alone?" The ugly way the man's lip lifted left her stomach sour.

"The rest of my family is sitting by the fire." She made eye contact with each person who watched her and Wade enter the tent. They had not given away her guest.

The man continued to stare at her. "Private, take a look in there." He pointed to the dwelling behind her. A soldier, carrying a light, walked past her, flopped the blanket up on the opening, and shone the light inside.

"Nothing, sir," the soldier said, pulling out of the dwelling.

Sa-qan did not want to make the officer angrier, but she could not hold back the smile of triumph tickling the corners of her lips.

Abernathy, as Wade had called him, stepped close, glaring down into her face. She caught a movement and put up her hand to stop the warriors at the fire from intervening. Her love for Wade could not endanger other Nimiipuu. She would suffer the consequences but not her people.

"I know you and Lieutenant Watts are up to something. I don't know what, but when I discover his treason, you'll both be sorry for consorting with the enemy."

"We are no longer enemies. My people have surrendered." She held her chin high and glared at him with all the disdain she held for evil mortals. The power surging through her when he took a step back tingled her insides and gave realization to the fact even though she was no longer a spirit, she did have mortal powers and strength. The revelation brought her a deeper core strength. One she had missed since becoming mortal.

"We will always be enemies until your people stop their heathen ways." Abernathy spun on his heel and stalked away.

Girl of Many Hearts shot to her feet and captured Sa-qan's hand. "Did you use magic to make your man disappear?"

Awe brightening the child's face filled Sa-qan with her newfound authority.

"No. He crawled out under the back of the dwelling. I do not have magic anymore." Until this moment, she had not realized she grieved her lack of txiẏak. Her grieving had ended. She now possessed mortal powers. Conviction and truth. These would do her well her remaining mortal years.

Silent Doe motioned to the dwelling. They entered and the woman did not give Sa-qan time to get comfortable before questioning her.

"What did your man want?"

Sa-qan smiled. "He has a name. It is Wade."

"What did Wade want?" The excitement in Silent Doe's voice brought joy to Sa-qan's heart.

"He wished to tell me he missed me and as soon as we are at the fort he will work to get out of the army." She frowned. It is a strange world when a person must ask permission to live his life as he wishes.

"We are going to a fort? What of our homes?"

"We will stay through the cold at the fort and travel to the reservation near our homes when it is warm. Our sick and wounded would not survive the trip home now."

"This is true. I find it hard to believe the soldiers are this kind."

The uncertainty in her friend's words dredged up her doubts once again. "Not all the soldiers are mean like Abernathy, the officer searching for Wade. There are those who wish us well."

"Like your man, Wade." Silent Doe teased.

Sa-qan's heart expanded and ached with happiness. "Yes, like my man, Wade."

The dwelling stirred. Girl of Many Hearts along with Lightning Wolf entered. Time to sleep. Tomorrow would bring another day. One with food for their bellies and no more fighting.

«»«»«»

After leaving Sa-qan, Wade joined in a game of cards with his men. Abernathy found him there a short time later. The scowl on the man's face proved he didn't condone fraternizing with the enlisted men any more than he condoned fraternizing with the Indians. But Wade knew his men would tell the colonel he'd been with them all night. They were loyal to him and didn't like Abernathy. The man had made a spectacle out of punishing enlisted men to receive any cooperation from the lower ranks.

Having lost two hands in a row, Wade returned to the tent he shared with other officers. The cold seeped through his clothes as the temperatures descended. He thought of the warm buffalo robes on the floor of the dwelling. Did they keep Sa-qan warm? Wade reclined on his cot and wished he could wrap his arms around Sa-qan, keeping her and their child warm. When they reached Fort Keogh, he'd head for Ft. Shaw, send a letter and back pay to Sergeant Cooper's family, and then submit his resignation. He hoped it didn't take too long for the papers to get to General Sherman. It wouldn't be soon enough for him to be on his way back to Ft. Keogh and Sa-qan.

«»«»«»

The following day soldiers and their captives stayed busy preparing for the trip to the fort. Wade spent the better part of the day overseeing the gathering of branches and dried grass to cushion the wagon beds where the wounded soldiers would ride. He'd spotted warriors cutting poles and lashing them together for travois to carry the Nez Perce wounded and their supplies.

After the camp settled for the night, Wade left the tent he occupied with other officers and meandered toward the area designated as the privy. To know Sa-qan was so close and being unable to converse with her had plagued his thoughts all day. He wanted to make sure she was fed well and the soldiers didn't mistreat the captives.

He walked past the privy area and into the darkness outside the camp's small fires. The snow on the ground would leave his footprints, but he doubted with the activity of pulling up camp in the morning anyone would worry over the prints.

He yanked the collar of his coat up around his ears and hunkered deeper into the wool garment. He didn't like the idea of the women and children being exposed to this cold while on the march to the fort. But he had little say over the ordeal.

From his visit the night before, Wade knew Sa-qan's tepee sat on the edge of the captives' encampment. He kept to the shadows of the structures and stood at the opening of her teepee, glancing around to see if anyone else remained awake. Darkness shrouded the camp but for coals glowing in fires sprinkled around the compound.

How did one knock on a hide-covered structure? He stood at the opening contemplating the best way to let the inhabitants know he stood outside. The blanket moved. He stepped back so as not to startle whoever emerged. To his delight a blonde head poked out, followed by the delightful body of Sa-qan.

She glanced up and stifled a cry of alarm as he wrapped his arms around her.

"How did you know I was here?" he whispered in her ear, savoring her curves in his arms.

"I grew restless wondering why you had not come to see me. I worried the mean soldier had detained you." Her soft whisper unwound the coiled apprehension in his gut.

"My work today kept me busy, and after dinner Abernathy's aide kept a keen eye on me." He kissed the top of her head and drew her toward the shadows of the teepee.

"I know we can both suffer to be seen together, but I also suffer when we are apart." She drew the blanket tighter around her body.

Wade wrapped his arms around her, enjoying her body next to his even if many layers buffered the effect. "I feel the same." He sat in the shadow next to the structure and drew her down on his lap, wrapping his arms around her to help stave off the cold.

She snuggled against his chest.

The action warmed his body from his toes to the tips of his ears.

"I'll be with the soldiers escorting you to the fort. After you're settled, I'll return to Fort Shaw and send out my resignation. I don't know how long it will take for the release orders to arrive, but I promise the minute they do, I'll be on my way to you." He smoothed her hair from her face. "Will you be all right with Silent Doe's family? Will they allow you to stay with them until I return?" He didn't want to think of her all alone until he returned.

"They have accepted me into their family. Silent Doe has been like a sister to me."

"Have you spoke to Wewukiye or Dove since the surrender?" He wondered what the two would do now that there was peace.

"Now my fear is not so strong, he has entered my thoughts. The Creator asked them to look after the Nimiipuu who escaped. They must find the free people and keep them safe."

The yearning in her voice tugged at Wade's conscience. "Do you wish you were free to be an eagle once more to help?"

She tipped her head to peer at him, her golden eyes glistened in the darkness. "No. I wish to be your woman in all ways, but I do wish more Nimiipuu had escaped. I fear your white leaders will not keep their promises. They have broken them so many times."

He, too, hoped this once the promises made to these people were kept. The moon crept higher in the sky. They couldn't sit here all night as much as he wished he could. Holding Sa-qan, talking about her people, and working together for their future was how he planned to spend the rest of his life.

She shivered as a cloud covered the slip of moon, throwing everything into darkness. The stillness of the night didn't surprise him given the light blanket of snow covering the ground and the people huddling under cover.

"As much as I hate to let you go, you need sleep and warmth I'm not providing." He tipped her chin up and touched her lips with his. How he'd waited this long to kiss her stunned him as warmth radiated through his body at the contact. She responded with a moan and pressed her body tighter against his, sealing every inch of her to him as the kiss deepened. He sought the sweetness of her mouth, encountering her tongue tentatively tasting him. The sensation of tongue to tongue shot another round of fire through his body.

How would he exist without his sweet angel until his orders came through? As if the same thoughts echoed in her head, her arms wound around his neck, clinging to him.

He lingered over the kiss, wishing it didn't have to end and he didn't have to walk away from her.

A sound registered.

They weren't alone.

Anger flashed hot and bright. Their interrupted moment quickly spun dead cold at the sight of Abernathy standing not ten feet away.

"Sa-qan, go back to bed," Wade whispered against her mouth. "Now." He set her on her feet. He knew the minute she spied the colonel standing in the darkness. She spun back toward him. "Go," he said firmly, willing her to obey and not get tangled up in his dispute with the officer.

She gave him one last long look before slipping through the darkness and disappearing into the structure.

He faced Abernathy, throwing his shoulders back, and waiting for the man to accuse him of treason.

"Lt. Watts. Leave this area and come to my tent at first bugle." Abernathy's tone radiated trepidation up Wade's spine.

Why had the man not thrown him in the detention tent? Would he instead retaliate against Sa-qan? Angst tore through his gut. He could deal with anything the man meted out to him, but should the colonel take Wade's behavior out on Sa-qan…the guilt would eat him alive.

Le'éptit wax kúyc
(29)

Sa-qan shivered wrapped in blankets and pressing her body against the sleeping child for more warmth. Cold did not cause the shivers. Fear for Wade shook her body and caused her stomach to be unsettled. What would the so·yá·po officer do to Wade after finding him kissing her? Did they kill soldiers who consorted with the enemy? Regret sliced through her, causing her to gasp and grasp her belly.

"Sa-qan, are you not well?" Girl of Many Hearts asked, sitting up.

"What is wrong, daughter?" Silent Doe asked, also sitting up.

The sound of people stirring and beginning their day filtered through the hide-covered dwelling.

"Sa-qan is not well." Girl of Many Hearts placed a hand on Sa-qan's shoulder.

Sa-qan could not utter a word. Her shivering rattled her teeth and froze her tongue.

Silent Doe placed a hand on Sa-qan's face. "You have fever. Girl of Many Hearts, fetch water and put it on the fire. We must boil willow bark for a drink."

Sa-qan raised a shaky hand toward the woman. She could not die of fever. She had to give Wade his child. Their child.

Through the morning her body flashed between shivers and heat-induced sweat. Silent Doe kept blankets wrapped tightly around her. The woman left her packing to make Sa-qan sip the liquid she had boiled from the willow bark.

"She needs the sweat lodge." Silent Doe's urging did nothing to persuade her husband.

"We cannot erect a sweat lodge. The soldiers are moving us this day." Lightning Wolf responded, loading their belongings on horses before taking down the dwelling.

Frustration gurgled in Sa-qan's body. She was a burden upon the kind family who took her in. She willed her body to heal, but instead, found herself loaded onto a travois and pulled behind a horse ridden by Silent Doe and Girl of Many Hearts. Where was Wade? She longed for his cool hand to rest upon her brow and take away her worries and sickness.

«»«»«»

Wade watched from atop a hill as the procession of mounted troops, wagons, herds of horses, and colorfully-clad Nez Perce made a vivid slash across the prairie as they set out for Fort Keogh. Colonel Abernathy had a lot to say that morning. One being, he, Lieutenant Watts would take his troops along with the Second Cavalry battalion back to the agency at Fort Belknap and from there return to his station.

"If I so much as see you breathing the same air as the captives before they leave I'll make sure that white-haired squaw has a hard road ahead of her." Abernathy's threat kept Wade from digging his heels into his mount and racing after the departing entourage. He hoped by staying away, Abernathy would ignore Sa-qan and she would arrive at the fort in peace. He knew she'd wonder about his disappearance and trusted she believed strongly enough in him to know he would return.

Heaviness squeezed his chest, making it hard to breathe. Deserting Sa-qan and their child plagued him with the same gut-wrenching guilt he'd harbored when he'd rode away from his family's farm to join up with the cavalry after the war. With one last lingering glance at the departing procession, he sent a silent prayer to his God and her Creator to look after her. He hunched into his coat, pulled the brim of his hat down over his eyes, and moved the group under his command toward Belknap. The sooner he arrived, the faster he could get back to his command and get out of the cavalry.

«»«»«»

Fuzzy images of Wade swirled in and out of Sa-qan's head as she endured being jostled on the unforgiving travois. The slowing pace of the animal pulling the travois proved they were stopping for the night. The sky darkened as the soldiers and Nimiipuu set up camp. Thunder rumbled in the sky accented by flashes of lightning angrily spearing the ground and shaking the earth.

Inside the hastily-erected dwelling, Sa-qan stared at the occupants. She did not blame them for keeping their distance from her. She had heard the other couple who lived with Silent Doe and her family arguing they should send Sa-qan to be with the old women and unmarried women.

"She is family and will be treated that way." Silent Doe stuck up for her as she knelt beside her with the bitter liquid the woman favored.

"Qe·ci·yew·yew," Sa-qan whispered her thanks through dry lips and drank the liquid. "You are putting yourself and family at risk helping me."

"You are family. Your body is weak because you carry a child. You will grow strong." Silent Dove, pat her hand.

"Did you see Wade today?"

Silent Doe's lips pressed into a firm line, and she shook her head.

Would he try to see her tonight? She did not want him becoming sick with the fever as well. She thought of their kisses the night before. Perhaps he was sick and that was why Silent Doe had not seen him.

The following morning, rain poured from the sky like the waterfall on Himiin's mountain. Everyone remained inside their lodges. Sa-qan relished the warmth of a fire in the tent and the bitter liquid Silent Doe plied her with all day long. By evening, Sa-qan no longer grew cold then hot. Her empty stomach growled and Girl of Many hearts brought her a bowl of soup.

"You are no longer sick when your stomach talks," the child said, sitting beside her.

She nodded and drank the soup. Her stomach welcomed the warm nourishment.

Wade had not tried to speak with her last night. Would he try this night if the rain stopped?

She finished the soup and smiled at Girl of Many Hearts. "You are good company."

The child smiled then frowned. "Your soldier is gone."

Sa-qan held back the fear circling in her stomach and souring her food. "He is busy and the weather keeps him in as it does us."

Girl of Many Hearts took her hand. "He is not with us."

The conviction in her voice stole Sa-qan's control. "How do you know this?"

The child shrugged. "I can feel things. Your txiẏak is stronger when he is around. It is weak now."

Sa-qan stared into Girl of Many Hearts's eyes. How did the child know about powers? Did she know her birth mother was a spirit now and had held txiẏak before becoming a spirit? Could she, Sa-qan, use the girl's powers to strengthen her body? She shook the thought away. She could not prey on another for her own selfish reasons.

"I am weak because of the sickness. I will be strong soon."

The next morning they continued on. Sa-qan rode a swaybacked, weary horse, but the ride was smoother than bumping along on the travois. She kept blankets wrapped around her and followed the procession. Her thoughts circled around the last night she found security in Wade's arms and the anger in the colonel's words. Had he punished Wade? Was that the reason no one had seen him?

《》《》《》

Five suns passed when they arrived at a large river. Sa-qan had spent the greater part of her days searching the mounted soldiers for Wade. He did not seek her out, and she could not hide from the inquisitive glances Silent Doe bestowed upon her each evening when all should be sleeping and Sa-qan sat up willing her ears to hear the approach of Wade's footsteps. Her heart yearned for his love and security. With each day that passed not seeing him, worry dug a deeper hold on her mind.

It took two suns for all the people and horses to cross the wide span of water. Again, she watched each so·yá·po cross. With each unfamiliar posture and face, her heart grew heavier. Why had he not told her he had to leave? Worry churned in her stomach. Had he been made prisoner by his own people? If so, how could she free him?

Seven suns past the river, loud noise, not as soothing as drums and singing, carried on the wind. Sa-qan stared ahead and saw a so·yá·po village. Many so·yá·po stood outside the walls. Cloth of red, white, and blue waved. As they approached, she realized the sound came from instruments the greeters held.

The Nimiipuu were allowed to set up their lodges on the sunny side of the river in a grove of cottonwoods. Now stronger, Sa-qan helped Silent Doe with the raising of the lodge and preparing their dinner. Filling the water bag at the river, she noticed the soldiers positioned around the Nimiipuu camp.

The next sun, many so·yá·po walked among their camp. A man with a box put his head under a cloth and a light flashed at the Nimiipuu who sat for him. Chief Joseph stepped forward, allowing the man to take his image.

Grumbling among the warriors caught Sa-qan's attention the following sun. She listened intently. The men grew more angry. The great white chief had once again lied. They were to be moved to another place farther from their homes. They would not return to their homes after the snow had melted.

Sa-qan's heart lodged in her chest. How would Wade find her? Would he learn of the so·yá·po's deceit and follow? Or would he decide she and their mix-blood child not worth the effort?

She stumbled and tripped.

"What's wrong with you squaw? You sick? Get away from me." The soldier she had bumped shoved her away with the rifle clutched in his hands. The disgust in his eyes shook her to her toes. How would she or any of the other Nimiipuu survive another journey at the hands of such mean-spirited men?

«»«»«»

Wade arrived at Fort Shaw after seven grueling days and a brief stopover at Fort Benton. He bathed and fell into his bed. He'd hoped being in his own bed he'd finally sleep without nightmares about Sa-qan, but he no sooner hit the straw mattress than visions of her surrounded by soldiers and being harassed woke him in a sweat. A good night's sleep would elude him until Sa-qan was legally his wife and safe in his care. He rose, wrote the letter to Sergeant Cooper's family, and then wrote his resignation.

His future now set, he returned to his bed and slept fitfully. The morning light streaming through a window and knocking on his door wrenched him from a dream of Sa-qan that had his heart hammering and his body throbbing.

Wade drew on the dark blue dress trousers he wore when at the fort and crossed to the door.

"Colonel Gibbon wants to see you." The colonel's aide saluted and waited for a reply.

"I'll be there as soon as I get dressed." Wade closed the door and poured water from a pitcher into a bowl. He shaved, glad he'd been to the barber after a bath when they arrived at the fort the day before. Adding the final touches, he buckled his saber belt and donned a clean hat. He stuck the letters he wrote the night before into his breast pocket and headed to the commander's headquarters.

Colonel Gibbon motioned for him to sit. After giving the man a lengthy rendition of Howard's dogged chase of the Nez Perce, Wade placed the letters down on the colonel's desk.

"Sir, this letter is to Sergeant Cooper's family. He died valiantly and I'd like them to receive this recollection along with his back pay."

Gibbon nodded.

"And this…" He tapped the other letter on the desk. "Is my resignation. I'd appreciate you sending it off quickly. I have private matters that need tended to."

Colonel Gibbon leaned forward and tapped the resignation letter with a finger. "This have anything to do with the last campaign?"

"Yes. I didn't agree with the army's tactics and wish to sever my relationship."

"It did get a little messy at times." Colonel Gibbon wiped a hand across his eyes. "I pegged you for a career man."

"At one time that was my goal, but not anymore. I see my future outside the military." Wade knew he'd have to move the colonel emotionally to get the results he wanted. "I met my wife and I'd like to start a life with her."

"How the hell did you find a wife while chasing all over God's green earth after Indians?" Gibbon narrowed his eyes.

Wade had known the colonel for several years. He wouldn't lie to the man. "She's Nimiipuu."

"Huh?" The colonel's perplexed expression would have given Wade a good laugh any other time but marrying Sa-qan was serious.

"Nimiipuu is the correct name for the Nez Perce. She's a Nez Perce woman I met and fell in love with." His heart raced, thinking of his beautiful silver-haired angel.

"Hell, that's consorting with the enemy!" Gibbon struck his fist on the desk.

"Whatever you want to call it, I plan to claim her as soon as I get out of this cavalry." Wade tapped the papers. "I'd appreciate your signing this and sending it on. I've given this country twenty years. I think it's time they set me free to have a life." He smiled ruefully at his commanding officer. "I'm not going to be much good to you wishing I could be living a simple life with my wife." The sooner his papers were advanced and signed the better.

"You really think you can survive outside the army?" Gibbon watched him closely.

"The minute we started shooting innocent women and children my stomach soured on this job." He stared straight into the colonel's eyes. "Your methods turned me away from this job. Finding my wife proved I made the right decision at Big Hole."

The colonel grunted. "I didn't like the outcome any better than you did, but I had my orders."

"I don't want to have the same orders if a campaign like that happens again. I want out."

Gibbon nodded. "I'll see what I can do. In the meantime this is what has been happening around here while you were gone."

«»«»«»

Sa-qan huddled against the cold wind rolling over the boat's short sides. Today she had taken the spot in the front of the oversized canoe to shield the others from the wind that poured over the front. The healthiest women took turns at the front each day. Five suns earlier, the women, children, and wounded had squeezed into fourteen boats with large cloths that caught the wind. They endured the cold river winds while the soldiers led the Nimiipuu men overland to their next destination.

The boat slammed into the riverbank.

"Out! Get out!" The man who had maneuvered the boat down the river flailed his arms and motioned for them to leave the large canoe.

Sa-qan willed her cold stiff limbs to work. With effort, she stood and climbed over the end of the canoe. She turned to help the others, her numb feet aching with each step she took. The older women and small children required more help than she could give. How much more could they endure? Many had thin faces and poor coloring.

"Welcome to Fort Buford," a soldier said, walking toward them. Another so·yá·po village stood back from the river.

With all these moves how would Wade ever find her? Each day she moved farther and farther from Fort Keogh, she grew more certain he would decide she was not worth the trouble to find. She wrapped her arms around her stomach. Could she survive alone with a child? She closed her eyes and pictured a baby boy, so like his father her chest ached. *Wade, I am waiting. Please find me and our child.*

Two suns later the warriors arrived. Sa-qan watched teary-eyed at the reunions of husbands and wives. Silent Doe and Lightning Wolf hugged, drawing Girl of Many Hearts into their embrace. Her arms ached to hold Wade. Her heart broke wishing she had warm safe arms to hold her.

Unable to watch any longer, she stepped away. Sadness swallowed her. Her loneliness grew greater than during her life as a spirit. If being mortal and experiencing all these emotions brought so much pain, she wondered how mortals had survived all these years. Could this be why they left this earth so soon, while a spirit, incapable of such emotions, lived on and on?

The men stripped out of their filthy buckskin leggings and blanket shirts to jump into the river and bathe. Their bodies bobbed in the cold water along with chunks of ice.

The cold night brought rustling and whispers from Silent Doe and

Lightning Wolf's area of the lodge to Sa-qan's ears. The sounds heightened her loneliness. Warm tears trickled down her face and pooled between her cheek and hand tucked under her head. *Wade, I miss and need you.*

Sa-qan occupied her mind with helping the people survive the bitter cold and yet another trip on the river to another fort. She and Silent Doe had become the keepers of the women and children, making sure those too frail received fair treatment and the children were fed and kept warm. Only at night when she lay alone wrapped in blankets did her heart and mind linger on visions of Wade. His heated kisses and loving arms. She asked the Creator to watch over him and her people.

They arrived after dark at another village welcoming them with loud music and tables of food. Word reached her as she sat and ate with Girl of Many Hearts and Silent Doe they would stay here through the cold. Relief swamped her tired mind. They had traveled a great distance but Wade was smart. He would find her.

Four days later, Joseph stood before them. His once powerful form slumped slack-shouldered. His face more wrinkled and sorrowful. "We are to be moved. When will these white chiefs tell the truth?"

Sa-qan helped Silent Doe, once again, pack up their lodge and belongings to be loaded on a smoke-spewing, earsplitting, screeching so·yá·po wagon.

The box on wheels had hard wood seats. They squeezed together, jostling and bumping along a special trail for the wagon the soldiers called a train. Four days they endured the trip. They stopped several times for food and water. Each day she wished the train to stop. To let this be the final camp. The farther they traveled from Fort Keogh her belief in Wade finding her lessened. He could not find her trail on the water and now on this black smoke-belching beast he would not know to follow.

Only her determination to help her people kept her from curling into a ball and letting the life slip out of her.

«»«»«»

Wade paced back and forth in his quarters. Two months had passed since turning in his resignation. When the hell would he get his release orders? The past week he'd snapped at privates and spent the nights preparing gear to leave, avoiding sleep for fear he'd have another dream that chilled his bones. The terror of the nightmare had yanked him awake. Sweat stuck his flannels to him and panic sat hard and heavy on his chest like a boulder. In his dream Sa-qan had been a silver-haired skeleton holding a dead baby in her arms. He couldn't close his eyes and see that horror again. He had to go to her.

Unable to wait any longer, he dressed and slapped his hat on his head. He strode to Gibbon's quarters. He pounded on the door. Gibbon's aide drew the door open dressed in trousers pulled on over his red flannels.

"I have to see Colonel Gibbon." Wade pushed his way into the room.

"He's sleeping. Like you should be." The man's usual curly mustache stuck out all askew.

"I can't sleep until I get out of the cavalry." Wade paced the room. He hadn't thought this move through. His tormented mind compelled him to confront the colonel.

"Sylvester, go back to bed." Colonel Gibbon stepped into the room, a night wrap drawn around his body, his underdrawers showing below the wrap. "This better be damn good, Watts."

"Sir, I can't wait for my release orders. I'm leaving tomorrow. I can't shake the feeling something is wrong with Sa-qan. I've read the papers and know the army is scuttling the Nez Perce all over causing them more grief than anyone deserves. I need to find her." He stared the man straight in the eye. "I'm petitioning for personal time and would request you grant it until my orders come through."

"What if I say no?" Gibbon settled his body onto a straight-backed chair at the table.

"I'll leave anyway." Wade dropped in a chair across from the colonel. "Sir, I've followed orders my whole adult life. Now I have to follow my heart and my gut."

The colonel stared into his eyes and grunted. "I'll not waste men chasing you around God knows where. But if I get wind you're causing trouble for the army, I'll have you slapped in prison and disregard any release orders that come through my hands."

"I only want to be with my wife and child." Wade stood.

The colonel's eyebrows shot up. "You didn't say you had children. How long have you and this woman been married?"

"We're married through the eyes of her people, but I plan to make it legal as soon as I catch up to her. And the child has yet to arrive." He extended his hand. "Thank you, Colonel." They shook hands, and Wade hurried back to his quarters. He had packing to do and a dress to purchase.

The last he read in the newspaper the Nez Perce were wintering in Fort Lincoln. He'd hire a mackinaw to take him down the rivers to the fort. Anticipation of holding Sa-qan in his arms before the week ended sent his heart thumping and spurred his packing.

Mita áptit
(30)

Sa-qan and the other Nimiipuu gathered around Joseph waiting for his words to soothe their tattered hearts. They'd been herded off the train at yet another fort and stood at the edge of a flat expanse dotted with soldier dwellings between a swamp and the river. She shivered. The moist cold seeped into her bones.

Joseph ordered them to retrieve their belongings and set up camp. She and Silent Doe put their blankets and few personal belongings in a so·yá·po tent. By the end of the week, they had taken down the so·yá·po dwelling, using the canvas to build a teepee. The Nimiipuu dwellings worked better for inside fires. The woman and children fell into the regular routine of village life while the men spent hours in council, talking over their bleak future.

Sa-qan spent her days tending the ill. Many did not handle the new country they lived in well. They had lost several on the journey, and she knew there would be many more deaths. Seven suns after their arrival, the local so·yá·po visited the village, walking among them, whispering and pointing. The boys cajoled nickels from the visitors, tossing them in the air, and shooting them with their bows and arrows.

As the days passed she gave up hope of seeing Wade. They had traveled too far for him to find her. He had promised his heart to her, and she kept that promise tucked in the recesses of her heart, but her logical head told her he would not be able to follow her trail. She would be lost to him.

Soldiers stood guard around their camp. A reminder they remained prisoners even though the townspeople came and went as they wished bringing food, medicine, and goods to exchange for bead and leather work.

Sa-qan held a dipper of water to a child's mouth when Girl of Many Hearts skidded to a stop beside her. Sa-qan glanced up into the girl's smiling face.

"He is here!"

Sa-qan stared at the girl. "Who is here?" She could not comprehend who would make the child so happy.

"Your man." The girl's eyes danced with merriment.

Sa-qan nearly drowned the child, her hands shook so. Wade was here? He had found her? "Are you sure?" Her voice cracked as her heart thudded in her chest.

Girl of Many Hearts bobbed her head up and down rapidly.

Sa-qan stood, smoothing her newly-fashioned blanket dress. Silent Doe had chided her for wearing a buckskin dress while the other women wore the warmer blanket dresses. If her light-colored hair did not make her stand out, her dress only worn for ceremonies did.

"W-where did you see him?"

"Right here."

Wade's deep voice washed over her like warm sunshine. She spun around. Her gaze beheld a wonder she had given up hope of seeing. The man she dreamed of every night since their parting. His face remained as she remembered, but his strong body no longer carried the soldier clothing. His tall frame wore the clothes of a so·yá·po who raised food and animals.

He opened his arms, and she dashed into them, wrapping her arms around his solid frame still trying to believe he had come for her. His comforting embrace brought tears to her eyes. Often the past three moons she had longed for his warmth and strong arms to hold her.

"Sa-qan, I've longed to hold you from the moment I watched the procession leaving Bear Paw."

She thrilled at the rumbling of his voice in his chest. "Why did you not say good-bye?" She peered up into his eyes. The sorrow in their depths formed a lump in her throat.

"Abernathy threatened to cause you trouble if I laid eyes on you again. Riding away from you that day was the hardest damn thing I've ever done." His arms tightened and his head lowered. "I've wondered ever since if he kept his word or if my not being with you left you vulnerable."

Their lips met and her heart soared. *He came for her!* Ignoring the gathering crowd, she kissed him back, reveling in the thought he was her home. She could be anywhere as long as he stood by her side.

And arm wedged between them. Her eyes shot open, and she watched in horror as a soldier shoved a rifle against Wade's chest.

"What do you think you're doing?" The soldier snarled.

"I'm kissing my wife." Wade shoved the man back. "Get the hell out of my way."

"Your wife?" The soldier scanned her body and stared at her hair and eyes. "These Injuns kidnap her?"

"No," Wade said at the same instance as she did. She smiled at her man, and he grinned back.

"She is Nez Perce, and she is my wife. I've been detained, and she had to travel with her people. Now, I'm claiming her." Wade stepped around the soldier, taking her by the arm. "Come on, I'm finishing my promise."

"She can't leave the compound," The soldier said, moving back in front of them.

"As far as I know there isn't a law that forbids a man to claim his wife." Wade stared at the soldier.

"I-I'll have to ask—"

"Go find your answer. I'm taking my wife home." Wade tucked Sa-qan against his side and strode away from the soldier.

Sa-qan allowed Wade to lead her over to where a young boy held a horse. She spun as he put his hands around her waist. "Where are we going? I must remain here and help my people."

"I have a preacher waiting to marry us. I promised we'd be legal by my people's traditions. Then I plan to make love to you in a soft bed. We'll deal with the rest tomorrow." He placed her on the horse as Silent Doe approached.

"I see your man has come." She smiled. "Do not worry. We will care for the sick until your return."

Wrinkles furrowed Wade's forehead at Silent Doe's words.

He swung up behind her. "We'll discuss that tomorrow. She'll be with me the rest of today and tonight."

His soft words ignited her skin. They would be together, just the two of them. Her heart hammered in her chest as he reached around her, grasping the reins in one hand and placing the other protectively over her stomach.

She leaned back against his solid chest and sighed. "I had started to believe you would not find me."

He kissed her neck. "Nothing would stop me from finding you. I read the newspapers. The public isn't happy with our government over the treatment of your people. The newspapers have kept the plight of the Nez Perce in front of them." He kissed her, again. "We'll discuss that later, too. Right now I want to concentrate on making you my wife and showing you how much I missed you."

The guard at the edge of the camp between the encampment and the town started to raise his rifle to stop them. Wade's arm around her stiffened and the man shifted his rifle to rest on the ground.

They continued into the town and straight to a white dwelling with a tall pointy top. Wade stopped the horse, dismounted, and raised his hands to her. The gleam in his eyes spread welcome heat through her body. She swung her leg over the horse and slid into his waiting hands. He lowered her to the ground slowly before his head dipped and his lips claimed hers.

She wound her arms around his neck and clung to him. Tears burned her eyes. Joy blossomed in her chest like a summer flower. She returned the kiss and broke loose from his lips to gasp for air.

"I've dreamed of that kiss so many times over the last few months." Wade rested his forehead against hers.

"I have dreamed of you as well. I worried I would never see you again and held my memories tight in my heart." She shuddered, cleansing her body of the anxiety she had harbored late at night.

"I'm here and don't plan to ever leave you again." He pulled a package out of his saddlebag and put an arm around her shoulders, leading her to the building.

At the door, he pulled it open and ushered her inside. The dark interior had candles lit at the far end. Many wooden seats like she sat on in the train lined the way to the candles.

"What is this?" she whispered, uncertain how she knew she stood in a sacred lodge.

"It's a church. It's where my people worship and talk to our Creator." His quiet tone matched hers. "This is where my people get married. Once we're married here no one can keep us apart. We'll be husband and wife in the eyes of all our people."

Her feet refused to move. What would the Creator think?

Wade tugged on her hand. "You still want to be my wife don't you?" The worry in his voice moved her into his arms.

"Yes. I do not wish to walk this earth without you."

He kissed the top of her head. "There's a room over there. It's small but will give you enough room to change. Take this and put it on. I'll go find the preacher." He handed her the parcel from his saddlebags.

"What is in here?" She squeezed the soft contents.

"A dress. I bought all the undergarments, but you don't have to put them on. In fact, it will make things a lot easier later." His eyes glittered with desire as his hand cupped her chin. "I plan to love you thoroughly as soon as this preacher declares us married."

He said the last so quiet she had to lean close to hear him. He took the opportunity to steal another kiss.

He spun her. "Go, before I forget we need a ceremony."

She walked toward the door in front of her. The small room had a bucket and a stick with grass on the end. A small colorful window up high on the wall provided the only light in the room. She unwrapped the package and discovered a so·yá·po dress. Small blue flowers scattered across the garment. She scowled. Why did she have to wear this to marry Wade? The soft cloth, while not as warm as the blanket dress she wore, did not scratch her skin. She raised it to her face. The smooth cloth skimmed across her skin.

Curiosity slipped her dress from her body. She ducked into the dress Wade gave her. It scraped the floor around her feet and caressed her skin. She stared down at the gapping cloth exposing her breasts. Gripping the cloth she held it together and frowned. So·yá·po women did not walk around holding their clothing together. She fingered the garment and found small round shell-like pieces sewn on one side. Memories of undressing Wade to heal him brought recognition of how to close the dress.

A light knock startled her.

Wade's head popped in. "Are you ready?' His eyes ran the length of her and ignited. "You're beautiful no matter what you wear."

"Why must I wear the so·yá·po dress?" she asked, fumbling with the next to last fastener.

Wade gulped down the knot of desire rising in his throat at the sight of Sa-qan. He stepped into the room and finished the last button, enjoying the silkiness of her warm skin against his fingers. She had to see he wasn't taking away who she was.

"You and I don't care that you are Nimiipuu and I'm a white man. But there are others that are going to be harder to convince. By wearing this dress, the preacher won't think twice about marrying us. I'm not taking away who you are. I'm making sure we're together."

His heart stopped, and he held his breath as she contemplated his words. A sliver of a smile tipped her lips and she held her hand out to him.

"Being your woman brings me joy. We must be together to help my people."

Air whooshed out of his lungs. He squeezed her hand. "After this ceremony, your people are my people." He meant the words as strongly as he believed the vow he was about to make to her and God.

He led her down the aisle between the pews. The preacher and his wife stood at the altar. The woman's eyes narrowed a bit. Wade glanced at Sa-qan. Her full breasts bounced with her steps, a movement the buckskin dress she wore when they first met had hidden. The curve-fitting dress she wore now revealed all of his angel's attributes. He hadn't realized the preacher's wife would know Sa-qan didn't wear the proper undergarments. Her beautiful hair also wasn't pulled back by combs or piled in a neat bun. He couldn't do anything about it now.

Wade tucked Sa-qan's hand into the crook of his arm and continued forward.

The preacher cleared his throat when they stopped in front to him.

The vows were short and binding. Sa-qan's eyes never left his face though they widened a bit when the preacher asked if he, Wade Andrew Watts took Angel Sa-qan for his wife. He'd had to give the man a first and last name for Sa-qan.

"You may now kiss your wife." The preacher didn't have to repeat the words he'd been waiting for.

Wade folded his arms around Sa-qan and kissed her with the reverence he held for their vows. He slowly released her, turned to the preacher and his wife and shook their hands. She also extended her hand to each one.

"Thank you, Reverend and Mrs. Mallory." Wade ushered Sa-qan down the aisle only stopping long enough to pick up her discarded clothing in the broom closet.

Outside, he untied his horse as Sa-qan wrapped the Indian blanket around her body. The thin dress he bought wasn't as warm as the blanket dress he'd stashed into his saddlebag. They'd buy her warmer clothing tomorrow. He had plans for her the rest of today and tonight. Wrapping an arm around her shoulders to help stave off the cold December air, he led her down the street to the waiting dinner, bath, and soft bed he'd arranged before riding out to the camp.

He stopped at the livery stable, paying the stable hand to keep his horse and grabbing his saddlebag. Wade held Sa-qan close to his side to help ward off the cold and walked quickly to Planters' House, the best hotel in Leavenworth. He'd already secured a room right next to the bathing closet on the second floor. He'd instructed the clerk to have the boiler in that bath closet heating in an hour.

Wade led Sa-qan up the stairs ignoring the stares of the men loitering in the lobby. He had one thing on his mind—warm his new bride. He pushed open the door of the bath closet, leading Sa-qan inside. She scanned the small room, her gaze lingering on the large brass tub sitting to the side of the room.

"What is this?" she asked, drawing the blanket tighter around her even though the room was warm from the boiler heating the water.

"We're going to take a warm bath. The two of us. Together." Wade dropped the saddlebag over the chair in the corner. He unbuttoned his coat and hung it on a peg.

Sa-qan stood where he'd left her, her eyes wide, watching him. He stood in front of her and unclasped her hands from the blanket. The cold of her fingers seeped into his hands and chased a shiver up his spine.

"Don't you want to get warm and clean?" He tossed the filthy blanket to the corner. He cringed thinking how many days and nights she'd been bundled in the dirty thing.

She placed her hands on his. "Nimiipuu bathe in cold water. It makes us strong."

"Right now, you need to be warmed up or you'll become sick." He unbuttoned her dress, exposing her smooth skin and full breasts. With care, he slid the garment down her arms, over her hips which looked narrower to him, and let it fall to the floor. Wade scanned her body. She'd lost weight since the last time he saw her naked. Her breasts were as full but her hips, legs and arms were decidedly thinner. His gaze dropped to her belly. The sight of a slight bump there expanded his chest. Their child grew in the woman he loved. He placed a hand on the bump and leaned down, capturing her mouth in a tender kiss.

Wade eased out of the kiss and started the hot water from the boiler flowing into the brass tub and pumped cold water to reach the desired temperature. Steam rose from the water. He skimmed a hand through the liquid and nodded. It would warm his angel without burning her.

He quickly shed his clothes and picked Sa-qan up, settling them both in the water.

"I've never had a warm bath." Her arms clung to his neck pressing her breasts against his naked chest.

He eased her back and spun her, slipping her backside in between the vee of his legs. "Let me wash your hair." He slid her down to wet her hair. Her large eyes peered up at him as she reclined in the water. The strands of her hair tangled around his growing arousal.

His fingers combed through her long, blonde, straight locks. He poured hair soap on his hands and worked it through her hair and massaged her scalp.

Her eyes closed, and she moaned softly.

He rinsed her hair and worked his hands down her neck, over her shoulders, and down both arms before cupping her breasts and gliding his hands down her body to her legs.

She slipped from his grasp, spun around, and knelt between his legs. "I will clean you." Her small hands started at his head massaging his scalp and tantalizing his skin as she moved over every inch of his body, becoming fascinated by his arousal. Her small hands rubbing up and down his shaft nearly shot his hips out of the water.

"Sa-qan, if you don't take your hands from me, I'm going to make love to you right here in this big brass tub."

She tipped her head sideways as he'd witness her do as an eagle and peered at him. The heat burning in her eyes told him she was his for the taking. He gripped her waist, raised her up, and slowly settled her over his arousal. Slipping into her fully dissipated all the dreams that haunted him at their separation. He drew her body flush to his and kissed her, sliding his tongue between her lips and tasting her sweetness. The sensation of her tongue and her hot body holding him tight sealed the last scars on his heart and his conscience. She was his home. His family.

He released her lips, allowing her to ride him as he raised his hips, plunging deeper and deeper until her eyes glowed and she whispered his name as her body gripped him. She collapsed on his chest and he released.

Wade brushed wet tangles of her hair from her face. Her eyes fluttered open. "I still owe you real love making." He kissed her cheek. "Can you stand? The water's getting cold."

She nodded and slowly rose off of him, stepping over the side of the tub. Water pooled on the floor, having splashed over the edges of the tub. He stood, grabbing cotton towels on the shelf. He started at the top of her head, drying every hill, valley, and nook of her body. Her face darkened as he spread her legs and dried her.

"Put on the dress I bought you to walk to the room." He dropped the towels on the floor and sopped up the water the best he could and pulled the stopper on the tub. With the floor drier, he donned clean drawers and denims, before gathering up their belongings in one arm and capturing her hand with the other.

He nodded for her to open the door, and they stepped into the hallway. An older couple exited a room across the hall. They both scowled, and the woman tsked.

Wade ignored the two and stopped in front of room 103. He released Sa-qan's hand and opened the door, ushering her in ahead of him. The room was large, clean, and well outfitted with a screened commode, dresser, large bed, and nightstand with a lamp.

He tossed their clothing on the chair by a small table and slipped the key in the lock. Sa-qan wandered about the room, skimming her fingers over the wood furniture, smoothing a palm over the quilt on the bed, and pushing on the downy pillows. Her motions reminded him she'd never encountered these things.

He caught her attention and together they sat on the bed. "I forget you've never lived in my world. Do you have any questions?"

"Where are we going to live?"

Mita áptit wax ná·qt
(31)

Sa-qan faced Wade placing her hands on his leg and stared into his caring eyes. She had enjoyed the warm bath. In her childhood, she remembered bathing in the cold streams with her mother. Recently, the women had washed with cold water dipped from the rivers and streams they camped beside. Sitting in this room on a soft bed, she was afraid to not live as a Nimiipuu she could no longer fight for them.

Wade continued to watch her, not answering her question.

"Where will we live now that we are man and wife and you no longer are a soldier?" Her heart began to ache he took so long to answer.

"I'd like to say in the camp with your people, but we won't have the freedom we need to move about." Wade placed a hand on her arm.

The heat of his touch reminded her of the quick mating in the bath. Her cheeks burned with the memory.

"I've talked with a man who writes for one of the largest newspapers in the East. He's willing to let us—you telling me and me writing it down—tell the Nimiipuu's story." He captured her hands. "If we can make the government see they aren't a threat they might treat the Nimiipuu better and send them home sooner."

Sa-qan started to shake her head. She had a duty to live with her people. She could not help them if she was not with them.

"You won't be able to help if you're confined and not allowed to talk with the white leaders." Wade ran a hand over his mustache and stared into her eyes. "You've seen how they allowed me to ride into the camp and back out with you. We can live in town and visit every day. We can write about the way the people are being treated and gain sympathies."

What Wade said made sense. But would the Creator believe her to be a traitor like her father if she lived with the so·yá·po? She would not be turning her back on her people or harming them as her father had.

"Sa-qan, angel, if I thought living with your people would help them I would. The only way we can help is by not being imprisoned and having the ability to move freely." He captured her hands, again. "Like when you were a spirit. You didn't live with the Nimiipuu. They didn't even know you existed, but you helped them. It will be like that only they will know you exist and will talk with you about how they feel. We'll put it down on paper for everyone to learn the strength and character of your people." Determination darkened his eyes.

Her heart opened completely to his love.

"And we will have the ability to travel to Washington and talk with the White leaders who give the orders." The conviction in his eyes and words rivaled her own passion for the Nimiipuu.

What he said made sense. She would be as her spirit, helping from the outer edges. "We can do this? Talk to the so·yá·po leaders? And have others learn of the Nimiipuu?"

"Yes. We can meet the reporter tomorrow. He's in town writing about how the army has moved the Nimiipuu farther and farther from their homes." He put an arm around her shoulders. "You can give him a firsthand account of the journey here."

Her heart sung with the knowledge her husband had thought this all out. It would be better if they could talk with the so·yá·po leaders. The soldiers guarding the camp and the one who shoved Wade when he kissed her showed proof she could be of more help outside the camp than inside.

She smiled at her husband. His intelligence and caring had first caught her attention. That he was pleasing to look at and made her body sing doubled her affection for him.

"Show me how pleasing it is to make love in a bed."

Wade's eyes gleamed like a big tawny mountain cat about to pounce. His hands slid into her hair, and he held her head gently, his face dipping toward hers. The softness of his hovering lips and tickle of his mustache rippled tremors through her body.

"I plan to love you thoroughly and completely."

The whispered promise tingled her woman parts and hitched her breath. He captured her mouth with his, nibbling and teasing her lips until she squirmed wanting his hands on her, his maleness in her.

He drew away, her body grieved the contact. She reached for him, but he took her hands, kissing the backs before releasing them and opening her dress. With each fastener he set free, he kissed her newly exposed skin. Each whisper of warm breath on her skin and moist kiss spun her senses. The slow delicious agony of his journey down to her belly quivered her legs, making her glad she still sat on the bed. No one had ever treated her in such a cherished way.

His rough-skinned hands slid between her shoulders and the dress. His warm palms moved down her arms slipping the garment off her shoulders and over her hands. Her bare upper body heated as his gaze drifted over her face, down her neck, and lingered at her breasts. Her nipples puckered and ached the longer his gaze lingered.

When her breathing became ragged with desire, she reached out to him.

He grasped her hands, holding them in her lap, and leaned forward, suckling a breast. The sensation sparked a bolt of lightning to her toes. He continued to give equal attention to both breasts making her squirm. His hand slid under her dress. The weight of his hand resting on parts of her that pulsed with need sent heat and light through her body. He stopped suckling and grinned. His eyes twinkled with the knowledge he had her body pulsing to the rhythm of ceremonial drums.

He captured her lips, caressing her tongue with his and leaned, lowering her to the bed. Settling into the softness, she wrapped her arms around his neck. He slipped out and grasped the dress, pulling it over her hips and tossing it across the room. Again, he sat beside her, his gaze traveling the length of her before he placed his hands on her thighs and spread her legs.

Mischief flickered in his eyes, before he leaned down, kissing her curls. Stunned by this action, she moaned when he took her into his mouth as he had her breasts. Having been still too young to experience the menstrual lodge or the women's lodge before being made a spirit she had not learned of the ways between a man and woman as other maidens. She wondered if Wade's magical touches were something other women experienced or if only the connection between she and Wade made her body sing, exalt, and yearn for more.

She clutched the cloth under her in her fists and rode the body shaking sensations, calling out his name as a clap of thunder jerked her body and lightning scorched her limbs.

"That my wife is being thoroughly loved."

The sensations ebbed. She opened her eyes and found an unclothed Wade holding his body over hers. His wonderful lips quirked in a wicked smile, and his eyes gleamed with desire.

"I wish to make our bodies sing together." She rose up kissing his neck and wrapping her arms around his solid middle, pressing her body to his.

"My duty as your husband is to make your wishes come true." His legs spread hers wider and he entered, taking her to greater heights than before. Making love with her husband brought as much freedom and joy to her heart as when she soared in the sky as an eagle.

《》《》《》

Wade lay on his side watching Sa-qan sleep. Before falling asleep, they'd eaten a cold meal he'd brought up from the dining room. While waiting for the food to be prepared, he'd telegraphed Colonel Gibbon giving his location so the colonel knew where to forward the release orders. He hoped it didn't take much longer. He didn't like the thought he could be thrown in jail if someone labeled him a deserter. If Gibbon didn't extend his leave until the release papers arrived, he could be a wanted man. He didn't see the need to explain all this to Sa-qan. She didn't need anything other than helping her people to worry about.

Sa-qan stretched. He stopped his hand as he started to reach for her. She needed her rest. Her condition when he found her yesterday tore at his heart. She wasn't eating enough, and the dark circles under her eyes proved she hadn't been resting either. When she woke, he planned to feed her well and insist she rest during the day. He knew Indian women were more resilient when it came to birthing, but he planned to make sure Sa-qan and their baby wanted for nothing.

He'd not let his new family down.

She scooted across the bed and flung her leg over his, pressing her naked body against him. Her lips skimmed across his chest, and her small soft lips nibbled at his nipple. His body, already aroused from watching her, throbbed.

"Are you sure? I don't want to hurt you or the baby." He'd do everything in his power to make sure neither one ever came to harm by him or anyone else.

"You would hurt me by refusing my wish." She ran the tip of her tongue around his rigid nipple and grasped his shaft in her hand.

He groaned and slid down to capture her teasing lips. In one fluid motion, he rolled her to her back and entered her slick, hot, waiting body.

«»«»«»

Sa-qan stretched as the sound of splashing water invaded her sleep. She opened one eye and spotted Wade, fully dressed, pouring water from a vessel into a large bowl. She rolled to her side and watched him scrape the scratchy hair from his face, leaving the hair above his mouth. She had wondered how so·yá·po men's faces could be smooth and have hair growing on them.

He turned from drying his face and caught her watching him. His eyes lit and the mouth that had taken her to great heights the night before tipped in a welcoming smile. "I'm glad you're awake. I'm hungry and I didn't want to leave you to go eat."

Hunger had become a constant companion since she became mortal. She had learned to ignore the pains and gurgles. But as his caring gaze scanned her face, her stomach rumbled.

"Come on. I'll help you dress, and we'll grab breakfast in the dining room before getting you more clothes and meeting the newspaper man." Wade crossed the room, grasped her hand, and tugged her to her feet beside the bed.

"I can dress myself," she said, glancing about the room for the clothing he gave her the day before.

"But I'll take pleasure in helping you dress." He led her to the table holding the vessel and bowl. Wade poured water on a small cloth and ran the cloth over her face, down her neck, all over her body, and even between her legs.

His detailed washing heated her body and started the pulse in her woman parts. The heat in his eyes proved he was aroused by his actions as well.

Sa-qan grasped his head, pulling him down to kiss and turn his thoughts to climbing back into bed.

He drew out of the kiss, shaking his head. "We'll never accomplish anything if you try to seduce me. And you need food. Your stomach told me."

"What does seduce mean?" She ran a hand down the front of his breeches.

He hissed and removed her hand. "Exactly what you're doing."

He led her to the chair and her clothes. "I'll help you layer on the undergarments. We'll also buy you a warm cloak as soon as we finish breakfast."

She stood beside the pile of clothes. "Why must I wear all of those?"

"Since we'll be spending a good part of today in town getting settled and meeting Baker, it's best you dress to not draw attention."

She started to protest.

He kissed her lips. "When we get a place of our own and folks have become used to the idea you're Nez Perce and we're married, you can wear whatever you like, but for now we have to make sure people don't have a reason to shun us." He tipped her chin up and gazed into her eyes. His pleaded with her. "I'm not doing this to take away who you are. I'm doing this to help people accept and listen to us."

He handed her white puffy breeches. She slipped them on. Then he pulled a white flimsy dress over her head and tied it at the neck.

"This is worn under the dress. And one of these. They're

petticoats. They help to keep you warm."

He held up the dress she wore briefly the day before. She ducked under it and slid her arms into the sleeves. The layers helped warm her, but she wondered how a so·yá·po woman wore all these clothes during the hot days of summer.

Wade fastened her dress and stepped back. "You can wear your moccasins. The long skirts will hide them." He handed her a comb. "Run that through your hair. We'll purchase pretty combs for you to pull it up out of your face."

She combed her hair and stared at her reflection in the large oval. She swallowed. With the so·yá·po clothing she no longer saw a Nimiipuu. Would her people still accept her dressed like a white woman?

Wade stood behind her, his hands on her shoulders, and his head above hers. "It's what a person feels on the inside that makes the person, not what they wear on the outside." He kissed the top of her head. Her stomach rumbled, again. "Come on. After our night we deserve a large meal."

Hand in hand, they descended the stairs. Wade nodded to the man behind a half wall and they passed through a large door. Inside the room, many tables and chairs filled the space. People already seated at tables glanced their way and returned to talking or eating.

Sa-qan scanned the room, taking in everything. Until yesterday, she had only witnessed so·yá·po ways from a distance in the sky. They had many things that while pleasing to look at and comfortable would make traveling hard. That would explain their need for the large wagons she watched enter the Nimiipuu territory.

A man walked up to their table. Wade asked him to bring them food called by names she did not know.

Wade watched Sa-qan. Her piercing eyes scanned the room, the people, and she listened intently. She cocked her head several times giving away her unease. He reached across the table and grasped her hand.

"You'll get used to these things. We'll only be in the hotel until we can find a house."

"How many horses does it take for a family to move from season to season?" Her wide curious eyes stared at him.

"We don't move like the Nimiipuu. Once a man and woman get married they move into a house and often live there all their lives or may only move one to two times in their life time."

She continued to stare at him. "Never move? Is this because they fill their dwellings with so many things?"

Wade couldn't stop the laugh bubbling in his chest. "I hadn't thought of that before. We do tend to collect a lot of belongings the longer we remain in one place."

Their food arrived. Sa-qan tasted it all with hesitancy, but in the end, she cleaned her plate.

"Now to buy you a cloak, order more clothing, and meet Baker." Wade placed his coat around her shoulders, tucked her hand in the crook of his arm, and set out for the closest dressmaker.

With his wife on his arm, Wade proudly walked down the street. They purchased a dark blue wool cloak to keep Sa-qan warm, and ordered three more dresses and another set of underclothes, before entering the Leavenworth Herald. Baker spent his time at the newspaper office writing when not out gathering information on the Nez Perce and government.

Wade spotted the man ten years his junior bent over a desk writing. Sa-qan's hand in his, he led her to the small table. He held a chair and motioned for her to sit. She eyed him and the curly haired man who watched them from behind round spectacles.

"Darrin Baker, I'd like you to meet my wife, Sa-qan. She's Nez Perce and will be helping me write the stories I suggested to you." Wade shook hands with the man.

"Mrs. Watts, I must say you're not at all what I'd imagined when your husband told me about your desire to help the plight of the Nez Perce." The man pushed his spectacles up the bridge of his nose and tipped his head to Sa-qan.

She didn't flinch at his comments. "I know I do not have the same hair and eyes of my sisters, but I am a true Nimiipuu in here." She placed a hand on her chest.

"Since we all have the same agenda, I think we're going to get along wonderfully." Baker didn't lose any time settling down to work. Wade admired how Sa-qan answered all Baker's questions even though the man's brows would bunch together in confusion at times.

Wade interrupted after an hour. "You'll have to continue this another time. I promised Sa-qan we'd visit the camp today, and she needs to rest." He took her by the elbow as she stood.

"Can you come by tomorrow morning?" Baker asked, obviously taken with Sa-qan.

She smiled and nodded. "If my husband says this is good for my people, I will be here tomorrow."

Sa-qan leaned against his arm as they walked out the door. "He is a man of great determination. I like him."

Wade smiled. The more White people Sa-qan felt comfortable around the easier it would be for her to function in both worlds.

He rented a wagon from the livery and drove Sa-qan to the camp. The guards and inhabitants gave them little more than a glance as they entered, believing them townsfolk coming to gawk.

Sa-qan hurried to a large structure at the far side of the camp. Silent Doe stepped out of the canvas tent. She stared at Sa-qan.

"Sister, you have given up our ways?" she asked.

Sa-qan shook her head. "My husband and I believe we can best serve my people if I am allowed to come and go as so·yá·po and not a captive. I can come here every day and help, but also leave and talk with the so·yá·po leaders and help my people return to their homes."

Silent Doe's gaze ran the length of Sa-qan. Wade stepped up beside his wife. He had to help Silent Doe understand only Sa-qan's appearance had changed not her inner strength and belief in her people.

"I haven't changed who she is in her heart."

Sa-qan nodded. "I am here to help with the sick. I will come after I have talked with Darrin. He is putting my story on paper and all the so·yá·po will learn of our love for the land and peaceful life we were forced to leave."

Girl of Many Hearts grabbed Sa-qan around the waist, hugging her tight. Silent Doe's apprehension vanished from her face.

"Your txiẏak is stronger," the girl said.

Did the girl know Sa-qan had been a spirit? Wade studied Sa-qan. She smiled down at the child before her eyes met his.

"Yes, my power comes from love." Sa-qan peered into his eyes. "Love for my husband and my people and love from my husband and people."

Hearing her place him in her heart next to her people dissolved any doubts he harbored about how she truly felt about him.

Wade leaned toward Sa-qan to kiss her. She smiled, her eyes dancing, and shook her head before she stepped through the tent.

Wade didn't know what to do with himself while she tended the sick so he sought Joseph. It wouldn't hurt to let the leader of the Nez Perce know what he and Sa-qan planned.

Mita áptit wax lepít
(32)

The months passed. Wade and Sa-qan traveled to Washington with Baker to speak to the government leaders about the Nez Perce. Though many sympathizers attended, General Sherman, the main adversary keeping the Nez Perce in Kansas Indian territory, could not be swayed. He remained adamant the Nez Perce would set an example to other hostile tribes.

On their trip, Wade encouraged Sa-qan to eat well and rest. It would be the only trip until after the baby arrived. Her expanding stomach would soon be hard to hide and the trip would become too hard on her. Even though she insisted Nimiipuu women could endure anything and give birth, rattling off the names of three women who gave birth while the group had floated down the Missouri River, Wade refused to allow her to do too much.

«»«»«»

On a hot humid day the end of June, Sa-qan stood at the kitchen table in their little house not far from the Indian camp. Her weight caused her feet to ache when standing too long, but sitting had become unbearable. Only lying in bed with Wade rubbing her back offered her comfort, but they could not stay in bed all day.

He had stopped taking her to the camp last week when she could no longer hide the discomfort of riding on the hard wagon seat. They spent the mornings at the table with Wade writing down her story of the Nimiipuu. Darrin helped them sell the stories to his Newspaper. The afternoons were usually spent at the Nimiipuu camp. Having half a day to herself, she grew bored. She knew little of the ways a so·yá·po woman kept a house. Wade had taught her to cook foods he liked. She had yet to learn enough of the so·yá·po scribbles to use a book the old woman next door gave her when she learned Sa-qan did not know how to cook.

Pain shot through her belly. The baby was coming. Silent Doe had counseled her on what to expect when her time came, but the slicing pain weakened her knees. She grasped the table to keep from dropping to the wood floor.

Wade, I need you. The pain subsided, and she shuffled to the back porch to drag the bathing tub into the kitchen. Their small house did not have the luxuries of the hotel they had lived in. She had insisted they did not need a large home. Just something to keep them warm and dry. As she tugged on the large brass tub, she wished she could simply turn a knob and have water.

The sound of a jingling harness lifted her thoughts.

"What the he—" Wade took the steps two at a time. "Why are you dragging—"

Another pain wracked her body. She clutched her belly and moaned.

"The baby?" Wade asked, scooping her up in his arms and heading to the bedroom.

"Stop." She panted through the spasm of pain and clutched his arm.

"You're having the baby. You need to be in bed." Wade pushed the bedroom door open with his foot.

"No…" She sucked in air as another pain spiraled though her back. "Nimiipuu give birth… in water… Need… fill the tub." She pushed at him, willing him to put her down. "Need… Silent Doe."

"I'm not leaving you for that long." Wade placed her on the bed. "Stay here. I'll have Baker ride out and get Silent Doe, and then I'll fill the tub." His brow furrowed as his worried eyes scanned her face.

"Will you be all right while I tell Baker?"

She nodded and wrapped her arms around her belly as another pain, not as hard, rippled through her belly. "Hurry."

Wade dropped a soft kiss on her lips. "I'll be right back."

She nodded and smiled. He would do everything the Nimiipuu way once Silent Doe arrived.

«»«»«»

Wade ran through the streets to the newspaper office. Baker sat slumped over his desk as usual. He glanced up as Wade slid to a stop inside the doorway.

"Baby's coming. Ride fast and get Silent Doe." Wade didn't stay to elaborate. He spun and ran back to their small house. His lungs ached, but he leaped onto the back porch and grabbed the edge of the brass tub big enough for two. He and Sa-qan had started a ritual on their wedding night of bathing each other. When they moved into their own home he ordered the large tub so they could continue the intimate moments.

Wade scraped the tub across the floor and into the bedroom. Sa-qan lay on her side clutching her belly. He dropped the tub with a loud bang and hurried to the bed, sitting down and rubbing her back.

"Baker is on his way to get Silent Doe. Is there anything I can do until she gets here?" Wade wanted to take away the pain he witnessed on her pinched features.

"Fill the tub. Silent Doe says it is easier to give birth in water. I have watched this as a spirit and while living with the Nimiipuu." The last words strangled out as she clutched her belly.

His body shook. He had taken away her powers and now his seed had grown and brought her this pain. "I'm sorry." Wade pushed the hair from her face and kissed her forehead. "If I could carry the pain for you I would."

"It is woman's work to carry the pain and bring forth the children." She placed a hand on his cheek. "It is your work to provide food and love us."

"I do love you." He kissed the palm of her hand.

Tears glistened in her eyes. "I know. It is your love that has given me strength." Her eyes dulled, and she clutched her belly.

Her pains came closer and closer together. Wade sprang from the bed and began filling buckets. First emptying the reservoir on the wood stove then refilling it and adding a bucket of cold water from the pump into the tub. He alternated buckets of hot and cold water until the tub stood full.

"Do you need help getting in the tub?" He sat on the bed and ran a hand down Sa-qan's back.

"Wait for Silent Doe." She breathed raggedly. Her face grew pale.

The sound of racing hooves approached and stopped. Within seconds Silent Doe entered the bedroom.

"Leave." She gripped his arm, dragging him from his seat on the bed. "No man is allowed when child comes to this earth." She pushed him toward the door.

"I want to be here to help." He sent a pleading gaze to Sa-qan, but her eyes were squeezed shut.

"You will not be helpful, only get in the way." Silent Doe gave him one last shove and shut the door behind him.

"Dammit, Silent Doe. She's my wife. I have a right to—" A hand rested on his shoulder.

"Let the womenfolk do what they know." Baker motioned with his head toward the kitchen. "You've got a strong wife. Between the two of them I'm sure everything will go fine."

Wade ran a hand over his mustache. Sa-qan was strong, but he'd helped dig too many graves at the camp the last few months and many of them for babies and children. As the heat grew, so did the deaths. He blamed the water and had ridden to the fort many times to pressure them about moving the group to a more hospitable area.

"Did you get the number of deaths last week from the Indian camp?" Wade poured coffee into two cups.

"Yes. I sent the story to the newspaper in Washington." Baker pushed at his spectacles with an index finger and stared into his coffee. "Deaths occur on reservations. Old age, births, accidents, and fights, but the numbers aren't as great as here."

The swallow of coffee didn't slide down easily. "It has to be the marshland and still water. The land where the Nez Perce come from has clear running water all year long."

"I agree, but getting anyone of power to listen…" Baker spread his hands and rolled his eyes.

Chanting drifted into the room. Baker rose out of his chair. "What's that?"

"Silent Doe urging the baby to come out and see his people." Wade had grasped an elementary amount of the Nez Perce language thanks to his patient wife and Silent Doe's family. He thought it necessary so he could communicate with his wife and children in her native tongue and it helped when working with the Nimiipuu.

Several hours later, a baby cried. Wade shot from the chair and lunged for the bedroom door. He shoved the door open and stepped inside.

Silent Doe handed a waxy, golden haired boy to Sa-qan, still sitting in the tub. He moved farther into the room.

The older woman spun, pushing him out. "I will get you soon." The door closed in his face, but the sight of his son in his mother's arms expanded his chest.

"Well?" Baker asked behind him.

"It's a boy." A boy. He'd prayed for a healthy child, but a boy…He now had someone to carry on the Watts lineage.

"What's his name?"

"I don't know. Sa-qan said we couldn't pick out a name until he arrived and showed us what it will be." They had both agreed the name would be both Nez Perce and English. "Then there will be a naming ceremony."

"Will I be invited?"

The wistfulness in Baker's voice added to Wade's good humor. He laughed and slapped the man on the back, leading him back into the kitchen where Wade poured them each a bit of whiskey to toast to the newest member of the Watts family.

«»«»«»

Sa-qan stared down into the puckered up face of her son. He had her light colored hair but his father's features and dark eyes. Silent Doe had cleaned up the boy and the room before she went to get Wade.

He stepped into the room, his eyes sparkling, a bright grin

stretching his face. Wade sat on the edge of the bed and put a finger under her chin, tipping her face up to his. His lips descended on hers, kissing her with aching tenderness.

"Qe·ci·yew·yew," he whispered against her lips.

"Why do you thank me?"

"For giving me a beautiful boy. A gift I will honor." He placed a hand on their child's head. The love shining in his eyes as he admired their son melted her heart.

«»«»«»

Two weeks had passed since the birth of their child. Sa-qan sat on the porch in the shade willing the wind to pick up and cool the air. Boy of Two Peoples or Toby, Wade's name for the baby, lay in the cradle Wade insisted they use. Silent Doe had given her a cradleboard, but Wade preferred she only put Toby in it when she needed to carry him and when they went to the camp.

Her heart grew heavy as she added two more beaded symbols to a flag she flew from their porch. Each symbol honored a Nimiipuu who died at the camp. Soon the beads would make the cloth so heavy it would only hang limp and unmoving as the people who had gone from this earth.

Wade rode up in the wagon. He drew the horses to a stop and stared down at her before his gaze drifted to Toby.

"I'm going to the fort to try and talk to the Indian agent, again. There are more sick people at the camp. Something has to be done."

Sa-qan stood. "I will come with you." She placed Toby in the cradleboard, tied the lacing, and handed him up to his father. Wade smiled and cooed at his son while she climbed up to sit beside him.

She took the cradleboard from his reluctant hands, and he slapped the horse's rumps with the reins. The wagon jerked into motion. She had not been to the camp as much since the birth. Silent Doe had told her things were well and to keep her baby away. Too many babies and old people died, she did not want Boy of Two Peoples to become sick.

"Who did we lose today?" she asked, fearing it would be someone she had grown close to.

"An old man and a baby. But nearly half the camp is sick."

258

The wagon rolled through the fort gates and up to the Indian agent's house. Wade jumped down and came around, raising his hands to take his son. He looped the strap from the cradleboard around his arm and lifted her down. Once her feet were on the ground she expected him to hand her the child. He tied their horse alongside two others at the hitching rail, and took her elbow, escorting her up the stairs.

He rapped on the door and studied her face. Worry had carved the creases around his eyes deeper.

"I can hold our son," she said.

A smile fluttered under his mustache. "I enjoy packing my boy around." He raised her hand to his lips as the door opened.

She squeaked at the same time Wade spit out a word she had never heard him use before.

Mita áptit wax mita-t

(33)

A Howitzer ball landing in his gut couldn't have knocked him as breathless as the man standing in the doorway.

"Colonel Abernathy." Wade finally said when the air returned to his lungs.

"Lieutenant Watts."

The man's eyes moved up and down Sa-qan, raising Wade's hackles. He'd never liked the man and seeing him now with a gleam of contempt in his eyes made Wade step closer to Sa-qan.

"We're here to see the Indian Affairs Agent." Wade didn't make any moves to enter the house. He preferred to speak to the agent without Abernathy listening.

"Lieutenant, why aren't you in uniform? I understand you've been here for nearly eight months and never once reported to the fort for duty." Abernathy's voice lowered to a mad dog growl.

Sa-qan drew in a breath. Her stare bore into Wade and seared his conscience.

"Colonel Gibbon gave me a leave of absence until my release orders caught up to me." Each night as he lay holding Sa-qan in his arms, he prayed for the orders to arrive in the mail the next day and each day he left the post office empty handed.

A condescending smile barely curved the colonel's lips as he held out a hand. "May I see the release papers?"

"They haven't arrived, yet." His gut soured as Sa-qan's hand tightened on his. Her fear raced through her palm and up his arm lodging in his heart. He had to remain free. He had a wife and child to care for.

"Sergeant Kemper," Abernathy called over his shoulder. A sergeant appeared. "Take this deserter to the stockade and lock him up."

"No!" Sa-qan stepped between Wade and the sergeant. "Tell him you are free."

Wade shook his head. He'd denied this day the last eight months. "Sa-qan, I didn't tell you the papers hadn't come to keep you from worrying." Wade placed his hand on her arms and set her out of the way. He slipped the cradleboard from his shoulder and kissed Toby's head.

Handing his son to Sa-qan, he stared into her eyes. "The papers will come, soon. You'll see." He placed a kiss on her head and walked down the stairs. He knew having Sa-qan for a wife and finally finding happiness couldn't last. He couldn't hold onto family and happiness.

Sa-qan stared at Wade's stooped shoulders as the soldier took him toward a large building. Why had he not told her the truth? Worry for him and for herself and Toby ripped up her back. He had ended his duty to come to her to help her people.

She spun and faced the smirking colonel. "Why have you done this? You do not need him to chase us anymore."

"He signed an oath to serve this country. Until his release orders relieve him of that oath he can't gallivant around pretending he isn't a cavalry man." He glared at her. "That's the White man's law. He's a White man and he has to live by his laws."

He stood in the agent's house. She swallowed hard. Did the agent and the spiteful colonel share a friendship?

Darrin. Sa-qan pivoted and hurried to the wagon. She untied the horse, placed the cradleboard on the floorboards, and climbed up. The reins smacked the horses' rumps harder than she had planned. They leaped forward. Toby gave a startled cry when the cradleboard bounced. Sa-qan grabbed her son and placed the cradleboard between her feet, driving the horses out of the fort.

The horses loped into town. Pulling back hard on the straps, she managed to stop them one building beyond the newspaper office. Darrin and several store owners poked their heads out to see why a wagon had entered town so fast.

"Darrin!" she called, dropping the reins and gathering the cradleboard. He ran to the side of the wagon and reached up to take Toby.

"What's wrong?"

She jumped down and clutched her child to her chest. "They took Wade away."

"Who?" Darrin led her into the newspaper office.

She started trembling. "The soldiers. We went to the agent's house to ask for more help for my people. So many are sick. An officer, Abernathy is what Wade called him, who did not like when Wade and I talked after the surrender, was at the agent's. He said Wade still belonged to the soldiers." Tears burned at the back of her eyes. "I thought he was free from the soldiers. Wade said the papers had not come."

Darrin took out a paper and writing stick. "Do you know the names of the officers and the fort where Wade served?"

"Gibbon I think." She shook her head. "I do not know the name of the fort."

He wrote then tapped the stick on the paper. "I better go talk to Wade and get all the information before I send telegraphs."

She grasped his hand. "I will go with you."

He peeled her fingers from his sleeve. "I don't know if they'll allow either of us in to see him."

"We must try." She led the way out of the office.

《》《》《》

Wade stalked the small cell. Damn, he should have waited for the papers to come through, but he couldn't let Sa-qan be alone that long. She would have had the baby without his help in that death infested camp. He shook his head. How long would he sit in here waiting? Not knowing if the damn papers would ever show up. He should have contacted Gibbon but had let keeping his family fed and the Nez Perce healthy override his worries about his papers.

"You have a visitor," the guard said, opening the large wooden door leading to the outside.

Sa-qan walked in with Toby and Baker. She put her hand through the bars trying to touch Wade. He walked close and took her hand.

"You and Toby shouldn't be here. Go home."

"I have brought Darrin. He will help us." Her eyes glistened with unshed tears. The sorrow drawing her pink lips into a frown twisted his gut.

"Who was your commanding officer and what fort were you attached to?" Baker poised a pencil over his small pad of paper.

"Colonel Gibbon at Fort Shaw." He clutched Sa-qan's hand. "Take Toby home and promise you won't ride out to the camp alone."

"Why?"

"I don't trust Abernathy. Promise me." She had to listen and not be so independent and stubborn.

"Abernathy? The man who tossed you in here?" Baker asked scribbling the name down.

Wade nodded. "He's had it out for me from the beginning of the campaign when I told one of his men to stand down and not shoot Sa-qan and her niece."

Sa-qan gasped. "The soldier who shot Silent Doe and was after Girl of Many Hearts was ordered by the mean colonel?"

Wade nodded. He'd kept this knowledge from her so she wouldn't say or do something to rile Abernathy further.

He saw her anger rise up her neck and darken her cheeks. Wade clutched her hand tighter when she pulled back. "Don't do anything or say anything. He'll only make our life hell."

"I agree. Let's keep inquiries between us," Baker added.

The guard moved away from the door and down the aisle between the two cells. "You have to leave."

Sa-qan drew Wade's hand through the bars and kissed his knuckles. A warm tear dropped where she'd kissed him.

"My heart and bed will be cold until you return."

He'd failed her. He'd promised her she would never sleep alone.

He slipped his hand from hers and stepped back.

Baker took her by the elbow and led her away.

«»«»«»

Sa-qan visited Wade every morning and with each visit he drew farther away from her in body and spirit.

"What are you not telling me?" she asked, gripping the bars.

"They've scheduled a court martial for next week. If I'm found a deserter they'll either make me serve out the time I've been gone or set me loose. But if the treason charges Abernathy has drummed up against me stick, I'll go to prison for five years."

The defeat on his face worried her. "What is treason?"

"Consorting with the enemy." A crooked smile lifted one side of his mustache.

"What does consorting mean?" She would not let him give up on her, their family, or her people.

"It means our times together during the war and the baby we made." His eyes softened. "Knowing you and making Toby are worth spending five years in prison."

"It was not treason. We were working to end the fighting. We did not care who won only to save lives." She clung to the bars wishing he would step closer, could hold her in his strong arms, and she could will her strength into him.

"They don't see it that way." He finally stepped to the bars and covered her hands with his. "If they put me in prison, tell your stories to Baker; he'll see they get published and you get paid. Don't move in with your people—stay free, so you can help them. I'll come for you when I get out."

She shook her head. He would not go to prison, but if he did she must stay with her people. "I must go where my people go."

"Please, it would help me knowing you're safe." He leaned to the bars and touched her lips.

Tears trickled through her tightly-scrunched eyes.

"Think of your people. The conditions they live in. You can help them by living apart, staying healthy, and giving voice to their plight. They will need you more than me."

The guard walked toward them. "Time to go."

Sa-qan picked up the cradleboard, turned her sleeping son to his father for a kiss, and followed the guard out of the building. She blinked at the brilliant sun and took several deep breaths to ease the tightness in her chest.

"We've got orders to move them Indians over to the Quapaw Agency." She heard a voice say. Sa-qan scanned the area and found the source. Abernathy. She had made certain she never encountered the man, but today, she had to know more details.

She slipped the cradleboard on her back and boldly walked up to the officer.

"Why are the Nimiipuu being moved?" she asked, catching Abernathy's attention.

"Because they're all getting sick here and they need to be moved to a proper reservation." His gaze scanned her body, leveling on her breasts full of milk.

The hair on her arms prickled. It took all of her courage to stand in front of the man. But she did it for her people and to show him she was not scared of him.

"Is the reservation near their home?"

The man sneered. "No. Farther away."

Anger bubbled in her chest. His eyes gloated knowing the Nimiipuu would be herded farther from the land that sung to their hearts. The farther her people moved from their home the more their spirits weakened.

"Why? They have done nothing to be treated so poorly." Her hands fisted at her sides.

"Because they made the cavalry look like fools. We'll show them who the real fools are now."

Sa-qan pivoted before she said or did something that would be harmful to her and Toby. She stalked to the wagon and climbed to the seat. Slapping the reins, she put the horses in motion and headed for the camp. At the edge of the Nimiipuu camp she pulled up the reins and stared. Wade told her to remain on the outside of the camp, but would she remain free to help her people if he were sent to jail? What if the mean Abernathy forced her and Toby to live with the Nimiipuu? The sickness could take Toby and then she would have no one. No husband and no child. Panic squeezed her throat and shook her hands.

Wewukiye, I need your help. She lowered her face into her hands and wept. Her people were only a short walk away yet loneliness consumed her. Her duty was to remain with the Nimiipuu and continue to fight for them, but how would she do that without Wade and her mobility as a so·yá·po wife? But how could she live if they sent her husband to prison? He told her Darrin would continue writing her stories and she would be paid but how did one pick up and move to a new place when you were an outsider? Wade's love for her showed the so·yá·po to treat her with respect—how could she gain their respect with him in prison and if she was alone?

She sat in the wagon frozen. Fear she would make the wrong decision held her in place. She did not want to be her father and hurt her people by being selfish. Her heart ached already for the loss of Wade, but her duty had to be to her people. To stay with them and help.

Silent Doe walked out to the wagon. "What is wrong, my sister? Your boy has strong lungs."

Sa-qan shook out of her fearful musings and realized her son cried for food. Her milk soaked the front of her dress.

"Come." Silent Doe led the horses into the camp. Lightning Wolf took care of the horses while Silent Doe held Toby as Sa-qan climbed from the wagon.

Silent Doe walked to their dwelling and entered. Sa-qan followed the older woman, who handed her son to her, and Sa-qan bared her breast. Her son suckled hungrily. The sensation of feeding her child brought tears to her eyes. Her indecision had caused him hunger. She had to shake her apprehension and push on.

"What troubles you?" Silent Doe asked.

In a torrent of tears, Sa-qan told Silent Doe all her troubles as her son emptied one breast and started on the other. She finished her story, wiped the tears away, and felt drained—void of happiness, joy, or even sadness. Hollow—as she had lived so many seasons as a spirit.

"You and your man must work together to help our people. You cannot leave him. You must fight to get him free then you will join our people where they send us." Silent Doe stated what deep down Sa-qan knew but had fought, fearing it made her like her father. Loving Wade did not make her selfish. Their love fulfilled her duty to the Nimiipuu.

Freedom washed over her. She no longer feared her father's curse. She could never be selfish and greedy at the cost of Nimiipuu lives.

Toby had fallen asleep with her nipple in his mouth. She kissed his forehead, popped the nipple from his puckered lips, and buttoned her dress.

"I must go home and change. Darrin and I must do more to set my husband free." She kissed her son's head and stood.

"May you find the wisdom needed to free your man." Silent Doe hugged her and motioned for her to leave.

Sa-qan hurried back to the wagon, to her house to change out of her milk-soaked dress, and headed to the newspaper office. Between her and Darrin they would get Wade free. She knew it with all her heart.

Mita áptit wax pí-lept
(34)

Loneliness seeped deep and cold into Wade's bones. After Sa-qan said she would stay with her people, she hadn't been by to see him. The loss ate at his growing fear for her and Toby. Abernathy made a point of telling him the Nez Perce had been shipped to Baxter, Kansas. *Sa-qan went with them.* That was why she hadn't been back to see him. The disease that killed so many here could easily take his family from him.

He'd been a fool to not argue with her. He knew her duty to help her people overrode all else. It was her conviction to her people that first attracted him and later won his heart. He also knew he came second to the Nimiipuu, but he still damned himself for not giving voice to his misgivings of her living among them.

Baker arrived earlier in the day with a uniform for the court martial to take place later this morning. He'd smiled and told Wade not to worry when he asked about Sa-qan and Toby. Baker was still looking for a good story. His court martial provided good fodder for the newspaper man. No wonder he was in a jovial mood.

Wade stood at the cell door dressed in a lieutenant's uniform, waiting for the guard to escort him to the trial.

The outside door creaked opened and the guard entered, strolling down the aisle between the other three cells. He stopped at the cell, jingled the keys unlocking the door, and swung it open. Wade had spent a month in the stockade waiting for word of his trial. Drunk soldiers had come and gone through the large wooden door to the outside world, but he'd remained imprisoned. Now the day had finally arrived for him to walk out that door, he wasn't ready. His court martial would begin, and he dreaded the verdict.

"Come on, it's a nice day." The guard motioned for him to walk on ahead.

A nice day to learn you'll spend the next five years in prison. And quite possibly have no family to return to.

Sunlight bright and blinding stopped him at the doorway. A small body lunged at him and clung tightly. He blinked and stared down at shimmering white hair. *Sa-qan!* His heart hammered in his chest. She couldn't be here. He grasped her arms, holding her away from him. Yes, it was his beautiful angel.

"What are you doing here? I thought..." Exhilaration spun his insides. She was here, not in some reservation far away. The light and joy glowing in her eyes wrapped around his heart. She'd stayed with him. Put him first. Her love for him was as strong as her love of her people.

"That I was far away?" She smiled and his world tilted, chasing away his fears.

"Yes." He hugged her tight and realized more people stood around. Wade scanned the military and non-military men standing in a line in front of him.

"I don't understand. Colonel Gibbon, what are you doing here?" He saluted his superior officer while clutching his wife to his side.

"When a newspaper correspondent starts asking me why one of my men who I'd given leave and signed off on his resignation was being held as a deserter, I followed the path of the papers and brought them here myself, to vouch for the fact you were not a deserter but following the orders I gave you."

Wade smiled at Baker. "I knew you were tenacious about a story."

"I called in a favor at the insistence of your wife." Baker said, winking at Sa-qan.

"But the other matter—treason." Wade found the word hard to spit out.

"According to your wife and statements by Sergeants Murphy and

Marks you didn't do anything that jeopardized the army."

"So I'm free of all charges? And discharged from the military?" He couldn't believe all the charges were dropped. He was free to love his wife and son and carry on advocating for the Nez Perce.

"Yes. All charges are dropped." Colonel Gibbon stepped forward. "I'm sorry for the mix up, and I congratulate you on an excellent choice of a wife." He smiled at Sa-qan.

"Sir." Wade extended his hand. The colonel took it and shook. "Thank you. For everything."

"You're welcome, son." The colonel motioned to the others present and they walked toward headquarters.

Baker stepped forward. Wade slapped him on the back. "I owe you, too."

"Just keep giving me good stories about the Nez Perce. I had to get one of my best informants out of jail." Baker shook his hand. "Your wife has you packed up and ready to head out to the reservation near Baxter, Kansas. Enjoy tonight, I have a feeling she'll have you on the road early in the morning." He walked away, leaving them alone for the first time in a month.

"You have us packed?" He captured her hand and started walking to the gate.

"Yes. We must catch up to my people and make sure they are taken care of." She stretched her stride to keep up with his long legs.

"Where are we staying tonight? And where's Toby?" He stopped outside the fort gate and drew her into his arms. He'd missed her soft lips and sweet mouth. He gazed into her sparkling eyes.

"The hotel. We have the same room near the bathing closet." Her eyes sparkled with desire.

"Toby?"

"Darrin is paying a woman to stay with Toby in the room next door for the night."

She stood on her tiptoes, and he couldn't refuse the offered kiss. Not after a month of missing her in his arms. Wade wrapped his arms around his wife and lowered his lips to hers. The spark of their bodies connecting no longer surprised him, he merely delved deeper and received everything her body gave him.

Sa-qan pressed against her husband, wrapping her arms around his neck as he lifted her off the ground, deepening the kiss and fusing their bodies as one. She had found her mate for all eternity.

Epilogue

May 1885

Sa-qan sat in the shade of the large post oak in the front yard. She studied the house she and Wade and their three children lived in a mile from the Quapaw reservation. The government finally stopped moving the Nimiipuu. They'd remained here for seven years. Seven-year-old Toby had ridden into town with his father. Five-year-old Grayson, known as Gray, kept guard over the squirrel he had caught in a snare and now had in a small cage. Their three year-old sister, Merry, played with a doll Girl of Many Hearts made for her from buckskin.

Sa-qan smiled at her two children and yearned to take them to the land she watched over as a spirit. She missed her brother and sister and hated how her people had become more cynical and more distant to one another. They had to return to the land of their fathers and grandfathers to learn to be at peace with one another.

Dust swirled above the oak trees lining the lane. Wade and Toby loped into sight, sliding the horse to stop by the barn and sending a gagging wall of dust toward the house.

"Cover your mouths, close your eyes," she told the two younger children.

Hands grasped her arms and pulled her to her feet before she opened her eyes. Wade's face came into view before his lips landed on hers.

"I-s, mother, they are going home!" Toby's excited voice filtered through the euphoria brought on by Wade's kiss.

She leaned her head back and gazed into her husband's gleaming eyes.

He nodded. "Word came while we were at the village. They're sending the Nez Perce back to their homes. "

Tears of joy trickled down her cheeks. She knew it would not end the dissension among The People but they would be back in the country of their hearts. All the years she and Wade spent following the Nimiipuu, writing stories about their love of the land, their deaths in a strange hot land, and trips to Washington had finally swayed the so·yá·po leaders.

She hugged Wade, then dropped to her knees and drew her children into her arms. "We are going home." She thought of Silent Doe, now a widow, and her beautiful daughter Girl of Many Hearts who married. Would they return? For her sister's sake, Sa-qan hoped the young woman would talk her husband into returning to the land of her mother.

"They're loading everyone on a train in three days." Wade knelt down beside her and their children. "Pack our clothes. I'm headed to the train depot to purchase our tickets."

"Will we be on the train with our cousins?" Gray asked.

"No, they'll be on a special train just for them. We'll take a regular passenger train and meet them at the depot when they arrive." Wade ruffled Gray's dark curls matching his father's.

"Yes." Sa-qan smiled at her husband. "We will be there to greet them."

«»«»«»

Author's Note

While the Nez Perce were allowed to return to the Pacific Northwest, Joseph and other followers of the Nez Perce Dreamer Religion were not allowed to return to the Lapwai reservation in Idaho, on land they once considered theirs. The government sent the non-treaty Nimiipuu to the Coleville reservation in Washington State. The officials were afraid the Dreamers would convert the peaceful Christian Nez Perce at Lapwai. Also, they feared fighting among the treaty Nimiipuu who remained on the reservation during the exodus and the non-treaty Nimiipuu who felt their land was stolen from them.

About the Author

Award winning author Paty Jager ranches with her husband of thirty-five years. They've raised hay, hogs, cattle, kids, and grandkids. Her first book was published in 2006 and since then she has published seventeen books, five novellas, and two anthologies. She enjoys riding horses, playing with her grandkids, judging 4-H contests and fairs, and outdoor activities. To learn more about her books and her life, or to click on links to take you to the ebook sales sites, you can visit her website.

http://www.patyjager.net

Other books in the Spirit Trilogy
Spirit of the Mountain
Book One - Himiin's story
Spirit of the Lake
Book Two - Wewukiye's story

Halsey Brother Series
Marshal in Petticoats – Gil's story
Outlaw in Petticoats – Zeke's story
Miner in Petticoats – Ethan's story
Doctor in Petticoats – Clay's story
Logger in Petticoats – Hank's story
Halsey Brothers Series – Box Set

Halsey Homecoming trilogy
Laying Claim – Jeremy's story
Staking Claim – Colin's story
Claiming a Heart – Donny's story (coming soon)

Other Historical Western Romance
Gambling on an Angel
Improper Pinkerton
For a Sister's Love
Christmas Redemption
Western Duets: Volume One
Western Duets: Volume Two
Western Duets: Volume Three

Western Anthologies

Sweetwater Springs Christmas: A Montana Sky Short Story Anthology
Rawhide "N Romance: A Western Romance Anthology

Contemporary Western Romance

Perfectly Good Nanny
Bridled Heart

Contemporary Action Adventure Romance

Secrets of a Mayan Moon
Secrets of an Aztec Temple
Secrets of a Hopi Blue Star

Thank you for purchasing this Windtree Press publication. For other
books of the heart, please visit our website at
www.windtreepress.com.

For questions or more information contact us at
info@windtreepress.com.

Windtree Press
www.windtreepress.com

www.ingramcontent.com/pod-product-compliance
Lightning Source LLC
Chambersburg PA
CBHW061533210726
48287CB00006B/1944